THE WOMAN
WHO ISN'T THERE

The Disappearance of Alice Martin

Geoffrey Lambert

Also By

GEOFFREY LAMBERT

The Morozov Chronicles

The Morozov Inheritance

THE WOMAN
WHO ISN'T THERE

The Disappearance of Alice Martin

The Morozov Chronicles

Book II

Geoffrey Lambert

DoctorZed
Publishing
www.doctorzed.com

First published 2013 by DoctorZed Publishing.

DoctorZed Publishing books may be ordered through booksellers or by contacting:

DoctorZed Publishing
IDAHO
10 Vista Ave
Skye, South Australia 5072
www.doctorzed.com
61-(0)8 8431-4965

ISBN: 978-0-9875445-3-7 (sc)
ISBN: 978-0-9875445-9-9 (e)

A CIP number for this book is available at the National Library of Australia.

Cover image 'Hidden Woman on Veil' © Jose Antonio Sánchez Reyes | Dreamstime.com

Printed in Australia
DoctorZed Publishing rev. date: 06/06/2013

For
Sophie, Olivia, Lucy, Tom, Chloe and
Lachlan. To enjoy in later years.

ACKNOWLEDGMENTS

As is the case with most books, they would not be the finished article they became without the assistance of others.

Thanks are due to Dr Scott Zarcinas, my editor and publisher. He persevered with good humour and constructive suggestions, and most of the time he was right.

To Zusje, for multiple readings of the MS, improvements to the language and many cups of tea.

To many friends and readers of *The Morozov Inheritance* who kept on my back with the question, "When is the next book going to be available?"

Well, here it is.

Geoffrey Lambert
Sydney 2013

"When I consider life, 'tis all a cheat;

Yet, fooled with hope, men favour the deceit."

John Dryden, *Aureng-Zebe* Act IV, Scene 1

1

The sun rose into a clear and timeless sky. Another sweltering day began. On the ground the air lay humid and lifeless. Within an hour the sun's raw heat would pierce the atmosphere and once more burn the skin. Summer's heat had begun early this year; it was only the first week in November.

The body started to go off. Bacteria and enzymes broke down its tissue. Bush blowflies laid their eggs in the decaying flesh. So far, no one knew it was there.

City commuters went to work with a spring in their step. Holidays of lazy summer days lay ahead. People smiled. It was a day in which most had every reason to expect all to be right with the world. But it wasn't.

Alice Martin was missing.

Professor Jack Martin woke just after dawn. The other side of the bed remained as empty as the previous night. His wife had become a missing person. He showered, dressed and poured a cup of strong black coffee before walking onto the balcony overlooking a tree-filled gully. Dank, lush odours rose from deep below.

He sipped the coffee. He doubted anyone would believe him. He would be sceptical of such a story himself. No one could vanish without trace from the middle of a function for one hundred and fifty people. Yet it had happened. Alice had disappeared.

Someone must have seen her.

2

With Alice still missing, Jack Martin decided to lodge a formal missing person report. Before leaving home to go to the police he made sure his son, John, left for school. As John walked past him in the hallway Martin caught a fleeting glimpse of their reflections together in the hall mirror. The differences in their appearance, he noted not for the first time, were more noticeable side by side. John's flatter nose, his high cheek-bones and broader face contrasted with Martin's thinner features. Not quite the filial similarities one would usually expect in a family. But then no one had commented on it for years. It happens in some families. When John had gone, he telephoned the university and cancelled his morning lectures. He then rang Sophia Hamil at her apartment.

Detective Constable Tom O'Leary remembered Jack Martin from the previous day. He had taken the initial report of Alice Martin's disappearance and told the professor to come back if his wife had not turned up in twenty-four hours. He looked at the man on the other side of the laminated counter. Average height, not overweight, light brown hair, and what appeared to be a scar just below the right-side hairline.

"Professor Martin. Morning," said O'Leary, speaking with a nasal thickness usually associated with a boxer. "How can we help?"

"I've had no contact from my wife, so I'd like to report her officially as a missing person." Martin spoke with the clear enunciation of a practiced talker, the DC thought.

"I see. You'd better come through."

The DC sat opposite Martin in the interview room, a blank pad open on the table. Two chairs on either side made up the whole of the furnishings.

"When did you last see your wife?"

"Two days ago at an exhibition opening at the State Art Gallery."

"What exhibition was that?"

"An exhibition of Pissaro's paintings. It was a charity opening. The university often gets invitations and they're shared around amongst the departments. This was History's turn, my faculty"

"And you took your wife?"

Martin nodded. "Yes."

"What happened then?"

"After we arrived, we moved into the main reception hall where drinks and canapés were served. We each took a drink from the waiter and moved into the general melee. I saw a partner of the law firm that sponsors the exhibition. We chatted with several other people who had also just arrived before the Professor of Law from the university waved to me. I spoke briefly with him and to about three or four others. At some stage, my wife must have drifted off in a different direction. I'm not sure when. I didn't see her again."

O'Leary nodded, making notes on his pad. He paused briefly, then asked, "So how do you know all these lawyers if you're Professor of History?"

"I'm Professor of Medieval History. I studied Law and Medieval History at Sydney Uni. I actually practised law for a couple of years before realising it wasn't what I wanted. So I completed a History doctorate and eventually got a tenured teaching position at Sydney that allows enough time for research."

O'Leary nodded as he wrote. "Does your wife have family locally?"

"No. Her parents are both dead."

"What about friends?"

"I've rung several," Martin said, "and they haven't heard from her."

"Can you think of any reason why your wife may have gone away, sir?"

Jack Martin shook his head. "No."

"Do you have any children, sir?"

"Yes, a son, John. He's eighteen and completing his last year at school."

"Does your son live at home with you?"

"Yes. He left for school just before I came here."

O'Leary stood up and excused himself, leaving Martin alone in the small room with its sparse furniture.

Several minutes later the door opened and a tall man entered, followed by O'Leary. Martin could have mistaken him for a lecturer, until he noticed the eyes, penetrating and interrogatory. *A barrister.* "Professor Martin, this is Detective Sergeant Nic Rysakov," said O'Leary.

For the next fifteen minutes Martin explained to DS Rysakov the sequence of events leading to his wife's disappearance. Martin's initial impression of Rysakov as a barrister was reinforced during the interrogation. His deep, authoritative voice commanded attention. The DS asked few questions while listening intently, his gaze rarely leaving Martin's face.

"Do you have any idea where she might have gone?" he asked.

"No, none."

"Is it possible she may have had an accident on the way home?"

"We arrived together in our car, and I drove it home, alone."

"Could she have been given a lift home by someone else? Perhaps they had an accident," said the DS. "Have you checked any of the hospitals in the area?"

"Yes. I rang St. Vincent's and Royal North Shore. Both said they had no patients under the name of Martin."

"We'll check again. Sometimes the triage nurses are more concerned with patients' welfare than their names. It can take a little time for the paperwork to catch up. Are you aware of any friends or acquaintances who were at the Gallery and may have had a motor vehicle accident?"

"No, I haven't heard of any, but some I see only occasionally."

"It'd be helpful if you can give us the names of people who

were at the Gallery and knew you or your wife, and how they can be contacted, before you leave."

Martin nodded. "Someone must have seen her. There were a lot of people."

"You said you searched for your wife when you decided to leave the Gallery. Could you run through for me again what you did?"

"The function started at six thirty but we arrived at around seven. It was scheduled to end at nine and by eight thirty people were leaving. By that time, I'd had enough. You're expected to stay until the sponsors and gallery directors have their say," Martin said. "That's when I started to look for Alice. I walked around the floor where people were still talking and drinking before going downstairs to the exhibition. I thought she might still be viewing the paintings. She wasn't. I waited about ten minutes, thinking she might be in the ladies toilet, which is on that floor. Then I went back upstairs and asked several people I knew if they had seen her. None had. I went outside to see if she was waiting for me. When I came back in, I spoke to the attendant at the door to see whether anyone had been asking for me. By this time it was nearly nine o'clock and most people had left. I went downstairs again, but attendants were clearing the area so they could close for the night. I explained to one of the female attendants that I couldn't find my wife and asked her to check the toilet. She came back shaking her head. I had one last look around the entrance then collected my car and drove home. Alone."

"And when you arrived home, there was no one there?"

"Only my son."

"Did he ask where his mother was?"

"Yes. I told him she must have gone to stay with friends."

"Did he think it odd? Or was your wife in the habit of going to visit her friends late at night?"

"No, he didn't say anything. We all get on, but we're each busy in different ways. John plays a lot of sport and, of course, studies."

"What did you do then?"

"I stayed up for several hours waiting before finally going to bed."

The next question Rysakov asked, Martin had been expecting for some time. "Had you and your wife had an argument recently?"

He paused, measuring his reply. "No more than any married couple."

"You don't think she might have gone off in a huff over something?"

"Not really. Though, I suppose it's possible."

"If she did, where do you think she might have gone?"

"Probably to a girlfriend's or her uncle's."

"Her uncle?" asked O'Leary.

"He's not a relation really, just an old family friend who came to Australia with Alice when she emigrated. She always refers to him as 'Uncle Henry'."

"She didn't immigrate with her parents?"

"No. Henry told me he had given an undertaking to her parents. Before they died he agreed he would look after her until she married. Apparently the parents had talked about leaving Germany for Canada or Australia, so he brought her here," said Martin.

Rysakov cocked his eyebrow, the first show of emotion on an otherwise expressionless face. "Does she see her Uncle Henry often?"

"Every couple of weeks. Sometimes she stays overnight, most times not. He must be around eighty now, but still mobile, and his mind is still sharp."

"Do you also see him regularly?"

"No. I never warmed to him. At first I thought it was because I'd married Alice, but he never mellowed. I find him cold and distant. Soon after I met her, over twenty years ago, I asked about Henry. All she would say was that he was fulfilling an obligation. She always ended by saying he was too old and boring to talk about, so I lost interest," said Martin.

"Can you give us his details and the names and numbers of her friends?"

Martin nodded.

"You said to DC O'Leary that you thought some harm may have come to your wife," said Rysakov. "Why is that?"

"Well, she seems to have vanished without a trace. At least, I haven't been able to find any," he said. "None of her clothes are gone. No one I've spoken to has seen her since before the Pissaro exhibition." He paused. "Her handbag and wallet are still in her wardrobe, even her credit cards are still in her bag."

The Detective Constable sat silently, looking at Martin with a questioning gaze. "How would you describe your wife?" asked Rysakov, eventually. "What sort of person was she?"

Martin thought for a few moments, before saying, "Attractive, always stylish in her dress, without being flashy. She enjoyed a party, we both did. She liked travel, particularly overseas, although she sometimes got a little serious once we arrived."

"What do you mean?" Rysakov asked.

"Serious in an academic sense," Martin said. "Like she was investigating a primary research source and needed her wits about her."

"Did she do any research?"

"Nothing of consequence. I would usually arrange to view a primary medieval source document at a library in say, Prague, and that could take up most of the day, so Alice would go off on her own to visit a village with an historic building, or some such. The arrangement suited us both."

"Would you describe your wife as a happy person?" asked Rysakov.

"I think so, though not the laugh-out-loud type." Martin paused. "She's a complex person, not easy to get to know well. A bit like a book really. To understand the whole book, you need to master each chapter. I'm not sure anyone's ever reached the stage of understanding the full book. Nevertheless, we had a comfortable relationship."

After several minutes of prosaic questions about himself, his family and his work at the university, Martin exited the police station. He had the distinctly uneasy feeling they thought he was hiding something. Which, of course, he was.

As he drove his XJ6 Jaguar though the city, he once again reviewed what had happened on the night of the exhibition. He became so engrossed he narrowly missed a small city-runabout in front when it braked suddenly at a traffic light. For the first time since the night of the exhibition, he had a feeling there would be no speedy resolution and that Alice's disappearance could turn into something altogether more serious. He had watched enough TV news reports of missing persons, and endured countless formulaic police shows – *CSI Miami*, *Inspector Morse*, even the German one with the clever Alsatian, *Inspector Rex* – to realise he would soon become the prime suspect in her disappearance. The police always suspected a close relative, particularly the husband, especially one with motive.

And he certainly had motive.

3

Next morning Jack Martin drove west though the city and down Broadway as he had a hundred times before. At the end of Broadway he turned in through the university gates and gently accelerated the Jaguar up the sweeping curve of the approach drive. Despite the events of the past thirty-six hours, the sense of belonging and satisfaction that he'd found his place in the world settled over him like a soothing mantle. The century old mock-gothic sandstone buildings of Sydney University spoke of permanence and stability. All the modern glass and steel buildings of the city he had passed through seemed to hang off their grandeur. In Martin's mind all universities, especially this one, provided leadership to the society in which they resided. Without them, the world would be a less attractive, more chaotic place.

Alice could never appreciate, really appreciate, the pleasure and excitement he derived from studying medieval history, particularly original source documents, and the thrill of uncovering the importance of a neglected manuscript. In her opinion, this type of work was the preserve of post-graduate students. Lately, she had begun chiding that he was more at home among books and students than with his family. In many respects, she was right. What she didn't know, however, was the added pleasure he derived from seeing and working with Sophia. At least he hadn't thought she knew.

Today, as he walked across the manicured grass of the central sandstone quadrangle toward his office he still felt the same sense of security, yet it had changed. The harshness of the real world had intruded. Just that one event. He tried to imagine what he would make of a colleague whose wife had disappeared, vanished leaving no clue. Although he might not voice it, even to close friends, he would certainly not rule out the possibility of murder. How could he?

As yet, thankfully, nobody knew what had happened. That would not last for long. Very soon he would have to tell the faculty Alice was missing. Within twenty-four hours the whole campus would know. Gossip spread faster than knowledge within these walls. He sat at his desk, littered with journals, books and papers. The phone rang, and before he realised it, the day's business absorbed him. Later in the afternoon, two graduate students called in for discussions on the progress of research for their dissertation, and when the phone next rang, it was his son.

"Hi, Dad. Mum's not home yet. Have you heard from her?"

Martin glanced at his watch. It was nearly six p.m. With a twinge of guilt he realised he had not thought about his wife since the morning. Tonight he would have to tell John his mother had disappeared. He stared, unseeing, at a bookcase bulging with volumes, realising he had no idea how to explain such a thing to a teenager.

If she'd left of her own volition it was an indictment of their marriage, of him. If she'd left involuntarily, they could be looking at accidents, kidnapping (although he considered that too far-fetched for serious consideration), assault, rape, maybe even murder. No doubt the police would look at all possibilities. The more he thought about it, the less he liked the probable outcomes. Before long, he could expect to be the primary 'person of interest'.

He packed a file of papers into his briefcase and left the office for the staff car park.

Twenty minutes later, as he weaved through the city traffic towards the Harbour Bridge and the northern suburbs, he wondered how much John had heard of their recent arguing. It had not really been a row, more an accusation by his wife some weeks ago. For more than six months his affair with Sophia had been so trouble-free he had reached the stage where he assumed Alice knew and passively acquiesced. They had not been romantically close for a long time. Whether she had actually found out about the affair, or just suspected, he did not know.

She began by asking yet again why he often stayed late at night at the university? Then came the direct accusation, the first time she had ever made it: "Are you having an affair?"

"What do you mean?" he said, knowing that as he spoke he might just as well have admitted the affair right there and then. He couldn't meet her staring gaze. He didn't have to. He could feel the triumph in her eyes.

"It's one of those graduate students, isn't it? The Lebanese girl you're always staring at."

When he did not deny it she persisted.

"Isn't it against the university rules for professors to take advantage of their students?"

"She's not my student." He felt relief in the tacit admission. It had been foolhardy to believe that his wife would not find out. "She already has one degree and she's working as my research assistant, a job for which the university allows a small stipend to be paid. We hope to keep her on staff when she gets her PhD."

He knew it was lame as soon as he said it. She had blindsided him. Not only had he not seen it coming, in a rather juvenile way he had convinced himself she didn't mind, even that she didn't care. He didn't believe she was jealous; it was something else. No one likes being made to look a fool. So, why should she? Maybe that was it. On the other hand, perhaps Alice had a quite different agenda altogether. Just what that might be he had no idea.

"Does she have a name, this assistant?"

"Sophia Hamil." Her smooth olive skin, shoulder length hair and the way she smiled up at him, especially when he put his arms around her waist, flashed into his mind. He had to make an effort not to smile at the image.

After a moment's silence, she said, "What would you do if I had an affair?"

Funny she should say that, he had thought then. *Is she trying to provoke me?*

The possibility of Alice having a lover had crossed his mind a number of times over recent years. It had only been a vague suspicion, not based on hard evidence, and rather than face the issue and risk causing trouble he had brushed the thoughts away, subsuming his concerns into the banality of everyday work.

That was when she said: "Maybe we should separate."

As he replayed the exchange in his mind, he once again had the impression he was missing something. Could she be the one hiding a secret? One thing he had no doubt about, she had enjoyed the confrontation.

That evening at home, without being too dramatic, he tried to explain to John that his mother had gone missing at the Art Gallery. He explained that he had gone to the police to report her disappearance and that the police had originally told him most such cases were solved within a few days. However, she may have had an accident, perhaps fallen over and was suffering from temporary amnesia, or she may have gone to a girlfriend's house and thought she had told us.

When he had finished, John looked at him, a mixture of confusion and concern on his face. "Do you think something serious has happened to her?"

"I don't know. It's possible."

Later that night, when John was in his room, Jack Martin went into the study and rang Sophia.

The next day at the university Sophia sat, silent, after Jack explained in more detail, how his wife had disappeared. They were behind the closed door of his office and, as it was now nearly lunchtime, he could count on not being disturbed for another hour.

"I don't know how, but I think Alice has found out about us," he said.

Sophia looked at him and smiled, a smile he could only describe as sensual. "Do you think she's simply gone away somewhere to make a point?"

"Possibly, but I would have expected her to have contacted John."

She nodded.

"Initially the police seemed to think she would turn up at any moment. Each day without word they become more concerned."

"But surely nothing could have happened to her." Her dark brown eyes that smouldered in the passion of love-making now looked concerned.

"It's bizarre," Martin said. "We were at a function with a hundred and fifty people and she vanished, without a trace."

"But someone must have seen her. No one can simply ..." She struggled for the right English word. "...evaporate. What about the security cameras, or the attendants. Unless she slipped out with an Old Master under her coat."

Jack Martin never tired of hearing her voice. The accent, partly Arabic, partly European, had a delicious sensual sound. He recalled again the first time he saw Sophia, her flawless olive skin and thick chestnut hair tumbling over her shoulders. She had initially been assigned to him for guidance in the preparation of her doctoral dissertation after completing an honours degree in Medieval History. The Dean had told him, "She's very bright, someone we would be pleased to retain on staff if possible." She had been the first of the graduate students to meet with him. Immediately, she seemed different. Smartly dressed, she had style, in the way of the European models he had seen on TV. Maybe it was the way she moved. Perhaps it was the impression of sophistication, of culture; whatever the reason he could not take his eyes off her. Over the months following their first meeting, as they got to know each other more intimately, he began to get glimpses of other issues, of a confidence more fragile than expected, and of something else, something a less infatuated man may have seen as a warning.

They had not made love in the first month after meeting, but by late in the semester he began to anticipate her visits with ever increasing desire. At about that time he asked her to join him for a coffee. While they were talking he mentioned he had approval from the faculty to take on a part-time research assistant, as a paid position. When she enquired if he had anyone in mind he'd replied that he hoped she might be interested. With that luscious smile he enjoyed so much she immediately accepted. The extra money would be very helpful, she said, and she would enjoy working with him. Not long after they became lovers, and he had a colleague assigned as her supervisor.

He snapped out of the reverie. She had asked him a question.

"How has John reacted?" she repeated.

"At the moment, he expects Alice to call or just appear. Maybe it's denial, I don't know. Last night I tried to explain that it might be more serious. I'm not sure he understood the reality of what I was saying. That, maybe his mother would not be coming home again, ever."

4

Gases began escaping from the body, sour, nauseating and colourless; gases that had yet to reach human senses. More finely tuned noses, belonging to two bush rats, caught the aroma of decay nearly half a kilometre away. Now they sniffed cautiously as they surveyed the rotting flesh in the darkness. Blowfly and flesh-fly eggs had begun hatching, their maggots wriggling inside the cadaver, to begin feeding.

Mid-morning on the following day, when Jack Martin returned to his office between lectures, he found a message stuck on the telephone handset away from the paper storm on his desk: RING DS RYSAKOV.

"I'm afraid we have no news, Professor," Rysakov said when Martin phoned. "Would it be convenient if DC O'Leary and I came out to the university? There are a couple of matters we'd like to discuss. Won't take up much time."

Half an hour later the two detectives sat in the cluttered room of the medieval historian, O'Leary in the old style leather upholstered armchair and Rysakov in the straight backed refectory chair Martin had bought when the old university library was rebuilt. It seemed a natural choice for the Detective Sergeant, Martin figured: the DS would not have looked comfortable in an easy chair.

Rysakov glanced at the jumble of books, journals and papers on the desk. "Looks like nothing has changed since my day."

"I don't think any academic would feel comfortable without piles of books, but I can assure you there is method beneath the impression of madness. Each pile has a reason." Martin smiled. "Were you at this university?"

"I majored in Criminology but included a few units of History;

15

American and Modern European, not Medieval. I tried to make it as relevant to the real world as I could."

Martin nodded. "You'd be surprised how relevant to the present much of medieval history is, and how it can help explain why certain countries and regions are as they are."

"A confusing mess."

"Not so confusing if you understand the history. Although I must say, understanding it does not make one particularly optimistic on the prospects for a solution. Take Israel and Palestine, for instance."

"I assume you haven't heard from your wife?" Rysakov said, getting back to the point of the visit.

"No," replied Martin, disappointed. For one brief moment he had hoped the policeman, as a fellow graduate in history, might have been interested in a discussion.

"Have you had any new ideas about where she might be, or where she may have gone? Could she have gone to a favourite holiday spot, or maybe overseas?" said Rysakov.

"No, her passport is still where we keep them. I checked. Other than going to see one of her friends or Uncle Henry, I can't think of anywhere she might have gone. It's bizarre."

Rysakov glanced at O'Leary.

"We're contacting the list of people who knew you and your wife and who were at the Art Gallery on the night. It would help if we had a recent photograph," Rysakov said.

"I don't have one here but I'll find one tonight and drop it off tomorrow."

"If it's not inconvenient, we'll call in tonight and collect it. Would six p.m. be alright?"

"Ah... yes, that would be fine," Martin said, realising the detectives were going to be knocking on his front door whether he liked it or not.

"Have you told your colleagues here?"

"No, not yet. I'll advise the Dean today. I've been hoping it wouldn't be necessary."

"That would be wise. At some stage the story is bound to be

picked up by the media and it's generally best if one's employer knows in advance what's happening."

Fifteen minutes later, Rysakov and O'Leary walked across the grass of the quadrangle outside the History Department, under the sculptured stone arch, and out of the university buildings.

"What do you think of our Professor, Nic? Do you think he had anything to do with his wife's disappearance?" O'Leary asked.

"I'm not sure. If he did he's a cool customer. At this stage I'm prepared to give him the benefit of the doubt. But only just. If it was your wife who was missing I reckon you'd be a bit more emotional about it," Rysakov said.

"Yeah. It probably doesn't mean a lot, but he didn't have a photo of his wife or his son on the desk. In fact, when you asked him for a photo he didn't have one in the room at all."

"Yes, I noticed. And he doesn't wear a wedding ring."

Later that afternoon, as the unmarked police Commodore crawled north in the heat through the peak hour traffic, Rysakov wondered what his great-grandfather would have made of modern police work. When you stripped out the advances in technology, there probably wasn't much difference. It always came down to people.

Years ago, in primary school, he had stormed home one day and demanded to know why he only had one grandfather. All the other boys in the class had two, so where were his? Later that night, his father told him for the first time the history of his family. Over the years he filled in more details in conversations with his father and an aunt in London.

His great-grandfather had been an Investigator, or Detective Inspector, in the civil police force of Imperial Russia. It had been he who solved the notorious 'Monster of Moscow' murders.

"Your grandfather, my father, was named Pavel. When the Communists took control of Russia after the Revolution many senior members of the old police force were dismissed or imprisoned. Your great grandfather, Maksim, had to flee. His son, Pavel, was arrested and kept in prison for six years. When Pavel left prison he tried to find his father but soon decided, if he were to survive, he must leave Russia. He eventually escaped to France. In Paris he met and married Danielle who was my mother," his father had said. "A beautiful and elegant lady. She came to visit us when you were about four-years old."

Rysakov could not remember his grandmother but had seen photographs of her. Elegant described her perfectly.

"When the Nazis invaded Poland," his father had continued, "we left France for London. Pavel volunteered joining the Special Operations Executive, the SOE, because of his fluency in four languages. He parachuted into France many times on secret missions and was killed one of the last missions before the end of the war."

O'Leary parked the Commodore outside a modern metal and glass house in one of the many tree-lined cul-de-sacs of Northbridge, interrupting Rysakov's thoughts. "We're here."

They stepped on to the front porch and O'Leary pressed the doorbell button. Jack Martin was expecting them. He led them down the hall and into the sitting room where a tall, broad-shouldered teenager stood in the doorway to a dining area. Nic remembered his own awkwardness at that age and felt sympathy for the boy.

"This is my son, John," said Martin as he introduced the two policemen. John regarded them with a mixture of curiosity and embarrassment.

"You live in a quiet, leafy suburb," Rysakov said as they sat down. In fact, it was so quiet he couldn't hear anything at all from outside, not even a crow cawing or a neighbour's car. "It must be a pleasure to come home to after the noise of the city."

"Yes, a bit of a haven. Although we're under one of the flight paths to Sydney Airport, so it's not as quiet as you may think Detective."

"This heat makes me thirsty," said O'Leary, standing up and facing the Martin boy. "Do you think you could show me how to get myself a drink of water, John?" he asked before the boy's father could say anything, and headed towards the doorway where the teenager stood.

"Sure," said John and disappeared toward the back of the house with O'Leary.

"I'll go and get the photograph for you," said Martin.

Left alone, Rysakov turned his attention to the room. It was comfortably furnished, if a little sparse. On one of the walls, at right angles to the window, hung a large plasma TV screen. Not as big as his own, Rysakov estimated, but adequate. Opposite the TV sat two couches upholstered in modern design, large floral patterns, one in shades of pewter, the other a burnished red.

Quite tasteful, he thought. It looked as though a woman with a decorator's touch had been in control but had to compromise her artistic flair, allowing the inclusion of a series of eclectic pieces like the New Guinea ceremonial mask with a snarling face and bone teeth. There were several other odd pieces and a strange metal sculpture that reminded Rysakov of a tortured soul writhing in anguish.

The detritus of the intellectual, he thought, as the professor returned to the room with a single photograph in hand.

"Alice didn't like her photo taken. This is the only one I have. It's a few years old."

Rysakov looked at the picture, showing a group of six at a social function.

"That's Alice," Martin said, pointing to a woman with blond hair. Rysakov saw an attractive woman, not remarkable, of average height, and a shapely figure. She could have been any one of the thirty-to-forty year olds frequenting the local shopping centres or cafés in Bondi Junction, Mosman, or in fact any suburb in and around Sydney, he thought.

"May we keep this? It'll be returned when we no longer need it."

"Certainly."

Rysakov paused, keeping his gaze fixed on the historian. His experience in law-enforcement had shown there were layers to reality, each progressively exposing harsher and rawer truths. At times this could be so confronting the person under interrogation might recall an event that threw new light on an investigation. At the other extreme it could, very occasionally, lead to an admission. He certainly didn't expect such a result here and now. On the other hand, he knew as well as any police officer that people were predictably unpredictable.

Then he said, "Where was the photo taken?"

"A university reunion dinner."

"Who is the man standing next to your wife?"

Martin looked at the photo.

"Oh, that's Clive Nestor. He and I worked together in the same legal firm before I joined the university. He left some years later to run an investment bank. Been very successful, I believe. Made a lot of money on the stock market. So he says."

"He seems to know your wife," said Rysakov, looking at the photograph. The man he now knew as Nestor had his arm around Alice Martin, his hand just under her breast. She looked relaxed and seemed to be leaning back towards him.

"They knew each other at university. They were a bit of an item for a short time before I met Alice," Martin said.

"What happened in your wife's childhood to give her a dislike of being photographed?"

"I never really got a satisfactory answer. She spent her early years in and around Prague, before the Communist regime collapsed. She was always a bit vague about it and said it brought back unpleasant memories. She got angry if I pressed it," said Martin. "Her mother was Russian, died just before they came out to Australia. Her father was Czech, I think, didn't look at all like her, she said. She took after her mother. Her father disappeared not long after she was born.

"She used to say she didn't photograph well and could get quite miffed with anyone trying to take her picture. Neither of us is into family photos, so it wasn't really an issue."

At that moment DC O'Leary and John Martin came back into the room.

"Great deck you have out the back, Professor," said O'Leary. "I could see myself sitting out there sliding into the evening with an ice cold beer on a day like today. Thanks for the glass of water, John," he added.

Rysakov stood up. "Thank you for the photograph, Professor. We'll be in touch as soon as we have any news."

As O'Leary drove the unmarked Commodore out of the cul-de-sac, Rysakov asked how he went with the Martin boy.

"Interesting. We chatted about his school, one of the expensive private ones, and sport; he's a keen rugby player. Then he asked me if we were going to find his mother. I told him we were doing our best and would continue working until she was found," said O'Leary. "That was when he asked, 'Did she leave because of the argument about Dad's graduate student?'"

Rysakov looked up from the photo.

"He said he'd heard his parents arguing about the professor having an affair with one of his students. He couldn't hear the name. Apparently this wasn't the first time they'd argued about his work. His mother often complained the professor spent too much time with his students. The kid's a bit confused. He can see his comfortable home unravelling and doesn't know what will happen then."

Do we have a motive here? wondered Rysakov, then filled O'Leary in on his conversation with the professor.

As the Commodore turned into the station, O'Leary said, "One other thing. Did we know Alice Martin worked for a company called ICI? It apparently invents and develops new industrial compounds and biotech products. John said she had always worked in the high tech industry. He was a bit vague about what she did there. One thing he was certain of was her computer skills. She's 'awesome', he said."

5

Sophia Hamil felt unsettled. She could hear the sounds inside her head again, words in that strange language, a tongue as ancient as the walls surrounding the village of her ancestors. She gently placed the fragile manuscript on the desk holding it with special cotton gloves for protection. She stared once more at the stained glass window of the Rare Book & Manuscript library. The soft gold hues of the old sandstone provided the perfect atmosphere for researching ancient documents. Several hundred meters away, the main library now resided in a huge purpose-built modern building, functional and without charm.

When she first heard of Alice Martin's disappearance her mind had filled with heady anticipation. Now she would have Jack Martin all to herself. She wanted him. She wanted his status. She wanted the security his money would provide. She would have her own children with him, she was sure of that. Last month she had stopped taking contraceptive pills; an unexpected pregnancy would force his hand. Recently, more so than in the past, she found herself imagining how their children would look: their mix of Mediterranean and Anglo complexion, his height, her dark hair and eyes; they'd be beautiful.

Wonderful possibilities ran through her mind until she realised, unless certainty existed as to Alice Martin's whereabouts, nothing could happen. The police were now treating Alice as a missing person. Did they think she was dead?

The yellow parchment manuscript lay unrolled on the desk in front of her. Above, the stained glass glowed as the mid-afternoon sun blazed behind it. She stared at it. In the intense light the figures in the glass began to shimmer and come alive. She had seen them before, the same figures. If she waited they would tell her what they wanted, they always did.

As she stared, bright beams from the afternoon sun pierced

the gloom of the old library, creating a glowing cocoon of light around her. The blue glass of the window dissolved into the endless, deep blue desert sky of northern Syria. The noble gold morphed into distant sand dunes. The Apostles became travellers. As she watched, they shook the sand from their white robes and headed towards the outline of an ancient city, the eleventh century Aleppo. On the horizon, the imposing silhouette of the city castle loomed fifty metres above the rest of the buildings. The travellers warily approached the city walls. The foreigners were non-believers. The men in robes on the other hand, were Believers and *Ismailis*, followers of 'The Old Man of the Mountain'. They were assassins and had no fear.

They spoke ancient Aramaic, the language of the time of Jesus, yet Sophia somehow understood their conversation. How, she did not know. Perhaps it was the language of dreams and visions. The assassins reached the door of a walled, two-storey villa in the city and knocked three times. The door opened almost immediately. Without doubt they were expected. They were shown into a cool, airy room looking onto a garden with date palms and fig trees. A fountain trickled water into a rectangular pond the size of an Isfahan tribal rug. The crisp tinkle of falling water filled the room with calmness.

A striking woman, her head partially covered with the customary *hijab*, entered the room and greeted the two men. Sophia knew this in itself was most unusual. For the woman to be alone, even in her own home, the meeting must be of great importance or delicacy.

After an exchange in which each treated the other with customary elaborate courtesy, they sat on cushions arranged to face the garden. Refreshments were offered before they broached the purpose of the meeting. Sophia strained to hear the conversation, something concerning the volatile political situation in Aleppo.

Finally, the woman said (and Sophia could now discern her every word), "I have recently had my husband secretly followed, and I have proof he is having an affair with a married woman whose husband is of a family who support the Seljuq caliph in Baghdad. I am told the woman is one of my husband's relations. This double betrayal brings dishonour on our families. If a solution to this problem could be found a property of particular interest to your leader would become available."

The two men remained silent for several moments before the taller of them spoke. His voice commanded attention. It was not much above a whisper, but had an accent as harsh and as sharp as the sand blown by the Sirocco, the desert wind.

"The Seljuq do not recognise the Twelfth Imam," he said. "It is truly said they do not show respect for the Qur'an or the true interpretation of Sharia."

"The family of whom you speak represent the Seljuq in the city," the other man said, in an equally harsh voice.

The woman nodded agreement.

There followed a lengthy discussion, which, to her frustration, Sophia failed to hear well enough to discern. Why she could hear some parts of the conversation and not others she did not know. Then, without warning, she could once more hear with clarity.

"Will Hassan Il-Ghazi attend the banquet?" asked the taller man.

The woman nodded.

The two men rose from the cushions and prepared to take their leave. As they did they turned their hawk-like visages and looked directly at Sophia. She gasped. The leader raised his finger, pointed at her and nodded. Sophia heard her name called, in the distance. For an instant she panicked. Of course they knew she was there, they always did. But they'd never before spoken directly to her.

"Sophia!"

The images of the *Ismailis* and the garden faded. She turned her head. The Head Librarian stood at the end of the desk trying to get her attention. Sophia no longer worried about other people seeing her visions. No one could.

"The library is closing and all manuscripts must be returned to their cabinets," the librarian said, exasperated at calling the young woman's name for nearly a minute. She turned and began tidying the next table.

"Sorry, I was miles away," Sophia said, handing the one-page document across with gloved hands. As she did she took one last look at the section she had been reading, a fragmentary document that was little more than a gossipy letter from an unknown writer in Aleppo to a merchant in Damascus. It was one of the original source documents the University had secured through bequests. It had been dated as coming from the twelfth century, the period she was researching.

> *'And Hassan Il-Ghazi did not return to his wife and his bodyguards were not seen again. You will be surprised to hear that his family wealth was less than was expected.'*

She quickly scanned down to the end of the single page, and there it was:

> *'Shihab al-Din, the vizier, was attacked and stabbed while he travelled. They are blaming the Old Man of the Mountains.'*

As she walked from the library she had difficulty focussing on the real world. The visions had happened before, but never had they pointed to her and beckoned. It must mean something.

"It's just my imagination," she said out loud.

The words sounded hollow, echoing in the cloisters of the quadrangle. Not even she was convinced. She now felt certain Hassan Il-Ghazi had been murdered by the two men of the desert, the assassins. That she had witnessed his wife commission the crime disturbed her deeply.

At the staff car park she sat in her blue Nissan Micra with the engine running, trying to make sense of the vision. *This is fanciful.* She shook her head and drove out the University gates onto Broadway. As she edged her way through the outward bound peak hour traffic, the images and voices of the vision remained. The conversation in Aleppo replayed over and over again through her mind. Was it possible assassins from nearly one-thousand years ago were communicating with her, trying to tell her something, something critical about the future?

It was ludicrous. She had been hallucinating. That was the only logical answer. Thirty-minutes later, she parked the car and went inside her unit, deep in thought. That night she found it difficult to concentrate. She tried reading, she turned on the television, she listened to her iPod; nothing seemed to work.

As the hours passed her anxiety gradually diminished, although she still saw the words and heard the voices. This had been worse than the first time, far worse. She had an inescapable feeling she was heading toward a critical point. The fact that the vision remained in her head must mean that they would tell her what had to be done. Why else would they stay there? Was it connected to the first time? What had happened that first time?

She had no recollection. It was a blank in her mind. If only she could recall what had happened. No matter how hard she tried, all that came to mind was an image of her grandma, a thunderous expression on her face. Yet all these years later, that same image of Grandma sprang in her mind whenever the visions appeared. How could Grandma be involved?

"Grandma was dead four years before the first time," Sophia said out loud to the empty bedroom.

She had never felt so alone, so scared.

6

DC O'Leary parked the Commodore outside the apartment block and placed a POLICE sign against the windscreen to discourage any overzealous parking attendant. Rysakov got out of the car. He found it puzzling that they still had nothing to indicate where Alice Martin might be, or what might have happened to her. And that included the three interviews so far that day.

The apartment was on the wrong side of the first floor, as far as he was concerned. No harbour view. Martin had told them that the woman who opened the door was now single. Ann Stratton, a university friend of Alice Martin, had a divorcee's cynical twist on life. She ushered them into the living room, a room with a view over the street and the unmarked police car.

"Alice was convinced Jack was having an affair. And she was right, I can tell you from experience, Detective Sergeant," she said. "My ex-husband acted as though sugar wouldn't melt in his mouth while all the time lying about the affair with his lawyer-lady."

Rysakov ignored her glance of appraisal. He saw her check the absence of a wedding ring on his finger, then give him the once over, crotch to crown. He knew what she was thinking, her expression said it all. Well, she would never know. "Did she tell you who he was having the affair with?" he asked.

"Some young Lebanese graduate student, I don't know her name. No doubt honey-coloured skin unblemished by childbirth, and big tits. Why is it that all men are drawn to big tits?" Rysakov could not resist a passing glance at Ann Stratton's well-endowed chest as he glanced down at his notebook. Her silk blouse had one too many buttons undone revealing a cleavage that promised much. From the corner of his eye he could see the direction of O'Leary's gaze too. He decided to change the subject.

"Were you at the Pissaro Exhibition where Alice Martin was last seen?"

"No, I'm not into art. I'm more at home at a rock concert." She said this with a touch of defiance which Rysakov ignored.

"Did you know Professor Martin at university?"

"In passing. In those days he was an interesting man, studying Law. If he'd continued as a lawyer he'd be earning a decent income by now, like Clive Nestor. Alice thought about marrying Clive, and then Jack turned up. At the time they married he wasn't a history professor. I told her it was false pretences. It was a huge drop in income for her."

"Did this cause any problems?"

"Strangely, no. Alice didn't seem particularly motivated by money. Can't understand why, doesn't seem sensible." She paused. "Yet she never appeared to be short of a dollar."

"What do you mean?"

"If we were all going to the theatre, Alice would buy a ticket. She never missed a new outfit for an important function. And they went overseas every year. But she wasn't into frivolous expenditure, if you know what I mean. Maybe that's how she made ends meet."

Ann Stratton stared out the window toward the street as if contemplating her explanation and finding it lacking. Rysakov didn't know whether this was relevant or not, so let it go.

"She said Jack suited her better, whatever that meant," she added.

"Can you think of anywhere she may have gone, perhaps for some time out, to think through her future maybe?"

"Not really," said Ann Stratton. "She might have gone to the beach, she loved the ocean, but I'm sure she would have rung someone to let us know."

There was a brief silence while the policemen waited. Rysakov did not think the last statement sounded as convincing as Stratton intended.

She looked from one policeman to the other. "You're worried, aren't you?"

"If you have any ideas please call me," said Rysakov, handing her a card with his contact details.

As they left the apartment toward the car, O'Leary said, "Sounds like we should pay a visit to this Clive Nestor sooner than later. Not only did he know Alice Martin, he was also on the list of people at the Exhibition."

Rysakov nodded. "Let's do it tomorrow. If he says he's too busy tell him we can meet in his office, his home or at the station. That usually focuses the attention."

7

The smell now made it impossible to miss. An early morning jogger, training for the Port Macquarie Triathlon, ran into what might as well have been the pain barrier. The putrid stench of rotting flesh hung like a curtain in the still air. He stopped as the first lung-full hit his senses. Involuntarily, he sucked in deeply to catch his breath, immediately knowing it was a mistake. He gagged and vomited.

Within an hour, local police, homicide detectives, a forensic unit, and a body recovery vehicle were at the scene, cordoning the area, preparing to remove the body and combing the immediate surrounds for evidence. Soon thereafter, media choppers hovered overhead and local television reporters scrummed for information on the body.

The office of Nestor, Nankervis & Co. on the fiftieth level of the MLC Centre had panoramic views over the sparkling blue water of Sydney Harbour. Even this early in the day yachts chased each other across the ruffled surface, weaving between ferries and container ships.

Rysakov and O'Leary had to wait ten minutes before Nestor, overweight and expensively dressed in suit and tie, came into the board room, still talking to someone they could not see. The impression was unmistakable: a successful businessman whose time was money; a man who commanded the sort of power women found seductive, despite the flabby stomach, balding scalp and double-chin.

"Gentlemen," he said, with the supreme self-confidence of a successful lawyer. Before he sat at the board table he made a point of glancing at his watch. Rysakov noticed the gesture. The watch looked expensive, maybe a Breitling, but it wouldn't tell the time any different from his digital Swatch. Regardless of what Nestor wanted, the interview would be over when he said so.

After introducing themselves, Rysakov said, "I understand you know Alice Martin."

"Yes, since university. Why?"

"She hasn't been seen or made contact with her family for about a week," said Rysakov. "We're contacting people who knew her to see if they can shed any light on where she might be." He paused before adding, "I understand you were at the official opening of the Pissaro Exhibition recently."

"Yes, along with a hundred or so others."

"Do you remember seeing Alice Martin there?"

Nestor thought for a moment. "I spoke to Jack, her husband, for a while. We used to work at the same legal firm many years ago. I assumed Alice was there but I can't say I recall seeing her." Nestor looked from one to the other. "Surely you're not saying no one saw her?"

"We're just trying to build a picture of that night."

Nestor stared out the window. "Amazing," he said, shaking his head.

"Why do you say that, sir?" asked O'Leary.

"Well, Detective, over one hundred people, a number of who would at least have met Alice, yet no one saw her? Wouldn't that mean she wasn't there?"

"Was the Exhibition a busy affair?"

"It was like any of these cocktail functions, a lot of people milling around in the forecourt area. All the sponsor's clients trying to throw down as many free drinks as they can before they have to go and pontificate about the art most of them know nothing about, and care even less about. So, to answer your question, yes it was busy."

"Did you see many people you knew there?"

"Yes, and I daresay missed talking to a number of others," Nestor said, before glancing at his watch again.

Rysakov nodded, ignored the gesture and tried a different approach. "You have magnificent offices here, sir. What exactly does Nestor, Nankervis & Co. do?"

"We're investment bankers. We advise clients on takeovers and mergers, we provide seed capital to help new enterprises grow, manage a hedge fund and sponsor IPOs." He saw the blank look on O'Leary's face. "IPOs: Initial Public Offers. Raising money for companies to list on the stock exchange," he said. "In fact I'm in the middle of one as we speak, so if there are no more questions I need to get back to work." Nestor stood up to indicate that, so far as he was concerned, the interview was at an end.

"One last thing, sir," Rysakov said before Nestor could escape. "What sort of person was Alice Martin?"

Nestor sighed and leaned against the wall. "Attractive. Great sex. We had a brief fling at university, though by the time we graduated the affair was over. She was ambitious. She liked status and position. She actively cultivated contacts that might be useful to her in the future. Funny thing though, she didn't seem motivated by money."

"Have you seen her since that time?"

Nestor glanced at his watch again, irked by the continued questioning. "Sure, from time to time. It was generally at functions like the art exhibition or lunches. We move in different circles."

"Were you and Professor Martin friends?"

"Not particularly. I generally only see him at functions," Nestor said.

"Are you married, sir?"

"Briefly, some years ago. It cost me a fortune. I won't make that mistake again. Look, Alice is an attractive woman, perhaps she got bored with academia, which wouldn't be hard, and ran off with someone more exciting. Have you checked with her employer? She told me some time ago that she travelled for them. She went overseas every year, maybe she went to scientific meetings or conferences."

O'Leary chipped in: "Do you mean her present employer?"

"Yes, International Compounds Inc., a bio-tech company. We raised some development funding for it a year ago on Alice's introduction. Has some very exciting intellectual property with rumours of a new breakthrough."

Nestor looked at his watch once again. Rysakov remained seated as if thinking. He did not move for a full minute, knowing it would seem like an eternity to the businessman. When he figured the message 'treat the police seriously and with respect' had been received he stood up. Nestor remained at the opposite end of the board table. He made no effort to show the police officers out. This was his domain.

Unmoved by the gamesmanship Rysakov turned towards Nestor. "Thank you for your time, Mr Nestor. If you remember anything else please give me a call," he said, placing a contact card on the table.

As they walked across Castlereagh Street to their car, O'Leary said, "Not particularly friendly. I wouldn't like to get between him and a dollar."

Rysakov nodded. "He needs to make a load of money to support an ego like that."

8

On the top level of the five-storey art deco apartment block, Warren Kay watched as the girl put the money into her purse. She said she was eighteen but he knew she would be three or four years younger, as he had requested. She performed well so he gave her a bonus. He liked to watch the young ones, with their unblemished nearly matured bodies. His father had preferred them even younger.

Kay stood on his balcony, looking at the spectacular city skyline in the early evening. He never tired of the backdrop formed by the sails of the Sydney Opera House and the graceful curves of the Harbour Bridge. If, for some unforeseen reason, he no longer had the view he knew he would sorely miss it.

He poured another glass of wine and put his feet on the chair opposite, stretching his long legs as his mind drifted back two years.

A run-in with a female lawyer, although costing him money at the time, had shown him a way to make spectacular amounts of money. And it was all legal. It pointed him in the direction of investment bankers and corporate dealers. The woman lawyer had caused the failure of the property deal he was pushing for. He couldn't remember her name. Anyway, she was dead now, therefore irrelevant. Once he had successfully retrieved his capital out of the deal, it had taken another six months before he understood what investment bankers really did. When you reduced it to its essentials, and cut away all the crap, it was very basic.

He shook his head in wonder. Investment bankers had money, and put it into businesses and deals. That simple. Where or how they got the money no one cared. It might be borrowed, managed on behalf of other people, joint ventured, and some, a really small amount, would be their own. What made these guys so wealthy, he discovered, were the fees, particularly the success fees, which they kept for themselves. The leverage was so spectacular he decided he had to get a slice of the action. For every dollar they risked, they stood to make more than ten times that amount. Even 'risk' was a relative term. It being something they managed to ensure the possibility of loss, to them, remained minimal.

In addition to his money, Kay had another asset. A talent no other investment banker possessed; and this made him truly unique. If a deal did not work because the parties genuinely misjudged the market, well, that was business. However, if the deal did not work for the wrong reason, for instance, if someone reneged on an agreement, and Warren Kay did not make the profit he expected, or actually lost money, then someone had to pay. His philosophy was simple: either he got his money or the guilty party paid the penalty. It's not personal, just business, he liked to say. But when someone crossed Warren Kay it became personal. He considered murder nothing more than the ultimate tool for making money. He rarely killed for any other reason. Yet Kay believed in flexibility.

Where capital and profit are concerned, nothing can be ruled out.

His workout before the girl arrived, including half an hour in the ring kick-boxing, had left him relaxed. He sipped the wine and applied his mind to what might be the emergence of a problem with one of his first investment banking investments; Nestor, Nankervis & Co. When the investment bank over-stretched its commitments he had been fortunate to be in the right place at the right time. He had agreed to provide the funds and negotiated a tough deal, one very profitable for Warren Kay.

All appeared to be going well, until the last few weeks, when he began picking up worrying vibes from Nestor, Nankervis & Co. Little things. Like a luncheon for select co-investors cancelled at the last minute; Nestor postponing a skiing holiday in Europe; long meetings behind closed doors; scuttlebutt and rumours in the financial market. Nothing specific mind you, maybe nothing at all, nevertheless he felt a developing sense of unease.

Tomorrow he would speak plainly to Nestor. Very plainly. He would leave the wanker under no misapprehension. If Nestor Nankervis had a problem, he wanted to know what it was. Now.

9

The next day Rysakov, O'Leary and two other detectives assigned to the Alice case assembled in one of the small briefing rooms at Police HQ at Redfern. With the peak period for summer holidays approaching, getting access to manpower was going to become more challenging. Uniformed officers had been co-opted to contact the less promising prospects to account for their movements on the night and to enquire if they had seen Alice Martin at the Exhibition, or anywhere else. Anything of interest was immediately referred to Rysakov. On the desk in front of him lay a file with a summary of the results to date.

Once the officers settled, Rysakov started. "Time to review what we've got."

He knew they were all experienced officers. They knew the procedure. They all knew that without a reasonable lead, the scope of the investigation would be wound down and manpower re-directed to the next high priority. So far this was not a case of each lead going nowhere. They had no leads at all.

"All the persons on the lists provided by Professor Martin, those he and his wife knew and who were at the exhibition, as well as the list of Alice Martin's friends and relatives, have been contacted, either by us or uniform. The result – we've drawn a blank. No one saw her. No one can even suggest where she might have gone.

"In fact, no one at the exhibition can positively remember seeing her there at all. One couple said they may have seen her, but as they were talking to a range of people they can't be certain. The clothes she was wearing, according to her husband, were a navy blue skirt, a cream blouse and a navy blue matching jacket. Hardly the sort of outfit that burns an impression in one's memory. The attendants can't remember either of the Martin's arriving. However, two remember the professor searching for his wife. One when she searched the ladies toilets and the other at the entry when he asked if his wife had left a message for him."

"What about the CCTV?" asked one of the detectives.

"We've been through them. No luck," Rysakov said. "If she was there she didn't look at the security cameras. In any event these cameras are there primarily to spot anyone trying to steal a painting. We'll run through them again, but it's not looking promising."

"Any luck with the friends and relatives?" another asked.

"Most of the people we contacted haven't heard from her since a couple of days before the exhibition. Most said she sounded normal, although several said they got the impression she was bit more tense than usual. They don't know what about. It could have been she'd found out her husband was having an affair with one of his students.

"One of her friends, Ann Stratton, said Alice was upset about the professor 'seducing', her description, one of his students. Some of them suggested a couple of places she might have gone and we're checking them out. I'm not particularly optimistic about any of them. The next step will be to go public and publish her photo."

He took the photo of Alice Martin off the white board.

"So far this is the only photo we have. Unless we get another, this is how everyone will remember Alice Martin."

10

Before Ryssakov left the station that afternoon he heard reports of a body in bushland off the Wakehurst Parkway, in the Manly Dam Water Reserve. He tuned into the twenty-four hour news radio as he drove through the city. It, and the latest footballer sex-scandal, made the lead items.

"A badly decomposed body has been discovered in Sydney's north. It is believed to be that of a woman although the police spokeswoman would not confirm this," the news reader said.

Rysakov made a mental note to follow-up the body in the morning. By that time forensics should know the sex, approximate age and time of death. If the basics matched he would get a DNA sample from the son. Perhaps Alice Martin would be found faster than he expected. If so, Homicide in their size twelves, would take over.

Rysakov walked under the sandstone arch of the State Art Gallery entrance for the second time that month. The first had been with Tom O'Leary before it opened for the day, not long after the professor reported his wife as a missing person. They had been more interested in seeing the foyer area, where the function had been held. This time, he went as a member of the public, to view the actual exhibition. Whether it would give him any fresh ideas he didn't know.

The grandeur of the foyer architecture impressed him once again. The colonial masters who built the original gallery over one hundred years ago clearly intended to make an impact, if not intimidate. For a brief moment he felt uncomfortable. Never having had much interest in art, he knew little about it.

If art becomes relevant to the investigation I'll be asking the questions, he thought, and relaxed. The cool constant-temperature of the Gallery provided instant relief to the hot humid air outside. *I think I'll like art just for the air-con*, he thought.

Looking around the foyer he could see why it was the perfect space for a meet and greet. He could easily imagine a hundred and fifty people talking, drinking and eating hors d'oeuvres. At least double that number could fit into the area, but, as had been explained to him by the manager, for smaller functions they cordoned off the rear portion of the room.

As he walked down the steps to the exhibition salons on the floor below he scanned upwards to find the security cameras. He located one. The others were not so easy to spot. They were there, he assumed, but discreetly placed.

"The main focus of security is on the art works themselves, of course," the manager had explained on his first visit. "The exits from the gallery are all alarmed, as are all the exhibits. Even exits you wouldn't imagine existed, including the air conditioning ducts."

He glanced at the back of the eight-page guide that came with the entry ticket. There were over one hundred pictures in the exhibition, arranged in chronological order to show the evolution of technique and style. Surprisingly, he found the exhibition fascinating, soon becoming absorbed, drifting along at the pace of the crowd.

As he walked through he identified the only exit at the end of the exhibition. That, and the way in, appeared properly secure. If Alice Martin had viewed the paintings, there were only two ways out.

Ergo, she must have been caught on camera, he thought. *Or she wasn't here.*

Yet, on the first two runs of the CCTV tapes they had seen no sign of her. He needed someone who knew her well to view the tapes.

As he neared the end of the exhibition he noticed that Pissaro had begun to paint city views and industrial landscapes in which static features were transformed by bustling crowds. Standing in front of the painting of a busy market town, *Rue de L'Epicerie, Rouen 1898*, he realised what fascinated him about these later paintings. All the figures were amorphous. They disappeared into the background. The buildings seemed to devour the stream of shoppers as they left the market. There could be no argument a large number of people attended the markets. Yet none could be identified, or needed to be. The artist had successfully conveyed the impression of a vibrant market town. He smiled: *Hence 'The Impressionists'.* Another thought begun to take shape in his mind. Perhaps Alice *had* been at the exhibition as the professor claimed.

The rear exit was via a one-way escalator up to the entrance floor. As he walked to the escalator he noticed a carpenter wearing a hard-hat and with a tool belt around his waist coming from an area to the rear. On impulse he caught up with the man.

"What's going on at the back?" he asked.

"They're building an extension over on the left hand side. It's a couple of stories high. There was talk about going lower into the sandstone when the freeway is extended, but that won't happen for years, mate," the carpenter said.

"How do they stop dust and noise getting into the gallery?" said Rysakov, fascinated that there was no hint of construction work from inside.

"There's a false wall over there," he said, pointing behind the escalator. "All the noisy, dirty work is done outside the gallery walls. When it's finished and the external walls are secure and weatherproof we connect it up and demolish the internal walls. We had a big concrete pour about a week ago to hold the new steel floor supports. We've had fans going flat out ever since to stop the moisture in the concrete getting into the gallery. Buggers up the art, apparently."

"What about security?"

"Nah, mate. The outer walls are alarmed and they turn the cameras on when we leave, and they've got guards there all day." As he turned away the carpenter said, "If you want to test the security try getting out that way during the day." With that he continued walking towards a door marked NO ADMITTANCE.

Rysakov had no intention of testing the gallery security, pleased it was not his responsibility.

By the time he exited the exhibition he figured the most obvious explanation remained that Alice Martin had not, in fact, attended the gallery on the night of her disappearance. So, if she wasn't at the function, where was she while her husband was here? More importantly, what had happened to her? If Jack Martin wasn't telling the truth, what were his motives?

There is, however, he thought as he walked out of the gallery, *one possibility, that hasn't been investigated yet. One with a motive.*

11

Next morning Rysakov called the head pathologist at the city morgue.

"The body arrived in late yesterday," said the pathologist. "As I told the detective in charge, if you want a faster analysis, find the bodies faster." Rysakov heard a slight chuckle at the other end of the phone. A standard pathology lab joke, he figured. Nevertheless, he laughed. He wanted cooperation.

"All I can tell you now is that the body is female. She was naked, which almost certainly suggests homicide considering where she was found. The detailed autopsy will reveal all the usual data such as time, manner and place of death."

"She didn't die there then?"

"I had a quick look at the crime scene report. Very unlikely."

"Do you intend doing a DNA analysis?"

"We'll try to pull finger prints but I'm not optimistic. This weather has accelerated decomposition, and there's been some animal degradation."

"What do you mean?"

"Small bush animals chewing on extremities like fingers and toes," said the pathologist. Rysakov remained silent, guessing the pathologist expected standard exclamations of revulsion. "High probability we'll do a DNA analysis as well."

"Including mitochondrial DNA?"

"You've been down this road before, DS Rysakov," said the pathologist.

"Past cases. As I mentioned, I have a missing person, female. In all likelihood it won't be her, but I'd like to send you swabs and hair samples from her son."

"If my body is your missing woman, the mitochondrial sequence of the son will be a close match for the mother's," the pathologist said. "It's tedious and labour intensive, but I'll see what I can do. Get me the samples when you can."

Rysakov despatched Tom O'Leary to collect the sample from Alice Martin's son. "Tell the professor we want to eliminate this body. If the guys at the morgue get onto it promptly, we should have the results within a week."

Later that day, after most of the city's workforce was at home or well on the way, O'Leary rang Rysakov on his mobile. "I've just had a call from the professor. He said John is upset about his samples being used in the DNA analysis. He said his son didn't fully understand when he gave the samples and withdraws his consent."

"You explained before you took them?"

"Of course. In fact the boy was very willing. There's no doubt in my mind that he understood exactly what it was about. He even asked if he could have his own copy of the results. Sounds like the professor's been in his ear."

"We could apply for a court order, I suppose," said Rysakov. "But I've got a better idea. Who did you give the samples to?"

"That chief pathologist."

"OK. Ring him and ask him to take enough out of the sample to get a result, and to then return the rest to you tomorrow. Then take that back to Martin. Let's see what happens." Maybe this was what he was waiting for. Sometimes a harmless bending of the rules led to the solving of crimes.

Mid-morning the next day, Rysakov took another call from O'Leary.

"Martin seemed happy to get the sample back. He asked his son if this was all. John gave me a quick look and confirmed it was. I got the feeling John was hoping we'd taken enough for a test, and was quite comfortable about it. I think he wants us to do the DNA."

Rysakov's curiosity was piqued. Why would the professor not want samples from his son used? Unless he knew what the result would show, and now for some reason he's worried about it.

Sophia did not tell Jack Martin about the conversation in medieval Aleppo. She had actually begun to think about it as a real event. Maybe it happened through some weird time-slip, she rationalised. Part of her mind told her that if she mentioned it to anyone that they'd say she was nuts, even her lover. Yet the atmosphere had been too real to simply be her imagination. Even dreams were not as real. She had felt the heat and dryness of the desert.

Sophia felt a familiarity with the woman, that she knew her somehow. She tried to remember the content of the document. Maybe it had stimulated her imagination. There was another explanation for her meanderings: that Jack arranged his wife's disappearance.

That's absurd. He wouldn't know how to do it and get away with it. If he had asked me, however...

A wave of panic coursed through her body. What did the assassins expect of her?

The strident ring of the phone interrupted the questions churning in her head. She agreed to meet the police at her flat at six p.m. When she got off the phone from DC O'Leary her heart beat a little faster. *It shouldn't*, she told herself, *there is no reason to be worried. He said the visit was routine.*

When she calmed down and thought about it more rationally she realised she should have expected the call. That Jack was having an affair was always going to come out. It also provided a motive, she realised. *I wonder whether that means the police will suspect Jack or me?* More likely they would suspect they conspired. What evidence was there? *None*, she said to herself emphatically. *There can't be any. I didn't do anything.*

Rysakov and O'Leary arrived right on time. The contrast between this young woman and Ann Stratton struck Rysakov immediately. Where the Stratton woman had an air of worldliness, Sophia Hamil still had an air of innocence about her. It took Rysakov only a split second to decide neither were his type.

The young woman ushered them into her lounge room. Once

they had gone through the preliminaries, Rysakov said, "We understand that you and Jack Martin are intimate. Is that correct?"

"Yes," she said. "Do you know where his wife has gone?"

"What makes you think she has gone anywhere?"

"Where else could she be?" she replied. "She found out about Jack and me and left him."

She watched the two policemen look at one another.

"Did you know Mrs Martin?"

"Not really. I only meet her briefly at several faculty functions."

"What did Professor Martin say about his wife? Was he planning to leave her?"

"We didn't talk about his wife." She paused. "But I know he would have left her if she hadn't left hm. He loves me."

When the two officers had gone, she stood in front of the mirror in her bedroom and smiled at her reflection. She had achieved what she had set out to achieve: *Alice left Jack because he loves me.*

"Not a bad looker. I can see what the professor sees in her," said O'Leary once they were out of earshot in the car. "Not all that keen on the Mediterranean type myself, though. Bit too volatile."

"She seemed very confident Alice Martin left her husband," said Rysakov. "Why is that? How would she know that and Martin himself not know?"

"Do you think they're in this together?"

"Too early to say. Could be. Wouldn't be the first time a husband does away with wife with his lover waiting in the background."

"Yeah. The Hamil girl is a bit hard to get a feel for. Did you get the impression part of her mind was elsewhere? Maybe it's an academic thing?"

"I'm certain there's something she's not telling us," said Rysakov.

By late evening the temperature had only dropped one degree. Sophia lay on the bed, naked, thinking of her brother. Vivid erotic images flitted through her mind. As she lay there, her mind began rolling over all the elements of her plan. She had no doubt she could persuade Jack to sponsor her brother's immigration, initially on a student visa and then to stay permanently. The last time they spoke, Josip told her two groups wanted him dead. Friends were hiding him. He would get documents in Beirut to support a student visa. Tomorrow she would ask Jack.

Once Alice was divorced or found dead she would marry Jack. In the meantime, after a suitable interval, she would move in with him. Her brother would also stay with them. She smiled.

12

When the police launched their media appeal all the local TV networks picked up the story along with the request for any information on the disappearance of Alice Martin. The daily papers ran the picture and a background story. A website with a Facebook link was set up by a local newspaper. The journalist who wrote the story could find little information on Alice. He relied on hearsay and whatever he received from the few of her friends he managed to track down. So far they had a lot of traffic and no hard data, as DC O'Leary put it. The same photo, the only photo, appeared in all the media.

"It's no surprise we're getting so many useless responses," Rysakov said to the policewoman on the next desk, a police constable who doubled as the station's incident manager. PC Ruby Walsh did a good job and made sure best use was made of the limited resources, subject to his overall approval. What's more, he noticed for the first time, she was attractive. "That photo could be any number of women. Yet every time there's mention of the story, out it'll come." He picked up the photo and peered closely at the indistinct image of one face among many.

He saw a female of average height, light brown hair fashionably cut above the shoulders. How would he describe the face? The media called Alice 'attractive'. But they always did, the story read better. Face slightly rounded, eyes, nose and mouth all 'normal', all in the right place, high cheekbones. The eyes blue, Martin had said. The lips were not full, they were… average. And that, Rysakov decided, was the most appropriate description of Alice Martin's appearance – average. How had Clive Nestor described her – great sex?

Shows you can't judge by looks alone, Rysakov thought. No doubt she was good at something else as well. Her son said she was awesome with computers. He recalled how no one suspected Sir Anthony

Blunt, art advisor to Queen Elizabeth and a Palace intimate. For forty years he doubled as a Soviet spy. Did Alice also have a secret life?

He placed the photo back into the file wondering if they'd ever find her. This was almost certainly a crime of passion, if a crime has indeed been committed. He pulled himself up. *Don't write her off yet, there is still an outside possibility she will turn up.* Yet the likelihood of that decreased as each day passed. He gritted his teeth in annoyance. Alice Martin frustrated the hell out of him. He couldn't get a feel for the woman, the wife, the mother, the person. He couldn't get a sense for what might have happened to her.

He sat back down. Without his second-in-command he found himself more desk bound than he preferred. Tom O'Leary's wife had caught a gastric virus and he had taken leave for the past week to mind their three children. Rysakov envied his DC, though he had no idea how Tom juggled his law enforcement duties with keeping a family together. That his wife managed to clothe and feed the kids on a DC salary only increased Rysakov's admiration. His own ill-advised marriage had ended two years ago citing irreconcilable differences. He discovered too late his wife had never really been in love with him. She had simply wanted to get married and he was the chump that was in the wrong place at the wrong time.

I was too dumb to see it, he thought. *No, that's not fair. I loved her and didn't want to lose her.* Even now, thinking about her hurt.

Rysakov closed the front door behind him. The small terrace-house in the inner Sydney suburb of Paddington overlooked a laneway, on the other side of which two large jacarandas shielded privacy for his rear patio. The house needed refurbishment and a coat of paint and although he toyed with the idea of renovating little progress had been made since he'd moved in after the divorce. He took off his coat, hung it on the back of a chair and poured a glass of iced water from the refrigerator.

"Never drink alcohol alone," he said out loud, eying the six-pack of ice cold beer. The incident manager would have made rather nice company tonight, he thought.

He felt like company, female company. Another of his rules, none of which were strictly observed – don't mix pleasure with work. Tonight that meant going out to one of the many pubs within walking distance.

The Lord Dudley was busy when he walked in – locals from the neighbourhood, arty types, students, ambitious executives, and members of the media industry. He ordered a sirloin steak, well done (no blood please, not off duty), from the barmaid, picked up his beer and searched for a table in the bistro. He had resigned himself to eating at the bar when he noticed a girl leave from a table near the window. As he got to the table he saw one seat still occupied by an attractive woman in a gray executive suit and what looked like a Hermes scarf loose around her neck. Hermes had been a weakness of his ex-wife, one his salary could not support, and it should have been a warning.

"Excuse me, is it OK if I sit down?" he asked. She stopped reading, closing the file and looked up.

"Yes, sure," she said.

He stood there, staring at her. She smiled. Embarrassed, he flushed slightly and sat, introducing himself.

"Hallo, Nic. I'm Sally McIntosh."

He told her he was a police officer, upfront. She didn't baulk. If anything, it made her more interested. She immediately wanted to know how the forensic teams worked. She had a degree in chemistry, she explained, and had almost become a forensic pathologist. She now worked as the PA to the research director of a pharmaceutical company. Two hours later Sally McIntosh looked at her watch. "Nic, I have to go. I've got to fine tune a Power Point presentation for tomorrow. I enjoyed talking to you."

Without hesitation he said, "What are you doing next Saturday night?"

"Not much, ordering a pizza probably."

"Why don't we go to dinner?"

"That would be fun," she said and wrote her phone number on the back of a business card. He put it in his pocket and stood as she left. He had no doubt that the business suit hid a superb body. As she reached the door she turned. Pleased she still had his attention she waved and, with a big smile, disappeared.

On an impulse he pulled out her business card, if only to keep the image of her lingering a little while longer. He glanced at the logo of the company: International Compounds Inc.

13

Sitting at his desk next morning reviewing the data, he barely noticed PC Ruby Walsh as she bent over lower than really necessary to place files on his desk. Rysakov pushed the Alice file to one side. After the media publicity and the inclusion of the photo in every newspaper and television news bulletin, they received nearly a hundred calls from people claiming to have seen Alice Martin. Most were dealt with by phone. Twenty-two he deemed worthy of using scarce manpower on. Twenty led nowhere. Of the balance, one woman claimed to have seen Alice Martin at the local supermarket regularly, and within the last week. He confirmed with the professor that his wife did in fact use this shopping centre occasionally. So the woman may well have seen Alice Martin at the centre – weeks ago.

Rysakov looked at the folder, unconvinced. When he last spoke to her, the missing person seemed a secondary consideration. It soon became evident that the woman's own importance to the investigation was her prime motivation. Attention seekers were not new, just monumental time wasters. On the hundred-to-one chance the woman had seen Alice Martin he put the file in his 'In' tray. That left one file, Sandra Blake, a woman certain she had seen the professor's wife at the exhibition.

"Ruby, who last spoke to Sandra Blake?" he called to PC Walsh.

"I think it was Tom O'Leary, Boss," she answered from behind her desk.

"Time I talked to her. Come on, you can stand in for Tom."

Sandra Blake turned out to be a Friend of the Gallery, someone who, Rysakov guessed, expected to be elevated to the upper stratum of society as a result. The modest two-bedroom apartment she lived in alone said it all.

"Do you attend all the gallery functions?"

"Yes. I'm frequently needed to oversee the ticketing and ensure it runs smoothly." She spoke in the precise manner suggestive of an exclusive private school education, not overtly superior, but leaving no doubt as to a cultured upbringing. "It's all volunteer work, of course."

"You told DC O'Leary you saw Alice Martin on the night she vanished. Would you mind going over it again?"

"Not at all, Officer," she said, business-like. "I had just spoken to Sebastian, the door manager. He told me he would be surprised if any more visitors arrived. Part of my responsibility was to go down to the exhibition area to make sure invitation tickets were being collected, and that no one entered more than once. As I went down the stairs I saw the woman in the photograph, also going down. I went past her to get to the entrance area. I noticed her in particular because she seemed to be keeping very close to a group, while not being part of the group."

"Why did you think she was not part of the group?"

"She had her head down and didn't seem to be taking part in the conversations the rest of the group were having."

"If her head was down, how could you be certain who she was?" he asked, looking across at Ruby as if to say, 'There goes the last lead'. "Perhaps it may have been another blond woman."

"That is possible Officer, but I don't think so. She looked alone, a feeling I am quite familiar with. I think that is why she stayed in my mind."

Rysakov nodded and remained silent.

"I understand that you looked at the CCTV footage for that area with a police officer about a week ago," said Ruby.

Blake nodded. "There is only one camera filming that staircase as there is no exit until one is off the stairs," she said. "It did surprise me that none of the cameras on the entrance to the exhibition showed the same woman. Though I do recall it was quite crowded at the time."

"And you're sure you didn't see her on any other footage of the various cameras?" PC Ruby Walsh persisted. "There appeared to be some blonde females on other cameras."

"None that I could be certain of. They all seemed to be in crowds, from what I recall. Although I couldn't see any of the faces, none of the figures looked familiar."

Rysakov could see nothing more would come of this interview. "Thank you for your time, Mrs Blake. If you think of anything else please give PC Walsh or myself a call."

"Do you think she really saw Alice Martin, Boss?" asked PC Walsh as they walked towards their car.

"It's a pretty slender thread. Yet so far, the only evidence we have that Alice Martin was there, is from her husband and the woman we just spoke to. Not exactly overwhelming. At this stage it's possible Alice Martin is not in the CCTV at all and never attended the exhibition."

Rysakov looked directly at Ruby Walsh as he spoke. He had been impressed with the way she conducted herself at the interview. Watching her as she drove the unmarked Commodore back to the station confirmed his previous opinion; she was an attractive woman.

14

Clive Nestor stared out of the Castleraegh Street office window down at the yachts on the harbour without registering – he might just as well have been looking at a brick wall. If he did not find a solution there was every chance he could end up hitting a brick wall, forcefully. The phone call from Warren Kay made that clear.

Nestor thought about the incongruity of names. Some names conjured up images of reliability, of leadership, such as his own name, Clive, after the great Clive of India, or the actor Clive Owen. It sounded solid and reliable. Others created a preconceived certainty of badness, before ever meeting the person. The name Adolph was an example he often quoted at dinner parties. He found it hard to think of a more prosaic, duller name than Warren. Yet, he now believed this man would give less thought to ordering a murder than to ordering a hamburger. Not that Nestor really believed Kay *would* order a murder. That only happened in fiction or on TV. He simply imagined his recent shareholder capable of doing so. Provided there was no prospect of being caught. He did not think Kay much of a risk taker.

Nestor met Kay by chance two years ago. Well, it seemed like chance at the time. Since that day he wondered more than once if he had been set up. After the call from Kay he felt sour enough to be certain. He cast his mind back.

An hour of what some might call deviant sex had left him relaxed that day. Probably too relaxed. Nestor and Alice had rekindled their past relationship after a chance meeting when both were entertaining business associates at the same restaurant. Two lunches later they began occasional daytime assignations. After twelve months of experimenting they knew each other's preferences well. At first he had been embarrassed and reticent and was pleased she had introduced him gradually. It hadn't taken long. After three meetings he brought along toys of his own, all reserve now gone.

As they left the apartment that day they literally bumped into Kay as they stepped into the street. Alice Martin introduced him. How Alice knew such a man he never really found out. She claimed a friend who bought and sold shares introduced him. Nestor thought that unlikely at the time, but hadn't considered it important.

"Warren is an investor," she said.

Those four words led Clive Nestor into a Faustian deal.

Not long after he met Kay he found himself over committed. The market had not risen as quickly as he expected and the firm found itself committed to a much larger investment in a new company than they had anticipated. Kay had provided the funds within a week. His terms had been tough, but Nestor had had no alternative. As a result, unless the firm could now repay the loan, he would lose control of his company to Kay. He would then become an employee of Warren Kay, an appalling thought. It had happened without him being really cognoscente of the potential consequences. And it was so easy. The market was booming. Money made money. Then it was too late. He had to successfully complete one large deal that would generate the fees required. The latest IPO the firm were working on would be perfect to get rid of Kay. But Nestor also had a secret agenda with this IPO.

Kay never threatened him directly. Nestor had nothing he could take to the police. Or to anyone, really, he knew that. As he sat in his luxurious office, in the distinctive MLC Centre, staring out at the harbour, he tried to examine when he knew for certain that Kay would not hesitate to use violence to get what he wanted. The answer remained elusive as ever. He just knew. If it suited him, Kay would use violence. Just when Nestor knew that could happen had become irrelevant.

Under Alice's guidance he discovered parts of her body Professor Jack didn't even know existed. She told him so. They met to satisfy a mutual physical need. Nothing else. The sex provided a pressure valve release for both of them. Beyond that Alice had no interest. Alice made it clear she had no interest in emotional closeness. No effort by him, and in emotional moments he did try, could penetrate the veil that hid the real Alice. She did not let her guard down. He, on the other hand, did lower his defences. He couldn't help it. Lying beside her on the bed after sex like he'd never experienced before, he could not resist boasting. A takeover to be announced next week, a capital raising at a give-away price, and others. Too many, including the forthcoming IPO to list the technology company on the stock exchange, his drop-dead deal. He had told her about the huge profit, how he would never need to work again and how it would all be tax free. So far as he could remember, he had not explained the detail of how he had structured his side of the transaction. She hadn't asked many questions, just enough for him to feel flattered. With the benefit of hindsight and because he felt flattered, he probably said too much. Perhaps she had taken it straight to Kay. He would never know.

"But hell, the sex was good," he said out loud.

He picked up his phone and called a number from memory. It could not be found on the phone SIM card. After five minutes alternately speaking with firm authority he didn't feel and listening at length, he said, "Thank you." As soon as the call terminated he deleted the number from the call log. Simplistic, perhaps, but it made him feel better. Perhaps he could get Kay off his back for good, and extinguish the loans at the same time. For the first time in years, the business would then be able to operate independently.

"Maybe I'll let him take a drop for insider trading," he said before immediately discarding the idea. *What would be perfect would be to frame him for a murder he didn't commit. That would be really sweet.*

He turned away from the harbour panorama and left the room, his attention re-focused wholly on the IPO.

"That bastard Kay is not getting any of this action," he muttered.

When the architect designed the building he must have known Macquarie Technology Park had already been the site of exciting biotech discoveries. It looked hi-tech. The current tenant, International Compounds Inc., had not disappointed. ICI operated at the leading edge of research into composite materials, including ground breaking work at the molecular level. Key components of the discoveries had been patented. Yet, unless the scientist knew how to deliver, express or create the concepts set out in a patent into a product, it is just so much theory – a written guarantee the inventor owns the idea. Not much else. The key is the knowledge of how, exactly how, to carry out every process to achieve the result described in the patent. At the frontiers of science, where new information is acquired daily, knowing how is critical. Without it the patent might only hold academic interest. Protecting a company's knowhow sometimes took as much time and money as getting the patent granted. Consequently, the value of the knowhow to a competitor could be huge. Occasionally, the knowhow is so critical a patent application is not lodged. Instead the company will often use other means to protect its assets, none of which are foolproof.

Sally McIntosh knew all this. The protection of intellectual property, or patents and knowhow, fell under her control. She also understood the value of such inside information to a potential competitor. Her ambition overrode any consideration of whether what she did was wrong. When she stole the first set of data a year ago she crossed the Rubicon. Thereafter it became easier. Calmly, she closed and locked the Director of Research's safe, holding the slim document in her left hand. As she walked out of the office she took the file of the week's results from his desk. She walked at a normal pace into the corridor and then to her own office next door. Anyone who saw her would not give it a second thought. She was the director's Executive Assistant. She often worked late.

No email of secret information, no fax, no ordinary memory stick or disc, no file, and no photocopy could leave the site under the security protocols she had helped establish. Yet Sally McIntosh knew that, in spite of ICI's best efforts, key secret information still left the premises. How it happened, only one person knew, Sally herself. A small conspiracy operated well hidden within the company. Only she knew all the details. Two others knew only what they needed to know. One, a security guard, unwittingly turned a blind eye to what he thought was an office romance. The other had disappeared.

She settled down to read the data she took from the safe. Few people knew she held an honours degree in molecular biology and a doctorate in the field of composite materials. No one in ICI had that information. She hadn't lied when she applied for the job. She told the interviewer she studied science at university and he had not enquired further as she wasn't expected to undertake any research.

For the next two hours she poured over the files, referring from one to the other. Finally she looked up and for some time stared unseeing at the wall. What she'd just read had caught her completely by surprise. She opened her office door. The rest of the floor lay in semi-darkness. No one else was around.

An hour later, she re-locked the file in the director's safe. He would never know it had been out. She walked out of the building, confidently logging her exit through the security detector, nodding good night to the security guard at the lift lobby. He winked to say, 'The romance is safe with me.' She knew that the memory stick she carried, with all the results on it, could not be detected. The ceramic technology it used did not yet exist commercially. It may be experimental, but it had never failed her. In exchange for the high capacity storage device prototype, she regularly reported the operational functioning of the device to the innocent researcher whose interest was wholly academic.

The last of the summer daylight had gone by the time she drove the company BMW out of the car park. Perhaps the fading twilight spurred her on, but by the time she reached her apartment she had decided. She would do nothing. Yet. The director would want a meeting with the scientists themselves to discuss a new round of tests. It was difficult to reconcile the full results with the limited early tests. The lab would re-assess the test process, and almost certainly order a fresh round. All of which would take time, time she would use to get a clearer idea of her own next step. The potential looked very clear. Here was the opportunity to make some serious money.

As she prepared a salad that night in her kitchen she let her mind drift. Nic Rysakov. She liked him. Saturday would be fun. *Clean sheets on the bed,* she thought. *How strange that of all the people I could meet, I meet a policeman. And the one investigating Alice Martin's disappearance.* Sally suspected Alice had run. To her it was simply the only sensible course of action.

She sat on the small balcony off the unit's living room and balanced the salad on her knee. Heat still radiated from the brick-work and she wondered if it may be cooler inside. Then the rich scent of jasmine wafted up from the garden below and she stayed. From where she sat she could see the TV in the lounge. A news update on the murdered woman found by the jogger was playing. For the first time Sally McIntosh faced up to the very real possibility that Alice Martin had not run, but was in fact dead. She wondered whether that could have any implications for her.

15

Jack Martin readily agreed to sponsor Sophia's brother Josip, particularly when she outlined her brother's extensive qualifications. As she described her brother, he gently traced his finger over her breast. They had already made love once and as she spoke he felt her nipples harden.

"Josip will live with us. It will be so good," she said, her hand sliding down over his stomach. He caught a glimpse of her face as he turned toward her. Her eyes looked unfocused. Before he had a chance to give it any thought lust took control.

As the days slipped by since Alice vanished, he thought of her less and less. When he did, the thoughts lacked the warmth he felt for the woman lying next to him. When they were first married he and Alice had experienced open, consuming passion. Love-making was pleasurable and they were good company with each other. As he progressed up the academic ladder they slowly drifted apart. He tried to remember when he first noticed what he now recognised as a progressive estrangement, but could not put a time or date on it. It had been too gradual. The demands for advancement in the often bitchy, sometimes bitter, politics of academia had absorbed more and more of his attention. Maybe it was more his fault. But he did not accept total responsibility. Alice herself had drifted away, becoming cooler over time. Now she had gone he came to accept the probability she had had a lover.

From the first year of their marriage he had sensed a part of Alice that he couldn't reach, something he couldn't identify or put his finger on. At times he seriously wondered whether Alice actually lived another, separate life, before telling himself that was ridiculous. He even briefly thought she might be bi-polar, before realising that she didn't really exhibit any of the symptoms.

The arrival of their son, John, stood out as a highlight. Although not aware of it at the time, but with the benefit of hindsight, Alice had seemed detached, as if she were acting out someone else's life. Still, she had been a good mother. *No*, he thought, *that's an inaccurate platitude.* Adequate better described her. An adequate mother, doing her duty with the right amount of attention, not love.

He wouldn't miss Alice. He gave his whole attention to Sophia as she slid her leg over his and pressed her breasts against his arm. No, he wouldn't miss Alice at all.

Once Martin had gone, Sophia showered and dressed. She felt relaxed and pleased with herself. Everything was going to work out according to plan. Soon the two men who were most important to her would be with her. And, of course, they would live together in the same house. She sighed and settled back in her chair, content. She did not ignore Martin's son. If necessary, she could manage him as well.

This time of day the sun blazed with furnace-like intensity through the west window in her apartment. She stared into the light, lost in her thoughts. As she did the window opened onto the interior of the house in Aleppo. Once again she heard the tinkle of water from the courtyard fountain. Once again she inhaled the arid aroma of the desert.

This time the two assassins appeared to be reporting to the lady. Sophia could not see her face. A head covering, folded down to her eyebrows and doubled back under her nose, like a *chador*, hid her features. She assumed it was the lady she saw when she stared at the stained glass window in the library, although it could be anyone.

"The transgressor is dead. It was Allah's will," said the leader, before half-turning to face Sophia. For a moment no sound entered the room. She sat frozen to her chair, terrified.

"Now another must die, one who brought disgrace on the family. To lift the disgrace, this you must do yourself."

The figure in the *chador* nodded acknowledgement. In that instant she knew the woman.

"Yes. I understand," said a muffled voice.

All three stared at Sophia as the Aleppo room faded.

Deep in her soul she knew what they wanted. She was just not yet ready to face it.

She ran her tongue over dry lips and looked away from the window.

16

Soon after Rysakov arrived at his desk, the morgue pathologist called.

"Thought you might like to know," said the pathologist. "Our Jane Doe is female, about forty, plus or minus a couple of years. Prima facie fit for your MP from what you told me. I should have the DNA analysis finished this afternoon. As long as I'm left alone." He paused. "I want to get another opinion, but I'm certain this female has not had children."

As he read through the file, Rysakov decided it was past time for him to visit Uncle Henry. Uniform had interviewed the old man, with no useful information gathered. He stood up and walked over to PC Ruby Walsh's desk.

"Ruby, find out Uncle Henry's full name and address, then arrange a time for us to meet."

PC Walsh leant forward as she wrote the name on her pad. Then she straightened her shoulders so her uniform blouse pulled tight. She looked up at Rysakov. "OK, sir," she said and smiled.

PC Walsh pulled the bright yellow patrol car into the driveway and killed the ignition. The garage had nothing else available on short notice, so they travelled high-profile. On the way she told Rysakov what she had dug up on Schmidt. According to the electoral roll, Uncle Henry's full name turned out to be Heinrich Gunther Schmidt. He arrived nearly thirty years ago from the then West Germany, apparently escaping across the border from East Germany. He held papers appointing him guardian of a juvenile, Alice Braun, mother deceased, father missing, presumed deceased. The Immigration Department had also added that Schmidt and Alice made regular trips to Germany until she married. Since then she mostly travelled to Europe alone. At irregular intervals her husband joined her.

"I am assuming she visited Germany. The EU has unrestricted internal movement, so Immigration said they can't tell which countries she visited," said PC Walsh.

Rysakov was impressed, but Schmidt and Braun, Smith and Brown? *I guess it happens, even in the GDR.*

Schmidt greeted them, a thin elderly man with cold pale-blue eyes and a firm handshake. He was dressed in grey slacks, white shirt and tie. Old style formality. From the first handshake Rysakov felt on guard, more so than he expected. This was a man accustomed to command and obedience. If Schmidt were to give the command to stand to attention, Rysakov thought, with some amusement, he might actually do it.

After the usual preliminaries, Rysakov asked, "Do you have any suggestions as to where Alice Martin may be, sir?"

"None," said Schmidt, his accent still thick even after living so many years in Australia. "It is my understanding she was not happy in her marriage. Have you considered the possibility she may have left Professor Martin for another man?"

"Do you know if she was having an affair?"

"It is likely," he said. "She found Martin rather dull."

"Did she tell you that?"

"Of course," said Schmidt.

"Can you suggest any names of possible partners?" said PC Walsh.

"Ja."

Rysakov and PC Walsh sat patiently in the silence that followed. Finally Schmidt said, "She was once very friendly with Clive Nestor."

Rysakov nodded and then, on an impulse, asked, "How well did you know Alice Braun's parents?"

If he was surprised the police knew Alice's maiden name Schmidt did not show it. "Her father I knew well as a colleague, her mother not so well. They have been dead many years."

"How did they die?"

"You ask how they die, why is that? They are dead. They can be of no interest."

"I'm not sure, it might be relevant."

"I do not think so," said Schmidt. "Her father disappeared. I suspect he had a heart attack and his body was stripped of everything saleable or useable before being buried to hide the evidence. The GDR had severe shortages of most goods at that time. Her mother had many lovers, but was shot in a civil disturbance."

"Thank you," said Rysakov. As he suspected, the information wasn't of much value. Then he tried something else on the cagey old German. "Before you retired, what was your occupation?"

"You ask strange questions."

Rysakov shrugged, not really apologetic.

"I used to work as an industrial chemist."

Rysakov had a hunch, one he thought was worth rolling the dice for. "One last question, how long did you work at ICI?" If he had not been watching Schmidt's face closely he would have missed the sudden tightening around the eyes and mouth, which just as quickly relaxed.

"It is many years since I worked there," Schmidt said in a flat tone. Silence followed. Then he said something that surprised Rysakov. "Alice told me Martin studies the similarities between Ancient Lebanese assassins and modern terrorists. He told her the methods are similar. She said his Lebanese assistant, who is also his mistress, has contacts with assassins in Beirut. How she knows this I do not know. Why she tells me, I do not know."

He could add nothing further.

Later, when the police car stopped at a traffic light, PC Ruby Walsh turned to face her boss. "How did you figure out the ICI connection?"

"Interesting isn't it?" Rysakov replied. They drove along in silence before Rysakov turned from staring out the window. "At this stage I can't see any connection between Alice Martin's disappearance and Martin's work, but Sophia Hamil's contacts with the Middle East might be worth following up."

17

Heinrich Schmidt was worried.

That policeman is clever, he thought. *And I am out of practice, and too old for these games*. Still, he was certain about one thing: Rysakov didn't know his real name, Dimitri Antonov, of that he would stake the rest of his days here on this Godforsaken planet.

He pondered on the policeman's name, Rysakov. Russian father, obviously. There are capitalists and there are good Russians. A policeman can be either. He stared at the library of books lining the living room wall with cold blue eyes. He had worked for the Party all his life. For years he moved steadily through the lower ranks, earning a deserved reputation for solving difficult personnel problems. And for tidying up loose ends. Contrary to Party policy, grease does make the wheel turn smoothly. Antonov smiled thinly. It helped get him into the Academy. Lack of connections at the right level, however, resulted in a posting to Sydney. With Alice.

His gaze strayed to a floor-to-ceiling wine rack crammed with bottles of the finest vintages. Yet, this city has its compensations.

These days, older, and with increasingly more time for reflection, he was sad about what they had done to Alice as a girl. Maybe they had had no choice. He liked to think that in today's world a different way would be found, though he could not think what that might be. While one could not change the past, sometimes one could, in some small way, try to make amends. She had always done what was asked of her, without complaint and generally with considerable skill. So he was comfortable he had made the correct decision earlier in the year, to tell Alice the truth about her family in Prague. It was little enough and should not die with him.

In all the years he had been in Australia he always achieved his objectives, either on his own or with Alice's assistance. He had no desire to retire to Berlin or Moscow. He preferred Sydney. The climate was indisputably better. The abundance of fresh food could not be compared, and – most importantly – the wine was infinitely superior. The only blot on his record had occurred recently. Ever resourceful, he had taken action which, if successful, might restore his clean record. He turned his attention back to the bookshelves covering one complete wall of the living room. The Russian-named policeman had focused the old man's mind on just how important his record was to him. He knew it was only ego, a matter of personal pride. That did not make it in any way less important.

I have sacrificed much and achieved positive results for the Party. Not a legacy anyone, except me, will care about, he thought. He cast his eyes over the books. Philosophy, political theory and history, all read at least once. "But I care," he said out loud, "and I *will* leave a clean record."

Within the hour, Schmidt made a phone call. He had learned over the years the necessity of being prepared.

The following morning the morgue pathologist called Rysakov again.

"I'm afraid your work's all still ahead of you, detective," he said. "I asked the Senior Lecturer in Anatomy at the university, he's a friend of mine, to take a look at Jane Doe. He agrees with me. She had not given birth. So, even without the extra DNA she isn't your missing person." He paused. "When I compared the DNA arrays she's not even a distant relative of the Martin boy."

Rysakov returned the handset to its cradle. Alice Martin remained a puzzle seeking a solution. *Wherever I look, she isn't there.*

18

"Welcome back," said Nic Rysakov as Tom O'Leary flopped into his chair.

"I think I'd rather chase an armed robber than look after those kids for another week," he said. "I don't know how she does day after day."

Rysakov laughed as he caught PC Walsh reaching for the telephone out of the corner of his vision. He was glad to have O'Leary back, but he had to admit he wouldn't have been at all unhappy if DC O'Leary had taken another week off. Now PC Ruby Walsh would be stuck in the office.

O'Leary parked the unmarked vehicle in the visitors slot and went with Rysakov to the reception to ask for Mark Archer, the CEO of ICI. Even the reception area had a clinical scientific atmosphere, which Rysakov suspected was both a consequence of their research and a deliberate effort to impress. Rysakov was also hoping to catch a glimpse of Sally McIntosh while he was in the building.

The man they met could have stepped from central casting: distinguished demeanour, hair greying at the temples, faint five o'clock shadow, blue-striped button-down-collar shirt, pin-striped tailor-made suit, and expensive black loafers.

"Gentlemen," he said, indicating a round table away from his desk. "Can I get you coffee?" His secretary took the orders as they sat.

"We're trying to build our profile of Alice Martin in the hope it may give us a lead that will help locate her. I understand a uniformed officer's already obtained from you details of her employment. It would be very helpful if you could give us an insight into what she did. Sometimes the little things can be helpful," said Rysakov. At least, he thought, he was making an effort to be encouraging.

"I'd be pleased to help if I can. The company's quite disturbed that one of its employees should disappear," said Archer.

Rysakov thought he detected a faint accent, but couldn't place it, maybe South African. He pressed Archer for more information.

"She seemed to have a good understanding of the science, but it was in computers she excelled. She seemed to understand how computers thought, as she used to put it. An absurd claim to make, I know. It simply illustrates the point. Modern science, particularly the work we do here relies quite heavily on computing power to implement and control the R & D, the research and development. Whether it's an electron microscope or a PC processing data, without computers, properly handled, we wouldn't get the results. Alice worked with the Marketing Manager in identifying potential new products, some of which may be years into the future. She also assisted in managing the overall computer systems. She helped design our data security system to protect the results of the R&D until patent protection is obtained. Many of our results are worth millions of dollars. ICI is a world leader in solar technology and power storage systems. Several overseas companies are working along similar lines but they're several years behind us." He made this last point with evident satisfaction.

"I assume some of these companies would pay large sums to acquire the technology," Rysakov said.

Archer nodded. "We get regular approaches."

Rysakov took that to mean an acceptable price had not yet been reached. "Does theft of intellectual property occur very often? I imagine the temptation to earn big money by selling to a competitor must be there."

"Industrial espionage is a constant concern," said Archer. "Fortunately, it happens less frequently than you'd imagine, and we take extensive measures to minimise the temptation."

While Rysakov and O'Leary pursued their investigation, on the other side of the harbour John Martin sat at home in his room, thinking. Not for the first time he wondered why he did not feel particularly close to either of his parents. Once again he confronted the obvious question: *If I think this way, are they my real parents?*

The idea had gradually taken shape as he came to the end of his teenage years. Now, with his mother's strange disappearance, he had begun to think about it more and more. In his year at school were two boys who knew they were adopted. Their parents told them. Either on TV or from his friends, but somewhere he had heard that not all parents told their children. Maybe his parents were among this group, embarrassed to admit it.

At the same time, in the inner-city, Sophia Hamil went about her day, her plan clear. One uncertainty remained: Who did the assassins mean? She still had no idea. Yet, the more she thought about it, the less concerned she became.

Strange, she thought, *but when the time comes, I'll know.*
For the time being she put it out of her mind.

As the day for listing the company on the stock exchange approached, Clive Nestor thought and talked of nothing else. His whole being seemed focused on this one deal. Although he had invested a respectable amount in REI – all disclosed in the Prospectus for Renewable Energy Inc. – no one knew the true size of his shareholding. The large nominee holding in the name of a European bank secretly belonged to him. The nominee held the shares on behalf of a hedge fund based in the Bahamas.

Nestor smiled as he doodled on a pad, jotting down a nine digit number. You only got the chance for a drop-dead deal like this once in a lifetime. The manager of the Bahamas hedge fund had made some bad calls and needed a no-risk deal to restore value for his investors. He had immediately agreed to Nestor's proposal last year, thirty-three thousand feet above the Mexican Gulf. For a percentage of the profit he would warehouse the shares. He was very sympathetic to Nestor's reason for offering the deal. No one liked paying tax. "Why else am I in the Bahamas?" he had said. They both knew that was only one of the reasons.

When the shares were sold after listing on the stock exchange, Nestor would be a very rich man, and pay no tax. *Then Warren Kay can go fuck himself,* he thought. As soon as the sale completed, Nestor planned to leave the country for good. *Kay can have my shares in this business. They'll be worth chicken shit!*

Today he felt more confident than he had for a long time.

Sandra Blake had never had any dealings with the police, not even a traffic fine. Though she did not show it at the time, she found the visit by the two police officers both exciting and worrying. She did not know whether she should get involved, but decided, as it could impact on the State Art Gallery, she should at least provide minimal help.

Try as she might, she could not get the CCTV images out of her mind. They continued replaying in her head. Perhaps she had missed something. The prospect of being a material witness finally overcame any remaining reservations. Important witnesses were often interviewed on television. She may even be invited onto the Gallery Committee.

She picked up the phone and dialled DS Rysakov. She waited as the phone rang. Maybe one more viewing, just in case, she would tell him.

In her office at ICI, Sally McIntosh looked blankly at the computer screen. What she saw in the Director's file the previous evening led to a sleepless night. The possibility of Alice being dead began to worry her. It could lead to the unravelling of her well-laid plans. If that happened, there could be serious consequences.

Across town, back behind her desk, PC Ruby Walsh wondered how she could entice Nic Rysakov to ask her out. Once they were free from the DS/PC relationship, she had little doubt of the direction in which she could steer him.

19

Overnight a southerly change blew through, cooling the overheated city. Sandra Blake arrived early at Redfern Police Head Quarters in fashionable but sensible clothes and sat in the small waiting area. People came and went in a steady stream. She glanced nervously at each, never long enough to catch their eye. Ten minutes after the appointed time, PC Walsh and Rysakov took her to the same room as her previous visit. The only change, Ms Blake noticed, was a large flat screen monitor. Although this made the picture larger, it didn't change the clarity of the grainy black and white images. She had them replay the stairwell sequence three times.

"Do you have another photo of Alice Martin?" she asked. "The face on the TV could be the same woman, but the angle is different.'

"I'm afraid we only have the one," said PC Ruby Walsh.

"I am sorry, each time I see the woman with the beret. I think it's her. But I could be wrong. The more I see it the less certain I feel. There's nowhere else on the film that I can see anyone like her. I thought I may have missed something else."

She looked embarrassed for wasting their time.

"It's much better to have a second look, Ms Blake, than to leave any uncertainty. If anything else occurs to you please don't hesitate to call me or PC Walsh," Rysakov assured her.

"Alice Martin is like a mirage, every time we look she isn't there," he said to PC Walsh when she returned from showing Sandra Blake out of the station. "If it wasn't for her son I'd begin to wonder if she ever existed."

Jack Martin decided to work at home that morning. He did so about once a month on days light of lecture load, ostensibly to catch up on administration and form filling, the mundane chores of University management. Like his colleagues, he far preferred to spend the time on research projects than justify his department's funding to state and federal politicians. But, it was a necessary evil in today's cash-strapped economy.

Martin pushed the pile of forms to one side and spent the next hour reviewing data on Lebanese assassins. Methods may have changed. The objectives had not: effecting political change through the use of fear or terror. That much was clear. What happened in Lebanon, based on the data he received, differed little to events in Syria, Iraq, or the mountains of western Iran in medieval times. In return for a fee, or promised reward, now or in the afterlife, lives could be extinguished.

Next on his to-do list was the offer from Lebanon. He sent an email accepting and giving instructions. He stretched. Another problem solved. He smiled as he recalled Sophia's excitement on hearing the news that the University would offer her brother entry as a student.

"Now he can get a student visa," she had said, jumping up excitedly. "Soon he will be here."

Then it struck him. For the first time in years he had complete flexibility. With Alice gone, and it appeared she had, he could do as he liked. Almost. With John's schooling all but completed they had discussed him taking a gap year as a teaching assistant in Wales or Ireland. In a month he would be on his way.

Martin could almost taste the freedom.

Heinrich Schmidt considered this his real name. He had used the identity for so long he considered himself more Heinrich than Dmitri. In any event, at this stage in his life, it had become immaterial. He knew he was considerably closer to death than most people. His cold, pragmatic outlook on life he applied to his own, as well as those he dealt with. He once overheard a labourer complaining to a friend, "Shit happens, mate." A crude sentiment, he thought, like most colloquial expressions in this country, but accurate enough.

No one will miss the white-haired old man next door, whatever his name. They will say to each other, "A quiet man, kept himself to himself. Had an old fashioned European courtesy about him. Wonder if he had any family?" That was how he saw himself. The neighbours did not know what he did not want them to know, that his courtesy masked a cold, remorseless focus, that the objective justified the means, that his determination to maintain a clean record was fundamental to his being.

The later had become an obsession, even. Such single-mindedness had proven a boon early in his career. It meant his superiors had confidence to leave him undisturbed for years, particularly as he produced results. At the department's headquarters in Europe the aggressive and more ambitious officials expected results quickly and regularly. Those who counted knew it did not happen that way, unless you got lucky. He had had his fair share of luck. But for the most part it required patience and diligence. Then there were times when the unexpected happened requiring decisive action. Schmidt came into his own at such times. This was such a time.

Alice's disappearance, without question, left a gap in his life. He had grown used to her over the years, and, he admitted to himself, to depend on her. In fact, in his own unemotional way, he liked her. Perhaps he felt some responsibility for the way she had been treated when the Party recruited her. They already had her cooperation to protect her parents. The way they had gone about it was simply boorish and lacking finesse. Not that he had any intention of raising the issue officially. Maybe he was getting soft.

In some ways her absence made decisions easier. He *should* retire. In the bathroom mirror an old face smiled bleakly back at him. Should being the operative word. One did not retire in this business, unless one got retired. Until that happened, he intended to keep his record clean as a matter of personal pride. An unquestioning belief in the State's philosophy that had driven them all those years ago now played no part in his thinking. Only youth could afford lofty ideals. Youth, with all of time ahead of them, and the certainty that where others had failed they would make a difference. They would build a new, more equal world.

He pulled on a brown and gray diamond-patterned cardigan

rather than turn down the air-conditioning in his living room. From the packed shelves of books he selected a volume, opened it at the correct page and sat at his desk. He straightened the blank sheet of paper next to the book and began. Such encryption remained unbreakable without the right key. Today he used Tolstoy's *War and Peace*, starting at page 300 in the Classics Edition, 1958. This would be a fitting book to end his career upon, a masterpiece, perfect for a man with such an exemplary record. With a smile, he nodded agreement to the thought.

He could not delay any further in advising headquarters that Alice had disappeared. For a brief moment of panic he had thought he would not be able to avoid having this major negative on his record. Losing an asset. Then the detectives had visited him and offered a way out. Today he would send the report, brief and succinct:

Alice Braun missing. Local police believe her murdered. Body not yet recovered.

Warren Kay recalled the old adage his father had brought with him from China: "Don't get mad, get even." He occasionally got mad and it was never profitable. Anger clouded one's judgment. One of the teachers at school explained the pitfalls of anger after Kay had beaten a tormenter with a garden stake: "Act in haste, repent at leisure." At the time he had thought it a stupid saying. He derived considerable pleasure watching the blood pour out of the boy's nose. When he left school, a very near miss with police convinced him he should treat the homily seriously.

He took a sip of wine and looked at the lights of the city reflecting on the still water, musing on the incident. Two detectives had visited him at the family home and Kay received them alone. His father spent his time visiting or procuring under age prostitutes, and managing his growing portfolio of residential properties. Only faint memories remained of his mother.

Two university students had been attacked on their way home, the police said. Someone had used a baseball bat and broken their kneecaps. The police gave the strong impression they believed he had carried out the attack. When they asked him if he thought the boys deserved such an attack, he knew he was safe. What a dumb question. He smiled at the memory. As if he would admit to the assault of his school-yard tormentors. He got even, no doubt about that. It had been just good luck he hadn't been seen, or that one of the boys hadn't pulled off his ski-mask. As it was, they suspected him. Too close a call. He had learnt a valuable lesson.

He took another sip of wine and surveyed his domain. The penthouse had been a bargain. The overstretched vendor had been a forced seller. For cash, Kay screwed the price down, getting an additional reduction after promising a quick deal. Although the dwelling had four bedrooms Kay lived alone. He preferred it that way.

He put the glass down and returned to his immediate problem, Nestor, and the substantial sum he had loaned Nestor, Nankervis & Co. when they got caught with commitments they could not meet, but could not avoid.

His mobile vibrated in his pocket, a text message. Having read it he pressed delete. If by an unlikely chance anyone else read the text it would be dismissed as the sort of message everyone received, trying to make an appointment and suggesting days and times. He flipped open his diary, checked a date, then closed it and stared out the window. A busy period loomed ahead, one requiring meticulous planning. He was a cautious, careful man. Having a reliable source inside Nestor's business kept him informed on any significant changes. It cost money, but the information he had just received more than justified the outlay.

20

As she slowly replaced the receiver on the cradle, Sally McIntosh breathed a sigh of relief. *If Nic hadn't rung I don't think I'd have remembered*, she mused. The last few days had been chaotic. *And without being too dramatic*, she thought, looking around the room, *a bit bloody terrifying*. For the umpteenth time she asked herself whether what she was doing was too ambitious, *too bloody dangerous*.

She needed a break and nothing could surely happen to her with a policeman.

Two suburbs away, PC Ruby Walsh looked around the large hall. With its four rows of tiered seating on opposite sides, and the rings at either ends there was no doubt that serious basketball was played here. She had never been in the hall before, even though it adjoined the gym where she trained. She refocused on the mostly male group spread around the matting. The unarmed combat-defence refresher was compulsory, and supported by the Police Union. No one in the force liked reading about officers being injured in the course of duty.

The instructor called for the next two participants. A large well-muscled man walked onto the mat. Ruby, like most of the others, knew of this sergeant. An overconfident blow-hard, and a bit of a bully, particularly with female officers.

"Next," the instructor said and Ruby realised he was looking at her.

She straightened her tracksuit and walked out. She knew she looked good in the soft fabric. She could hear a murmur of anticipation and several wolf-whistles. The sergeant walked toward her with a big smile on his face.

"Nice tits, constable. I'll give 'em a workout," he said barely loud enough for her to hear.

She smiled demurely and backed away. The sergeant immediately pressed the advantage advancing in a confident, loose boxing stance. Ruby stopped in the centre of the mat. He took another step, feinted with his left, followed by a half-strength right at her chest. She slid back and to her left so that all he hit was air. The audience laughed.

"Good girl," the sergeant said, a forced grin on his face. "Now give me your best." With that taunt he dropped his guard and stood in front of her, chin sticking out. The instructor shook his head and re-gripped his whistle.

In a blur of speed Ruby swivelled on her left foot and chopped down on the sergeant's left trapezium muscle, temporarily numbing his shoulder. Then she backed away to her left.

"Oh, a smartass, eh?" said the sergeant. He came at her fast, his powerful right arm ready to hammer her. She knew that if he connected she would be knocked out, perhaps with a broken bone or two. She also knew that that was not going to happen. She leant back, gripped his wrist, and threw her weight backwards. The sergeant, half expecting this move, immediately pulled against Ruby's weight. As he did Ruby kicked her right foot hard against his chest, winding him. She pulled on his arm with all her force, rolling him on top of her. As her back touched the mat she shot her left leg onto his chest and the sergeant cartwheeled over her head, landing heavily on the mat. She jumped to her feet in one movement and stood ready over him.

The instructor blew his whistle to end the bout as surprised clapping burst out around her. As Ruby offered her hand to help the slightly dazed sergeant to his feet, the instructor said, "I want you to remember, never take an opponent at face value. It is better to survive, without heroics. Ruby, incidentally holds several black belts in karate and has trained with some serious people, including the SAS." He looked at Ruby, who, embarrassed, dropped her eyes to the mat.

"Thank you, sergeant, for assisting in the demonstration," the instructor added diplomatically, implying they had set it up for instruction.

Later that day, Ruby took a call at her desk that puzzled her. When Rysakov appeared, she picked up her notes and stood up.

"I hear you defended our Section well, PC Walsh," he said. "Well done," and he left it at that, for which Ruby was grateful.

"We have another case involving the State Art Gallery, Boss. A possible theft. It looks like we're now the experts on the Gallery."

"Uh-huh. Probably because they remembered my name. What do we know?"

Immediately following the closure of the Pissaro exhibition, the gallery within a week opened a new exhibit – Egyptian Antiquities. One reviewer, Rysakov later found out, called it a 'mishmash of minor items of limited interest'. These 'minor items' included gold beakers, engraved tablets, several ceremonial spears and other weapons, a number of mummies, and various items of domestic use from Egypt of the Pharaohs. Rysakov also learned that these mummies were not real ones, but facsimiles, according to the bill of lading that accompanied the airfreight documents. They travelled in non-air-tight containers and were to be shown in the open without the usual glass casing.

"To provide a more dramatic impact," the Gallery curator said.

DC O'Leary had a number of matters to follow up on Alice Martin, so PC Walsh accompanied Rysakov.

"Normally these exhibitions, though a lot of work, run quite smoothly. This is different. Because it seemed a bit unusual, I called the police," the curator said.

"I understand you have two concerns," said Rysakov. "Firstly, there are apparent discrepancies between the bills of lading and the actual goods unpacked. Secondly, the insurance cover of fifty million dollars has made you suspicious an insurance scam may be underway."

"That's correct. And on top of that, at the preview, a group of protesters somehow got in and tried to destroy the items, particularly the mummies."

"Who do you think the protestors were?" he asked.

"At first we thought they may have been Coptic Christians

protesting over the treatment of their church in Cairo. But the Copts destroying artefacts doesn't make sense. We're now fairly certain it was Muslim extremists, like those who blew up the giant Buddhas in Afghanistan several years ago. They shouted slogans about blasphemy and destroying the graven images. Before we could get enough security personnel down to stop them they grabbed whatever they could reach. I think we recovered all the items," he said. "Some were found on the next level. However, with inadequate paperwork, who knows if it's all accounted for. We can't be certain there is anything missing. We just suspect there may be, or at least a claim will be made for items that may or may not exist."

Rysakov nodded. "We'll take a look around, but there's not a lot we can do without clear evidence of theft."

The Antiquities were being shown a level above the Pissaro and towards the rear of the State Art Gallery, adjacent to the construction area for the extensions. From a vantage point on the scaffolding, Rysakov peered down on the workings. Directly below him and heading off some fifty metres to his left, a new concrete support wall had been built to match the thickness of the original stone wall. It had been veneered with thin sandstone and he watched briefly as riggers dismantled the scaffolding. He asked Ruby to draft up the notes of the interview and then review the file. He did not see much for them to do. Uniform could handle the riot and wilful damage charges.

21

When Nic Rysakov arrived at Bondi Beach early the following morning he changed his mind. Instead a north-south run along the sand, he stood watching a medium sized southerly swell bend around the headland, following it until it washed over his feet on the beach. He slipped his flippers on and began swimming out beyond the break. For the next hour he joined half a dozen bodysurfers catching wave after wave. At the end of every third or fourth set he noted a ten foot monster rear up and roll from the top onto the deep water. That meant if he got dumped he wouldn't get hurt. He swam out another fifty metres and waited. Only one other surfer went with him.

"We'll have it all to ourselves," he said, grinning in anticipation.

"Yeah," the other guy said. "Oh yeah."

It came at the end of the second set of waves. It began to rise further out than usual. This was a mother of big waves. The problem, Nic knew, was not getting on the wave. The problem was keeping up with the speed of the break and not getting run over.

At ten foot, it was near his limit for bodysurfing. Both surfers started swimming hard. As they picked up speed the wave caught them. He felt the swell lift, propelling him forward. He knew full well the trick to big wave bodysurfing was to temper his slide down the face. Too fast, as he could testify from painful experience, and he'd get smashed with the weight of breaking water. He stretched his arms down beneath his body to act as hydrofoils. Once the break started he brought them forward, almost to right angles, slowing him down until he sensed the front of the break go under him, a matter of seconds. Immediately he dropped his arms back under his body and raced towards the shore near the top of the froth. He kicked hard to keep up with the speed of the water. To his right he saw the other surfer, still with him. He grinned with sheer pleasure and received the same look back. They washed up on the sand at the same time, panting. A wild one-hundred and fifty metre ride to shore.

"Man, what a blast," the other guy said.

"Nothing comes near it," agreed Rysakov.

He might be fit, he might be strong, he reckoned, but enough is enough. He picked up his towel and headed for a coffee.

The chief pathologist sat in his office in the city morgue looking at four sheets of results, side-by-side on his desk. He didn't want to be here on the weekend, but circumstances demanded it. With continuing local and international crises, the NSW State Government's Health Department budget never seemed sufficient to enable him to order enough updated equipment, or anywhere near the number of qualified staff he needed. So he waged an ultimately successful campaign to take in limited commercial test work, at full rates, and to dedicate the earnings to new equipment. DNA analysis was in highest demand and could be charged at a premium rate. However, the work often had to be done out of normal office hours, which was why he was here now, missing Saturday lunch with his family.

Six months ago one of the first commercial clients had been a successful investment banker, Will Callaghan. Callaghan wanted to know whether he carried the recessive gene causing cystic fibrosis, CFTR. He did not, and his DNA profile had been added to the data base along with every analysis undertaken using the equipment. Soon after, there had been a rare outbreak of collegiate cooperation between the State Health Departments. Each agreed to share DNA profiles to create a national database, not only for criminal cases, but for any purpose. Prosecutors in each State hoped this might make their job just a little easier and speed up the pace of criminal justice.

The DNA analysis of the body found in the bush did not match the sample provided by young John Martin, so the pathologist had been surprised to subsequently get a letter from the young man.

"This package came with the letter," the admin secretary told him. The letter mentioned him by name and thanked him for ringing personally to explain the DNA process.

> *I am not sure what has happened to my mother, or if I shall ever know. One thing I would like to know is whether my father and mother are my biological parents. I have had doubts for several years as a result of lots of little things. I would be very grateful if you could use your DNA machine to settle the matter for me.*

> *I am enclosing a hair brush of my mother's. I can't find anything else that might have her DNA on it. It all seems to have gone. Also a comb of my father's and a letter he licked to seal. I hope this will be enough.*

> *Please let me know how much the DNA tests costs. I have my own money in a savings account.*

> *I hope you can help me.*

The letter was signed, *John Martin.*

Whether it was the language of the letter, or whether he was overtired and emotional, he decided to follow through on the boy's request.

When he ran the analyses the result for his father came up negative. So did the result for his mother. They were not his biological parents. After some consideration he decided to invite the boy in and give him a copy of the analysis. What the kid did would be a matter for him.

On a whim he then ran the boy's profile through the national database, to see if he could get a match. He did it for no other reason than he could. He then forgot about it. When he checked the results before leaving that day he found, to his considerable surprise, he had a result. It matched the mitochondrial DNA (mtDNA) profile of Will Callaghan, his first DNA fee paying client. The two had a common female ancestor.

Now he had a problem. Without Callaghan's permission he could not tell the boy. The mere fact he had done the tests without permission could present a problem, though he thought it unlikely. On the other hand the information might be relevant to the police in an ongoing investigation. After rolling the issues around in his mind he picked up the phone to ring DS Rysakov, before remembering it was Saturday. He would decide how to approach Callaghan later.

At the time the pathologist picked up the phone to tell Rysakov the results of the DNA analysis, Jack Martin drove to Sophia Hamil's apartment.

22

A sense of unease had begun to infect his psyche. It started slowly and gathered momentum. He'd glimpsed the potential for problems several weeks ago. The conversation with Nestor during the week increased the feeling. The call from his source inside the company now put Kay on high alert.

The bastard is going to try and trick me, Kay thought. *He's going to keep my money.*

As it was, the loan fell due for repayment that week. Kay put down his copy of the loan document. It did have a clause giving the borrower an option to extend the loan for another two years, subject to both parties agreeing. He stopped wrestling with the problem. Whichever way he sliced it, he came to the same conclusion.

"Mr Clever Banker is going to use the option clause to keep my money for another two years," he said to himself. *He'll probably offer a higher interest rate to get me to agree*, he thought. *If I don't, he's got the cash, and it'll take me two years to go through the courts.* One last time he went over in his mind everything he knew. The same answer kept coming up, and he did not like it. *Why do people think they can take my money and get away with it?*

"That is not how it goes, Clive Nestor," Kay said out loud.

His own lack of experience with the detail of finance documents, as he now realised, had provided the investment banker with the opportunity. Hard business negotiations he could handle. Some you won, some you lost. That was life.

Calculated and deliberate breaking of a written agreement, one he had confirmed only last month, he would not tolerate. *Bloody Nestor knows very well the loan is due for repayment.* He cast his mind back several years to another banker who reneged on a commitment to a project Kay had heavily invested in. *Every morning when he shaves he can see what happens, from one side of his face to the other.* Kay smiled coldly.

He always got his money back. The female lawyer who advised the banker had died in a motor vehicle accident. His mind jumped. Could that have happened to Alice? No, he would have heard.

Alice Martin.

A rare kindred soul, he thought, *not constrained by conventions. No inhibitions.* He smiled at the recollection. *Buggered if I know what she saw in Nestor.*

Alice Martin was also the first person he had come across, after asking dozens, to explain the biotechnology industry to him, honestly. "Only bet what you can afford to lose," she said. "The chances of success are very small." So he didn't invest. Instead he tried to get a name to invest. That way he could do what the investment bankers did, keep a small free equity. When the name investor, Will Callaghan, declined the deal, Kay put biotech to one side. Instead he pursued an intermittent liaison with Alice.

"Not your fault, Alice, that your friend Nestor is an asshole, but you should have warned me. You really should have warned me," Kay said to the memory. He walked outside onto the balcony, wondering if they would ever find her.

Somehow he doubted it, certainly not alive.

23

The harsh faces of the two assassins stared at her intensely, their eyes unblinking. To one side sat the woman, her *hijab* loosely draped so it covered much of her face. Sophia did not understand if that represented appropriate modesty or an unwillingness to be identified. The frequency and urgency of the visitations had increased. She now saw them at least once a day, and they were becoming more insistent. She sat still on the couch in her apartment, waiting.

"It is important to send the correct message to other transgressors. Such is the righteousness of the Master's teaching that a personal message will be sent to other family members tempted to follow this path." The assassin stopped, waiting.

A mild panic gripped her. *They want me to respond,* she thought. She should just ignore them. An abstract part of her brain wondered what would happen if she did. But she couldn't, her head moved, nodding understanding. Any possibility of inaction withered when confronted with the brutality of those stares. Silence.

Finally, the woman stirred. She half-turned on her seat to face Sophia. As she did the *hijab* slid off her face. Sophia gasped. It was her grandmother, dead for many years.

"What happened was not right, but," she shrugged both bony shoulders, "we have to deal with it. With you it is not so straightforward. He is encouraging you, seducing you. You know it is wrong. You must act. Now! To do otherwise will damn you for eternity."

Grandma could not be ignored, even the men of the desert were wary of her.

"Do as they say," she said, pointing a bent arm at the men, both of whom continued to stare with undiminished intensity. For the first time a feeling of terror began to curdle in her stomach.

She nodded and had opened her mouth to ask a question when the doorbell rang. All three residents of Aleppo vanished. Sophia concentrated on the sound of the bell and tried to get her mind back into focus.

24

Rysakov thought the city skyline view justified the restaurant's name, City. When you thought about it, you had to be several kilometres out of a city to see it, rather than be in it. The atmosphere was low key but sophisticated, not too romantic for a first date. Nic Rysakov looked across the table at Sally. She looked gorgeous.

So tell her, he could hear his ex-wife saying, *women like compliments, you oaf.*

He couldn't be absolutely sure, but he thought the perfume she had on smelled like Dr Pratt's Original. "I've never had such good table service, Sally," he said. "At first I thought they were just angling for a good tip. Then I realised they're coming back to get a look at you." She gave him a wide smile and mouthed, "Thank you".

During dinner he discovered Sally's family background to be very similar to his own. Hard-working parents keen to provide an education that gave their children choices in life. Both their parents actively encouraged them to secure professional qualifications. They were rewarded in Sally's case, he pointed out, and a little disappointed in his case, when he entered the police force.

"I made up my mind a long time ago that I won't go through the privations my parents put up with," Sally said. "I want to see them spend their retirement free of money worries and in a new apartment, near a golf course."

"I think my own parents are happy enough their kids can support themselves. My old man reckons he'll have his mortgage paid off in a couple of years," Rysakov said.

"I want more than that. I want a house close to the city with water views, a holiday place up north, overseas holidays every year, and enough money to live well." She laughed nervously.

Rysakov decided to change the subject before he got out of his depth. A policeman's salary didn't stretch far. "From what you said earlier, with all ICI's projects, would you have the time? I mean to use a holiday house and travel."

Rysakov could sense Sally realised she had started to get a little intense and was grateful for a chance to change the subject.

"The market usually thinks of biotech when ICI is mentioned and we do have some really exciting products being developed. But the project with the most potential, I think, is in solar energy. It looks as though we may have made a breakthrough in generating solar power *and* in storing it. The key appears to be in using cobalt in a novel way, and no one yet seems to realise how big this could be."

The conversation meandered throughout the evening, neither getting bored with the other. Several bottles of wine were consumed, by which time Rysakov was confident enough to ask her if she would like to share a taxi home. "Just to make sure you arrive safely," he said.

To his surprise, she invited him in for a coffee. As they reached the door to Sally's apartment neither spoke as she fumbled with the key. Once inside, Nic kicked the door closed behind him. Within a minute clothes were being clawed off unceremoniously, the coffee forgotten.

The sun was well up when Sally lifted her head off his chest. "I've got some bad news. I have to get up and meet some friends for lunch," she said.

"Cancel," Nic said, before embracing her again.

"I wish I could."

He asked the taxi driver to go past the beach at Bondi before heading home. The swell looked good enough to get his gear and come back for a swim. Back to reality.

He would have to keep busy till next Friday.

"Sophia, it's me," Jack Martin called through the closed door. He pressed the bell for the tenth time, heard it echo inside the apartment, then silence. He could have sworn he heard sounds coming from inside. He wrapped his knuckles against the flat panel that may have once been glass. Still nothing. Maybe, he figured, she had gone to the deli for food. Had they arranged to meet for a quiet dinner today or had he mixed up the days? She had a light work load on Monday and often spent time in the library, researching. His work ended mid-afternoon, no lectures after three o'clock. They often met up at that time. Were they going to meet today? Perhaps, he couldn't be certain.

Therefore, he told himself, *logic dictates I come back at five.* The initial disappointment at finding an empty flat resolved into heady anticipation. He turned and walked out of the entranceway to the apartment block.

Inside, Sophia Hamil heard the retreating footsteps and looked up to see the *hijab* covered head of her grandmother. She must have also heard the footsteps going away. Sophia remained silent as a lop-sided grin formed on her face. An idea began to form.

"It must be done," said the figure, the voice clear and insistent in her head. She nodded again, but the odd grin remained. She would obey the voices, but in a way that suited her.

Jack Martin continued walking across the tree-lined campus park, thinking about the conversation he needed to have that night with Sophia. He would have preferred to get her explanation before they met tonight, but she'd been out. After an absence of a week he wanted nothing to interfere with their love-making. However, he had to find out what the facts were. She couldn't have made a mistake. That would not make sense. There had to be a good reason, he was sure of it.

The reply he received from the email enquiry he sent to Beirut last week, seeking the information he needed on Sophia's brother, was totally unexpected. He hadn't expected to get everything by return, more like "get me what you can now and the rest as soon as you are able." He had anticipated some of the information would be unobtainable, given the conflict that had devastated Lebanon over the years.

He was not prepared for the answer he received. He sent back a immediate query. Within twenty-four hours he had confirmation. There was no mistake, these records were intact. Sophia Hamil had no living brother. She once had an older brother, many years ago. The investigator recommended by the Australian Embassy wrote:

> *One person I spoke to, who appeared knowledgeable about the village and the family, said the brother disappeared more than ten years passed. It was widely suspected in the village that the two siblings had inappropriately close relations for a long time, though I have no evidence to support this story. All signs lead me to believe the brother has been dead for years, since before the family emmigrated to Australia.*

That was all, no further amplification or explanation. Several follow-up enquiries by Martin received the same answer: "He is dead." How or when, no one knew, only that he was. He left the email print-outs on his desk. He did not need them for the conversation with Sophia. No doubt there were other Hamils in Lebanon, perhaps records had become compromised or confused.

25

Soon after Rysakov arrived at his desk the following Monday the chief pathologist rang to advise him that the DNA results showed Alice and Professor Martin were not John's biological parents.

"What does that mean, if anything?" Rysakov asked.

"It would explain why Alice Martin could leave, if that's what she did," said PC Walsh.

Rysakov nodded. "Ruby, check out where the boy came from, what State and what age he was. Anything else you can get. Probably just another adoption, with the parents unwilling to tell the child the truth." He shrugged. "Call the professor first, it'll save time if he's cooperative." He turned to DC O'Leary. "Anything more on the Jane Doe in the bush?"

"Nothing I've heard, boss. Are you expecting something?"

"Not really, it's just the coincidence, the time of death being around the time of Alice Martin's disappearance." As he said that an outside possibility occurred to him. "Tom, I suppose the pathologist did go back and check the Jane Doe's DNA now they've got Alice Martin's."

"I'll check."

Rysakov turned back to PC Walsh. "Ruby, I'd like to have another run through of the State Art Gallery CCTV tape. I want to have a closer look at the woman Sandra Blake initially thought could be Alice."

"I marked the time sequence for each of those segments Ms Blake commented on," said PC Walsh. "It won't take long."

"Good, then don't bother getting her back in."

An hour later Rysakov sat watching the CCTV footage play and then replay. After the lunch break he called Tom O'Leary and Ruby Walsh into the room with the audio-visual equipment.

"I'm going to show you two sequences of people on the stairs at the gallery. The second sequence is the one where Sandra Blake initially thought she could have seen Alice, but became less certain every time we ran the footage. The first clip is from earlier in the evening. Tell me if you think there is anyone, male or female, that appears in both clips," he said.

He ran the sequences through twice before stopping. "Well?"

"There are a few people in each whose faces you can't see clearly. You always get some who don't want to be on record, want privacy, or just don't want to be recognised and stored," said O'Leary, adding, "We can eliminate the men."

"Only those that are indisputably male," said Rysakov. "What if she was disguised?"

"A really good disguise could present a problem," said O'Leary.

"I agree," said Walsh. "But that would require a bag of clothes, and make-up. Someone would have noticed the bag, and we would have seen it on the CCTV of the stairs."

"Maybe I'm starting to see things," said Rysakov, "but what about these two?"

He pressed PAUSE, freezing the frame on a group walking down the stairs. There were seven, one of whom seemed to be bringing up the rear. There was no clear view of any of the faces, particularly the seventh, who was almost certainly a woman.

"Keep that picture in your mind. Now look at this." He fast-forwarded to the shot of a woman walking up the stairs wearing a beret, with her face averted from the camera. "This was the image that Sandra Blake thought could be Alice."

Once they had time to absorb the images he asked, "Could they be the same person? Could Alice have carried a beret in her handbag, and – this is where I may be way off target – could the jacket she wore be reversible?"

"The first woman has a dark coloured jacket," said Walsh. "The beret woman has a light, probably beige or cream coloured jacket, and I think the style is different. The beret jacket has a tie. The other one looked as though it was open." She paused. "But she could have carried a tie in her handbag, I suppose."

Rysakov flicked back and forth between the clips without reaching a satisfactory consensus. "What we need is a software expert to take the two images out of the sequence and compare the physical characteristics, and the jacket. Ruby, can you see if you can find someone to do that? If we get some sort of match then it's possible Alice used a simple disguise to exit the function early and disappear. No one was expecting her to leave, so no one was watching. A simple switch of a couple of items and maybe some makeup and she walks out."

"In theory," said O'Leary. "What we need is evidence."

Ten minutes later, PC Walsh put the phone down and said, "Prof Martin has agreed to see us first thing tomorrow, at his home. Apparently he occasionally works a part day at home on a low load day."

"Good," said Rysakov without looking up from the file he was reading.

Jack Martin arrived later than he intended that afternoon. He smiled in anticipation as he pressed the bell. Sophia had sounded pleased when he rang to tell her he would be delayed.

"Gives me more time to prepare, Jopi," she had said. After he hung up he wondered where the new nickname came from. He could hear soft footsteps approaching the door. He decided he would raise the issue of her brother after they had made love. The door opened and Sophia stood in front of him, stark naked. She had an odd expression on her face, half smile, half leer.

Instantly aroused, he kicked the door closed behind him and put his arms around her. She pressed her body into his and began thrusting her hips rhythmically against him. In the back of his mind a question mark flashed weakly. This was a different Sophia. Something seemed out of balance. He looked at her face. Her eyes were half closed with a pleasure glaze as she became more and more aroused. She took him by the hand and led him into her bedroom. Any vague misgivings he may have had vanished.

"I'm ready like you told me," she said. He wondered if this might be a new game she wanted to play. By now he was so aroused it didn't matter.

She had never been so uninhibited. It momentarily occurred to him that soldiers departing for the front line probably spent their last moments with their sweethearts with similar abandonment. He did not seem able to satisfy her. No sooner had they recovered than she had something new to try. Eventually, exhausted, they both fell asleep.

"Rysakov," he said into his phone the next morning, only half awake. *Shit, it's only six a.m.*, he thought after a quick glance at the radio alarm alongside his bed.

"Mike Smith, Nic. You still running the Alice Martin disappearance?" said DS Smith.

"Yeah," Rysakov replied, now wide awake.

"You better pull on your pants and get over to the Hamil girl's place," DS Smith said, rattling off the address. "Don't stop for breakfast."

Rysakov closed his phone and rolled out of bed. He had worked with Mike Smith in the past. They got on well. Smith still worked in Homicide. For Smith to call him this early could only mean bad news. It was not going to be a good day.

26

Sophia woke suddenly. Jack Martin had not moved. He lay where he had gone to sleep, breathing regularly. She did not think she had slept for long. Gently, she climbed out of the bed and tiptoed into the kitchen where the full moon bathed the room in enough light for her to see. She found what she wanted and a minute later eased back into bed, careful not to disturb Martin. She slid her right hand under her pillow and lay down.

Suddenly, she sensed someone else in the room. She sat bolt upright, Martin stirred in his sleep and rolled over. Her grandmother stood at the foot of the bed, behind her stood the two hawk-faced assassins. They stared at her, censorious faces, silent and severe. Then her grandmother smiled, a hard, bleak expression, wholly devoid of warmth.

"I know," Sophia whispered. "I am ready."

The ancient head nodded slowly. "You must do it, there is no alternative," the voice said. "It is your duty."

"Will you stay?" she asked.

The three figures stared silently at her, and did not move. Sophia slid her hand under the pillow.

On his way out, Rysakov rang PC Walsh to tell her to meet him at Sophia Hamil's address.

"OK, boss. Martin's not at home anyway. I rang to confirm our appointment and his son said he didn't come home last night," Walsh said.

The light early morning traffic pulled to the side of the road at first sight of the flashing blue light on his car. Rysakov arrived at the Hamil apartment fast, minutes before the forensic team. Two police cars stood at the curb outside the building, red and blue lights spinning. Mike Smith met him at the entrance. They stepped under the blue and white police tape and went inside, careful not to disturb the scene. As they did Rysakov pointed to what could only be a dried pool of blood.

"Is that what I think it is?" he asked.

"Yeah," said Smith, "come in and I'll run you through what we think happened. In fact there's little doubt about it. No suggestion of outside parties."

They stopped at the entrance to the bedroom. Through the door Rysakov saw a bed with sheets all askew. At the head lay a broad flat pillow soaked in blood. Just off the pillow sprawled half across the bed, with his neck bent at an unnatural angle, lay Professor Jack Martin. Blood covered most of the mattress. There were even splashes on the carpet.

Probably carotid artery spurts from the side of his neck, thought Rysakov, scrunching his nose. "Christ!" he said. The cloying-sweet smell of recently spilt blood overwhelmed his senses in the airless room. "Open a window."

"My guess is that the weapon was a very sharp narrow-shaped blade, easy to force through flesh. Probably a chef's kitchen knife. My guess is that the victim..."

"It's Professor Jack Martin," said Rysakov. "That's a positive ID."

"OK," Smith nodded. "I reckon the professor was asleep on his side, neck exposed, and the perp, almost certainly the Hamil girl, stabs down into the neck..." He lifted both hands above his head to simulate the action, continuing, "...severing the carotid artery completely, which is consistent with the distribution pattern on the bed and the floor. He would have lost consciousness within a minute, dead in four to five. He never woke up properly. The blade might've cut his trachea as well."

"Who gave the alarm?" asked Rysakov.

"Well that's the funny thing. It was the girl. Maybe she had second thoughts, or snapped out of whatever trance these whackos get into. She stays here, on the bed, until the professor's blood stops pumping. She's got blood splatters all over her breasts, face and arms. Then she walks out into the corridor, stark naked, yelling,

'It is done, grandma, it is done!' The woman next door, who says she's a light sleeper, opens her door and sees a blood covered naked female wielding a knife. So she does the sensible thing, slams the door and calls the cops."

"What happened next?" asked Rysakov. He saw PC Walsh speaking to one of the other uniformed police and beckoned her over.

"Best we can figure, the girl snaps out of her trance, turns to go back into her apartment, trips and falls on the knife. It penetrated her heart. It should've bounced off a rib or gone in at an angle, but it didn't, just bad luck. Anyway, she's dead before anyone arrives. That's the pool of blood you saw coming in. We removed her body first, being in a public place."

Rysakov nodded. He would leave the rest for Mike Smith to attend to. Nothing further relevant to Alice Martin would be learned here.

"Mike, you OK if we have a look at Martin's office today? We've still got no lead on his wife," said Rysakov. He motioned for Walsh to follow him as he left.

"Sure," said Smith.

"These deaths don't seem to have anything to do with Alice Martin's disappearance, but the professor's death leaves an eighteen year-old without parents," he said as they headed toward their cars.

"Adoptive parents," corrected Walsh.

"That's right," said Rysakov. "Any progress in tracking down his biological parents?"

"I've sent out the usual queries, but the privacy laws mean John Martin would have a better chance himself."

"Get your enquiries back, but don't spend any more time on it," he said. Walsh nodded. No point chasing a dead-end.

When in Sydney, Will Callaghan lived in what had been his family's home in Narrabeen, by personal choice. He sat staring out the window at the surf, finding it hard to focus. What an extraordinary conversation. It bordered on the bizarre. The chief pathologist at the city morgue, of all places, had called and informed him he had a blood relative in Sydney. One with whom he shared a common female ancestor. After swiftly giving approval, retrospectively, for use of his DNA profile, he told the pathologist, "I'd like to meet this young man. When you give him the information, please ask him to call me."

Now, twenty-four hours later, John Martin sat on Callaghan's balcony drinking a beer. As he listened to the teenager, Callaghan wondered how far back their shared heritage went. He liked the boy. They seemed to get on well. When he heard that John had lost both parents in such quick succession, he immediately thought, could he, or more importantly should he, offer to become his guardian? He had no children, but he did have substantial wealth.

Plenty of time to think about that, he thought. *And of course his mother could turn up at any time.*

So he decided to watch and wait. Experience suggested more was still to come. It could be anything, up to and including murder, based on recent events. Until there was clarity, he decided he would give John Martin whatever help and support he needed, legal, financial or emotional. They were related after all.

"It's difficult to know how far back our common ancestor is, but there's a strong possibility it's my great-grandmother, Katya, who I only discovered myself in recent years."

"Where did she live?" John asked.

With many interruptions, Callaghan told him what had happened after his chance discovery of a letter in a violin case his own mother, one of Katya's granddaughters, brought with her from China. A couple, who became his own adoptive grandparents, found his mother as a young girl wandering alone in Shanghai just before the Japanese took full control. They came to Sydney on the last boat out of China as Japan entered World War II. Another of Katya's children, Anna, had married a Czech and gone to live near Prague in the 1920s.

"In all likelihood Anna is your great-grandmother," said Callaghan. "You're going to need a lawyer to help you with your adoptive father's estate, maybe even to look at your position as potentially his sole heir. I can recommend a good one, or you can choose one of your own. I'll guarantee payment of their account. That way you can choose anyone you like." He paused. "So, it looks like we're related, John," he said after a while. "That makes you family."

For the first time since he arrived, John Martin's face opened in a broad smile.

27

Warren Kay did not like being photographed. Anonymity offered protection. Once lost it could never be regained. So far as he knew the police had one photograph, from the year after he left school. He had never been charged with the assault, so he did not know if it remained on file.

Funny, Alice didn't like having her photo taken either. Wonder why?

He sympathised. He never discovered Alice's real reason, except that it was almost certainly not his. The same logic meant he never succumbed to the new media. No Facebook page, no Twitter account, no Google email, in fact he only had one ISP and email account, in a false name. That was his only concession; and he had to admit, the internet proved very useful at times.

He crossed the street and hopped onto the curb. It looked like a media scrum in front of the office block on Castleraegh Street. Flashing cameras confirmed it. Whoever they were pursuing, he would not be walking in that entrance. He checked the side door was clear and stepped into the first elevator that opened.

Ignoring the receptionist and spectacular harbour view, he walked through the office foyer, past analyst's work-stations, opened the door to a large office, and strode in.

"I'm sorry, sir," said the receptionist following him as fast as her high heels allowed. "Mr Nestor is not in. Please wait in the foyer area."

"I'm a shareholder in this business," Kay said. "I expect Clive will be along as soon as the media have enough photos. I'll have a black coffee while I wait."

As soon as the secretary left he closed the door and hurried behind Nestor's desk. No papers, no files, too clean. He tested the drawers down the two sides, locked. A small filing cabinet, also locked. Finally, he pulled at the door to a credenza. It opened to reveal a selection of glasses and several bottles, whisky, gin and one other. He heard the door opening and stepped over to the window, to look at the view.

"Hello, Warren, I wasn't expecting you in the office today," Clive Nestor said, bursting into the room.

"I'm sure you weren't. On the other hand, I *am* expecting my loan to be repaid, Clive. I get the feeling you may not be intending to. That would be unwise."

Kay stood directly in front of the banker. Three inches taller, broader shoulders, obviously stronger, Kay intended to intimidate. He wanted to leave no doubt in Nestor's mind. His money must be repaid; the consequences for not doing so would be severe. As Kay stood there, his expression cold and uncompromising, he saw fear flit briefly across Nestor's eyes. The banker almost suppressed it before turning his face away. Now Kay had no doubts. Nestor had been intending to keep the money.

"The public issue for Renewable Energy Inc. is nearly complete," Nestor said, rushing his words. "But it could take a couple of weeks to a month, what with lawyers, investors and so on, before it's finalised. Then we can arrange repayment." When he received no response he went on. "There is no doubt that REI will be a roaring success on the stock exchange, a lot of fund managers are keen to invest. It'll give speculators a good profit and longer term holders an even better return."

"The loan is due now and will not be extended," Kay reiterated, his voice ice-cold.

When Kay left, Nestor unlocked his desk, took out a file, found a phone number and dialled the Bahamas, clutching his chest.

The banker in the Bahamas answered the phone. It was the second call of the day on what he had expected to be an inactive account. *Interesting*, he thought, *that I now get a call from Mr Nestor.*

The call went longer than usual. Finally, he hung up, making a file note to increase the handling fees. He made no mention to

Nestor of the earlier call he had received. However, according to his instructions, he now rang the earlier caller to tell them of Nestor's call. They were paying him a far larger fee than he could ever get from Nestor. With half paid up front. Very generous.

28

As she entered the café, Sally McIntosh still didn't really fathom why she had agreed to have coffee with the old man. Maybe that was it, he was old and she felt sorry for him. He introduced himself as Alice's Uncle Henry. Although Alice had not referred to any uncle in all the time Sally had known her, Sally did not consider querying whether he was Alice's uncle. His strong European accent helped convince her. She sat across the table in the local Gloria Jean's Coffee shop and listened as he told her that all the information she supplied to Alice had in turn been passed on to him.

"For further research purposes," he said.

He told her enough technical information for there to be no doubt about his connection to Alice. And he knew exactly how much Alice had paid her, and of the large sum promised on delivery of proof of concept. None of these payments were traceable to him, he said, or to Alice. Sally sat listening to her actions being recited back to her. For the first time the seriousness of what she had done sank in.

It only took several minutes for Sally to realise she did not like Uncle Henry. It had been a mistake to meet him. She had not realised how much personal information Alice had accumulated about her. Now this man knew it all.

"You will continue to send me the information you would have given to Alice," he said.

"There are problems with some of the test work," she said, knowing full well she would never do as he asked. Dealing with Alice was one thing. Dealing with a foreigner who treated her like a vassal was another. "There will not be any more data for some time. I'm not even sure if these projects will go any further."

Sally added to herself, *Maybe if I tell him the project's failed, then there is nothing to hand over, and I can end any contact with Alice and this odious creep.*

"Alice told me before she disappeared that full test data would be available within two weeks. There were no problems," he said.

His eyes looked ice-cold. "I'm afraid I have to go back to my office now," she said, standing up.

"This is my telephone number," he said placing a business card in front of her. "Ring me when the data is ready."

Sally barely glanced at the card, noticing only the name Heinrich before striding out of the coffee shop, leaving the card on the table. As she turned the corner to exit the shopping centre she glanced back. Heinrich had not moved. He caught her eye, causing her to miss a step before she rounded the corner.

Schmidt did not move for quite some while after Sally McIntosh left. He sat, immobile, staring at the space she had vacated. He felt like the old man he was, lost in the past. A pretty girl who had been there, was now gone. It could be a metaphor for his life. And he was thinking about the girl who had just gone, about life, about her life and how it could affect his. Unfortunately for Sally, none of these thoughts were in her best interest.

Her refusal to cooperate did not come as a complete surprise. On the other hand, if he had been a betting man he would have wagered she'd at least have tried to negotiate her way out by giving him the latest data, asking for more money and then saying, reluctantly, that would be the end. But she had shown no interest in money. He had confidently expected to threaten her with exposure. She had not given him the opportunity. For some reason she did not appear concerned about exposure. That worried him.

If I send the details of her spying to the ICI Board she must surely go to gaol, he thought. *What have I missed?* A sliver of doubt entered his mind, a feeling to which he was unaccustomed.

What could have possessed Alice to disappear at such a critical time? The police appeared to expect foul play. Schmidt thought that unlikely, but possible. In any event, with each day's passing it became more irrelevant. His flawless record stood as testament to a lifetime's dedication. Now, in the twilight of his career, two young women were about to blemish his record. And one of them knew how much that record meant to him. The more he thought about it, the angrier he became.

He stood, slowly. Two arthritic hips only one of a number of age related medical issues. The decision made, he knew what had to be done. He felt confident again. Meticulous planning would be required, an area where he could claim, with all due modesty, to be amongst the best. One last field operation.

Later that day, as PC Walsh drove him back to the station, Rysakov called DS Smith.

"Mike, we had a look through Jack Martin's files and desk. He had received several emails from the authorities in Lebanon stating that the Hamil girl did not have a living brother. Apparently she had one years ago, but he died. So she was either scamming the professor, or a sandwich short of a picnic," he said.

"It was the latter. Forensic found pills for schizophrenics in her flat. They spoke to the prescribing doctor. She went for long periods where she took them conscientiously, then stopped for no discernible reason. Not unusual I gather," Smith said. "From what the doctor said he couldn't rule out the possibility of psychotic episodes in her case. We'll see what the coroner thinks, but it looks pretty straightforward to me."

As the car turned into the police car park, Rysakov noticed a smile on PC Walsh's face before he realised he'd been staring at her for the last five minutes.

29

Sally McIntosh hurried out of the smart apartment block where she lived. She could see the trees at the end of the block. They reminded her she had not been in the park to see the gardens for months. She nodded briefly to the casually dressed man who passed her going in the opposite direction. A break in the traffic appeared and she hurried across the road.

Not until she sat on the stool at the bench covered with daily papers, and a hot coffee in her hand, did she wonder who the casually dressed man could be. She figured she must have seen him on a number of occasions to have automatically greeted him. *Must live around here*, she thought and picked up the newspaper.

As she opened the front page she thought of Schmidt. She had little doubt he would try, at least once more, to induce her to maintain Alice's flow of data. Having had time to think over the alternatives, she decided to sever all contact with him, and Alice. If Alice ever returned. What could he do? If he reported her to ICI, she had only exchanged information with a colleague who worked for ICI.

In breach of the rules, sure, she thought. *I'd get a reprimand, and any prospects for promotion would be gone. Then again, maybe he doesn't want it known he's been receiving confidential information. How can he report me, and make his accusation credible, without admitting his involvement?*

She knew instinctively that old man Schmidt hadn't bought her lies. What he didn't know was how close they really were. Her boss, the director, had ordered a new series of tests to confirm the results. If the original results proved correct, the discovery would revolutionise the use of solar energy. They had created a completely new type of battery.

This'll be worth billions, she thought. *The tests will take a week at the outside, then, they'll have to announce it. No way they can keep a lid on it.*

"Bugger Alice, bugger Schmidt, this is too good," she said as she stood and stepped off the pavement. A frantic horn and screech of rubber shattered her thoughts. She jumped back in fright as a courier van swerved around where she had been seconds before. A Ford sedan, which had been following the van, came into her peripheral vision and, still in shock, she again jumped backwards. Her heel caught on the kerb and she fell hard onto the pavement.

The first person to offer to help her up was the casually dressed man she had greeted earlier. "Are you OK? Let me help you up."
"Thank you," she said, tears forming in her eyes..
As she steadied, he pressed a tiny tracking device to the underside of her handbag, into a fold in the leather, excused himself and headed back down the street, job done.

One of her heels had snapped during her fall. Taking off her shoes, she checked the traffic and crossed the road. By the time she sat down in her apartment tears were flowing freely. When the phone rang she dried her face and composed herself.
"Hi, Nic," she replied into the receiver.
"I'd love to go out on Saturday."
"See you then."
She hung up.
For one brief moment she contemplated telling Nic Rysakov about Schmidt. Immediately she realised how impossible that would be. To seek his protection from any imagined harm that might come from the old man she would be forced to tell him the full story. That would see the end of her freedom. Could a policeman ignore what his lover told him? She didn't know. For the next hour she sat, paced the length of her living room and made notes on a legal pad. The shock of the near miss with the van focused her mind. She ran through all the conversations she could recall having with Alice. At first their interactions had been minimal, but, as they came to know each other Alice had opened up, just a little, sufficient to give Sally a picture of a woman with a plan. The picture was far from complete

and Alice had not confided any part of a plan. For Sally it was not so much what was said, but how it was said. Sally got the impression revenge formed an integral part of whatever the plan entailed. What Alice intended and why, Sally had no idea.

Even though it might help his search for Alice she could not risk telling Nic that in her view Alice was not coming back, ever. *Dead or fled*, that's how she thought of it. Either way, Sally believed, whatever Alice had planned almost certainly remained in place. But she had no proof, so most of the next hour she spent trying to piece together just what Alice may have been intending. Revenge, for a woman, would most likely take an emotional or monetary form. For some reason she didn't think it would be emotional, that did not fit the Alice she knew. To inflict monetary pain, on the other hand, almost certainly required help.

She came up with one more certainty. Whatever help Alice may have required, it did not come from Heinrich Schmidt. *He'd only help if he personally got a benefit*, she thought. The only other names Alice had mentioned were her husband, Jack, and a friend from university with whom she'd had an affair. None of that helped.

John Martin answered the phone.

"Will Callaghan, John. I've just heard from the lawyers we briefed. They'll ring to arrange a meeting for you to go through it all in detail. In fact, I asked them why they didn't contact you first. I reminded them you are their client, just because I'm paying the bills doesn't change that," Callaghan said. "Firstly, your father left the bulk of his estate to be divided equally between you and his wife, Alice. The lawyers believe you can sell all the assets if you decide to. However, one half of the proceeds must be placed in trust for Alice. If she is confirmed to have passed away, her share will go to you, unless a new will of hers is discovered."

"What if there is no trace of her?" asked John.

"Death in absentia is usually declared after seven years," said Callaghan. "Secondly, the lawyers had more luck than I expected in tracking down your personal history. The papers lodged with the Immigration Department in Australia show your place of birth as Prague in the Czech Republic. They also had a copy of a birth certificate which they will give you when you meet."

The names on the birth certificate meant nothing to Callaghan. He stopped speaking and for a short time John remained silent.

"So, I'm really Czech?"

"Looks like it," said Callaghan. "Maybe you should think about going to Prague one day. When you've spoken with the lawyers and feel like a beer and a meal, give me a call and I'll tell you a bit more of my story."

As he was about to disconnect, Callaghan added as an afterthought, "I'd suggest you don't discuss this with anyone at this stage. At least, not until you have all the information."

30

Rysakov listened to the chief pathologist while he read a report on his desk. It took him several seconds to realise the scientist had stopped speaking.

"Sorry, I was thinking," he said.

"In summary then," the pathologist concluded, "the female found in the national park was murdered, almost certainly asphyxiated as she lay on her back on a firm flat surface, based on the traces of livor mortise in the body. I'd also wager the death was accidental, possibly part of some sex game. We found tiny traces of two different types of semen. Chances are that the last client, realising the girl was dead, put her in his car and dumped the body where it was found."

The pathologist stopped. Rysakov had the distinct feeling that there was more.

"That's impressive, but this is now a homicide," said Rysakov, "over to the heavy boys."

"I've already told them," said the pathologist impatiently. "You showed some early interest so I'm just keeping you informed."

"Nice."

Rysakov waited.

"I know who she is," the pathologist said.

"Now that is impressive," said Rysakov, his interest piqued.

"She was arrested for soliciting in a city hotel foyer a year ago. The arresting officer took finger prints and got a DNA sample. So, when I ran her DNA through the data-base, bingo! She's a sex worker and the vice boys know who she works for so they can track down her last client."

Rysakov understood the pathologist had not called him for flippant reasons. There was a remote possibility the murder of the call girl may have some connection to the disappearance of Alice Martin.

He made a short hand-written note for the file and returned it to the current pile on his desk.

The lawyers for John Martin had sent him a copy of their assessment of the terms of the will and copies of the documents from Immigration. They noted this was at the behest of Will Callaghan, Martin's adviser, and with Martin's consent.

Rysakov pushed back in his seat. He only had a vague recollection of Callaghan, so he Googled him. An ex-investment banker and hedge fund manager who had bet the farm and lost, now rumoured to be back on his feet with private UK backing.

"These reports give us the background on John Martin, but they're probably not much help in finding Alice," he said, handing the file from the lawyers to PC Walsh.

He decided to go for a long walk to clear his head and review the Alice Martin case. He exited the police station and bought a chicken sandwich at the kiosk by the corner, eating it as he walked. The route he usually followed on these excursions covered a circuit of about three kilometres from Redfern down the length of Hyde Park and back.

His thoughts seemed to flow more freely as he walked. Alice seemed to have vanished without trace. None of the usual leads; no use of any of her credit cards, her passport left at her home, no airline or interstate train tickets, no contacts with any of her friends or with Heinrich Schmidt, no admittance to any hospitals in Australia. The media campaign had drawn a blank. None of the sightings had checked out. However, there was the CCTV tape from the State Art Gallery. He still had a question mark over that. What if the Blake woman had been right and the figure in the beret was Alice? Then she must have gone to the exhibition intending to disappear. If that were the case, she could have used a disguise and false passport to leave the country. If she had access to funds in another name, anything was possible.

There was of course one other explanation. It too often turned out to be the correct explanation in these cases. She was dead. Her body disposed of in a way they would never discover. Like the barrister rumoured to have been dismembered and fed through a mulching machine. And the lime bath that ate away everything except the teeth and finger nails. He finished his sandwich.

The simple, straightforward answer was often the right one. Complicated solutions were not usually the norm, because, well, they were complicated. As he walked back into the station through the glass doors, out of the heat and back into the air-conditioned cool, he suspected the case of Alice Martin had a few more surprises in store before it was done. So far there were two dead, three if the Jane Doe turned out to have some connection to Alice.

He had just sat down when PC Walsh appeared on the other side of his desk.

"Sir, what if Jack Martin killed his wife and disposed of her body. I've read that some of the Lebanese crime groups are very successful in making bodies disappear, and he did have all those contacts with people in Beirut," she said. "Now he's dead. I don't fancy our chances of finding Alice Martin, dead or alive."

31

Clive Nestor sat in his office looking out the window at the harbour, only minimally aware of the yachts in full sail, the ferries docking at Circular Quay. The smile hovering on his lips had nothing to do with the magnificent view. The pre-marketing hype for the new issue of shares now exceeded even his most optimistic forecasts. Fuelled by rumours, rumours he himself had leaked into financial markets, interest had reached a level where fund managers were competing for allocations of shares. Today he had briefed a journalist, on an exclusive non-attributable basis, that the company had cornered the market in a rare commodity, one essential to a revolutionary new technology. Even cynical, seasoned market veterans sniffed the air and decided they could not ignore the rising ground swell of interest. If it turned out to be only half as good as the rumours, they wanted a piece of the action.

He figured the company could probably double the equity they intended raising and still have a huge unsatisfied demand for the shares. After a few moments consideration he decided to recommend that the directors increase the amount of cash raised. It would make Renewable Energy Inc. a much stronger entity, and more attractive to investors.

With the extra funds REI would be in a much stronger position to purchase stock of, contracts for, and mines producing, cobalt. By increasing its financial strength REI would be in even greater demand in the market. The greatest danger in the new issue, however, was for interest to peak too early. If that happened all the hype could collapse like a pricked balloon, the shares would never reach the price at which he intended to sell. He had expected ICI to announce their discovery two days ago. If it was going to be any later than a week he needed to know. His timetable revolved around the information Alice had given him. While one had some flexibility with speculative companies, once the real promotion began that flexibility contracted dramatically. He needed a source in ICI who could tell him when their announcement would be made. Only then would he know if he had a problem.

He continued staring at the harbour for some time before swivelling his chair to the desk and typing a three letter name onto his iPad. Potentially this was a far more serious threat. Warren Kay had called him that morning. He explained again to Kay that the REI share issue should be completed within weeks, a month tops. At that time Nestor, Nankervis & Co. could repay his loan. Not before. When Nestor finished speaking, Kay said not a word, he simply ended the call.

That worried Nestor.

As for Kay, he held a lien over a controlling interest in Nestor, Nankervis & Co. as security for his loan. After his call to Nestor he had no doubts, by the end of the week, one way or another, he would control the business. At least he would attempt to. The fact that he had clear rights to get repaid or exercise his charge over control did not mean he would get it. Not easily, not without a fight. Nestor would fight, and not only with legal manoeuvrings. Kay was convinced Nestor intended to keep the money and avoid repayment. Kay discussed the problem with his lawyer, Joe Garand. Garand suited him to a tee, a practitioner who believed the law was there to be exploited and that the statutes were simply guideposts around which to negotiate.

"If I was acting for you to keep this guy's money, I could tie him up with proceeding, delays, appeals, and counter claims. If you finally did have to pay the money back it would be years down the track. In the meantime, you'd run the business down so that there's no value left and no assets to sell to repay the loan," said Garand.

"So how will he pay the bills in the meantime?" asked Kay.

"I would set up another company, not owned by you, that would employ you to do whatever it is that you did before," said Garand. "However, I still think you'd be better off trying to persuade Clive

Nestor to honour the loan agreement in some way. It'd be a lot less drama and cost."

By the time he returned to his penthouse, he'd made a decision on Nestor's debt. That done, he hit MESSAGES on his phone. He didn't get past the first message.

"Mr Kay, this is DS Smith from Homicide. Please call me as soon as you get this message."

He remembered Smith from a previous encounter, a tough, straightforward cop, one to be wary of. Someone who took pride in careful planning and attention to detail. So what Homicide could want with him he couldn't imagine. Kay had two rules regarding the police: Keep a low profile and never volunteer information. On the few occasions the police had cause to question him, those two rules had stood him in good stead. So far.

32

Nic Rysakov walked the short distance from his office to the police training facility at Redfern thinking about Sally. He thought about her a lot in fact, more than he expected. Training sessions always seemed to him, and to most other senior front-line officers when they discussed it, as nothing more than attempts to formalise the bleedin' obvious.

A sign INTRA-FORCE TRAINING – DIVISIONAL CO-OPERATION directed him to one of the smaller rooms down the corridor on the fifth floor. As he looked for a seat he saw DS Mike Smith.

"Couldn't get out of it either?" Smith said.

Rysakov smiled. "None of the old excuses work these days."

As they queued for coffee at the mid-morning break Mike Smith turned to Rysakov. "Looks like we have a possible starter for the Jane Doe in the National Park."

"Yeah, so I hear."

"Oh, we know who she is. Good chance we also know who killed her."

"They only give you the easy ones, Mike," Rysakov said, pouring coffee from the urn.

"One of the sources we spoke to said in passing that our suspect mentioned one Alice Martin when making a booking. Some sort of comparison I gather. The publicity about Alice triggered his memory and when we asked about our man he made the connection." Rysakov cocked his eyebrows. "Like to come along when I interview him?"

Will Callaghan forced himself to refocus on the spreadsheets in front of him on the laptop. Investment decisions had to be made today, like every other day. Often the decision was to do nothing.

Without the right amount of thought and planning, even that decision could be as expensive as the wrong buy, or sell. After many years managing his own business Callaghan had developed a strong self-discipline, initially as a sought-after investment banker. Then, deciding to act as a principal, he borrowed a large amount of money to buy and sell businesses. Several spectacular successes led to over confidence and the whole pack of cards collapsed. He lost the lot.

Once he had settled his creditors he had the luxury of time on his hands. Without the enforced leisure he would not have made the discovery that led to an extraordinary inheritance, one of which he was certain not even his mother, when she was alive, had any knowledge. Callaghan now owned a very private multi-billion dollar investment trust. He ranked among the elite of international private equity investors. Only three people knew just how wealthy he really was. He lived comfortably, but not ostentatiously.

He completed the phone call, sent an email confirmation and pushed his chair back from the partner's desk. An early mentor in investment banking had impressed on him the adage that one did not have to like the people one invested in, just be sure they could make money. When he first met Clive Nestor, he didn't like him, too brash and showy for Callaghan. So be it, he had thought, the market says he is a money maker so they went ahead and invested.

As a shareholder he received the information on the forthcoming new issue, Renewable Energy Inc. It looked exciting. It could be a game changer on a global scale and he intended to take the maximum available stake. He already held a major position in hydrocarbon fuels. If this new technology worked, it could be a long term replacement and without doubt establish solar energy as a prime energy source.

That was not what exercised his mind now. A conversation with a well-informed lawyer alerted him that a recent shareholder had begun action to take control of Nestor Nankevis & Co. Callaghan immediately sought detailed background on the shareholder. What he discovered about Warren Kay made him uneasy, very uneasy. The name prompted his memory. A check of the files in his office showed Kay had proposed several deals two years ago, neither of which Callaghan had invested in.

Now he faced a more complex decision. *Do I put up the money to pay Kay out, and buy his shares as part of the deal, or do nothing?* First step, speak to Nestor.

33

With PC Ruby Walsh's down-beat assessment in the back of his mind, Rysakov pulled out the photo of Alice Martin, that slightly fuzzy group picture from university days. He was still perplexed as to how there existed only one photo of her.

"But there is another photo," he said, loud enough for PC Walsh to look up from her desk. "Ruby, ring John Martin and arrange to pick up his mother's passport. Damn, we should have thought of that before. There'll be a recent photo in it."

"I think the passport's in one of the evidence files, sir," she said.

A short time later she returned and opened Alice's passport. The hair had been tinted and pulled back in a rather severe style, which had the effect of flattening and broadening the appearance of her face. Her lips were thick, accented by a deep red lip gloss. This was a different person to the other photo.

"Maybe this is what she looks like now."

"If she didn't she wouldn't get through passport control," said Rysakov. "Check with Immigration. If she went out like this, she's long gone. Or she's used another passport."

"Or she's dead," added Ruby.

Several hours later Rysakov rang Sally to confirm their date for later in the week. He ended the call as Mike Smith walked in.

On the drive across town, Smith briefed Rysakov on what they knew about Warren Kay, his reputation as a dangerous man to wrong-side, his apparently successful business deals and, based on information the call girl's madam had provided, including his appetite for unusual and twisted sex. "Her words," said Smith.

"He's a teflon target," Smith added. "Never been arrested, no convictions. But, he's clever and, in my opinion, dangerous."

Kay opened the door to the penthouse himself, leading the

officers through to the living room. He gestured to two lounge chairs set facing the harbour view, taking in the Harbour Bridge, the Opera House and a steady stream of ferries going in and out of Circular Quay. He then sat with his back to the view, and to the light, still and silent, waiting for the policemen to commence the interview.

This is one cool cat, thought Rysakov. *He actually looks like an innocent man.*

He was pleased Smith began exactly as he would had it been his interview. The guy clearly didn't want any small talk, so don't give any.

"Mr Kay you know a woman called Honey French," Smith said.

"I've used a call girl who trades under that name. If that is who you mean, then I know her," Kay replied, surprising Rysakov with his frankness.

"You hired her on the twenty-eighth of November. What time did she leave?"

"Are you certain on the date? If not, I can confirm it," Kay said.

As no doubt intended, the offer demonstrated Kay's confidence, a matter not missed by Rysakov.

"No need, we already have independent confirmation," said Smith.

Clever, Rysakov thought, *now he knows the source.* Kay nodded and stayed silent.

"Honey French's decomposing body was found recently."

"Where?"

"Why is that important?"

"I may have seen it on the news."

DS Smith remained silent for a moment. He continued looking directly at Kay who calmly returned the stare. *Unperturbed*, that's how Rysakov thought the suspect appeared.

"The body was found by a jogger in the Manly Dam Reserve," Rysakov said, allowing Smith to watch for any reaction. There was none.

Kay nodded, "I saw that on the news a week or so ago."

"The forensic evidence says she died on the twenty-eighth of November. What happened? Wouldn't she do as you asked? Some of these rent girls forget who's paying don't they," said Smith. With no response from Kay, Smith continued an increasingly aggressive line of questions.

Finally, Kay leaned forward and said, quite calmly, "Detective Sergeant, we both know that Honey French may have died then or on the twenty-ninth. In this hot humid weather the speed of decomposition may have increased, at least I remember hearing something along those lines in a TV series. One of the *CSIs* I think. From what I recall, none of the methods used to determine time of death are one hundred percent reliable or precise." He paused, before adding. "The last time I had Honey around, whatever the date, I kicked her out by nine p.m. There was a fight special on TV, cage fighting, I wanted to see. Where she went when she left here," he shrugged, "I have no idea. Maybe you could check the cab companies, the local ones or Silver Service. I recall her using them in the past."

Smith wrote something in his notebook before looking hard at Kay. "We have evidence that places you where the body was found."

"I don't believe you," said Kay, "particularly since I wasn't there."

"The evidence is very persuasive."

"If you're talking DNA, I had sex with her earlier that night. That's all it proves. You do know she's a call girl?" Kay asked with just enough sarcasm.

Rysakov sensed Mike Smith had gone as far as he could at this meeting. He was going to need additional hard evidence to have any chance of shaking Kay.

"For the record, DS Smith," Kay said, "I did not kill Honey French."

"Mr Kay, I wonder if you could help me, on an unrelated matter?" Rysakov said. Kay shifted his centre of gravity slightly to the left so he faced Rysakov more squarely. For the first time in many years Nic Rysakov felt cold, naked power. He returned the gaze with a hint of amusement. He was in no way intimidated.

"When did you last see Alice Martin?"

Rysakov felt pleased when a flash of surprise registered fleetingly on Kay's face. *He wasn't expecting that.*

"I don't recall offhand, we met irregularly."

"How well do you know her?"

Asking a loaded question without warning nearly always worked. Rysakov could now concentrate on extracting any information that might point to the whereabouts of Alice Martin, or what happened to her.

"We had common personal interests."

"When you last saw her did she mention going away?"

"Not that I recall."

"You've known her for some time," said Rysakov, making an assumption he was sure would not be contradicted. "Where do you think she would be most likely to go if she had gone away?"

Kay stared at Rysakov. "No doubt you have checked the obvious places," he said. After a pause he added, "Maybe she went overseas. Maybe to Europe, she'd been there before, I recall."

"Where in Europe would be her most likely destination?"

"I have no idea," Kay said.

"We're coming to the view it's more probable she's dead."

Kay remained silent.

"Did she have any enemies, or had she received any threats?"

"Not that I am aware of."

Rysakov watched Kay intently. Mike Smith was right, this was a very dangerous man. A man with no soul, a man who dealt with the devil. He saw in Kay's eyes an acknowledgment. Neither would give any quarter.

34

Saturday morning and Sally McIntosh felt lazy. Already the early heat promised another scorcher. She lay naked in bed thinking, not of her date that evening with Nic. Instead, she tried to work out why Schmidt wanted the information she had supplied to Alice, and what he might use it for. He was a foreigner, so the chances were he worked for a foreign government or organisation. Once she accepted that, the full implications of her actions hit her. She broke into a sweat. She had committed industrial espionage, not only against her employer's interests, but probably also against her country's interests.

If she stopped now, as she had already decided to do, perhaps no real damage had been done. *Who am I kidding?* she thought. Theft is theft. A prosecutor could rightly argue it had been systematic and occurred over an extended period of time. It was not a one-off, isolated incident.

She could, of course, tell her new lover. Though, as soon as it occurred to her, she dismissed the thought. As an officer of the law he would have no choice but to report her. That had to be the correct thing to do.

But maybe, *If he loves me enough...*

Warren Kay met with his contact inside Nestor, Nankervis & Co. at a secure location in a nondescript suburban café, a location they had never used before and would never use again. He gleaned little that was new, until the insider mentioned in passing, "This new issue must be good, the firm is cashing out all our other investments and putting the lot into it."

When she also mentioned she had collected a new passport for Nestor, Kay decided the time for action had arrived. Nestor had had more than enough warnings.

During dinner on Saturday night, Sally decided she might be falling in love with Nic. It seemed their table floated alone in the universe. The other patrons in the restaurant provided only background hum and she barely noticed their presence. She decided to gently raise the subject of Alice.

"Nic, did you meet Heinrich Schmidt in your search for Alice?"

"Yes, do you know him?"

"I've met him once. He's Alice's uncle."

"He said he came out with her from East Germany, but I think she was born in Prague."

"He came to my office during the week, wanting some of Alice's books. He's a bit creepy," she said. She decided to go a bit further. "When he told me he wanted Alice's books he made it clear that included her lab notebooks. But they're company property. I got the impression that I had better do what he wanted, or else," she said.

"Did he threaten you? Because if he did I can put the frighteners on him," said Rysakov.

This was exactly the protective reaction she was hoping for.

"No, he didn't say anything. It was just his tone of voice and the way he looked. I'm probably being a bit dramatic. I doubt I'll see him again."

"If he bothers you again tell him to call me."

They left the restaurant about ten, catching a taxi to Sally's apartment. She stood on the sidewalk as Nic paid the cab. When he turned towards her she threaded an arm around his waist, squeezing against the muscular chest. Nic placed a hand in the small of her back, pulling her closer.

When they came up for air after a long goodnight kiss Sally said, "I'm desperate for a real coffee. Stay here."

She smiled and before he could protest hurried across the street to the coffee shop, still open and busy. He waited at the doorway to her apartment block watching the queue into the coffee shop shorten. She reappeared, carrying two large polystyrene cups, her favourite handbag dangling from her elbow. She stopped at the kerb to check the traffic. Rysakov could only see two vehicles, one driving slowly past her. The other, fifty metres up the street, seemed to be double-parked with its lights off. Sally started to cross the road. At the same time, in his peripheral vision he saw the parked car began to move, its lights still off. As she reached the centre line on the road the car entered his field of sight, accelerating rapidly. The motor roared as its speed increased. Sally heard it and hesitated, momentarily unsure whether to go back or forward. She turned to go back. The car veered towards her. Rysakov yelled at the top of his voice, "Look out!" He saw her drop the coffee and try to make safety between parked cars. She was almost there when the car hit her at speed.

The impact whipped her upper body back, slamming her head into the windscreen. The car skidded sharply to the left, flinging the limp body off the bonnet and into the bull-bar of a parked Range Rover, snapping her neck. Now nothing more than a tangled pile of flesh, Sally slid onto the asphalt.

Rysakov froze, his eyes wide in shock. It had happened so fast and with such deliberate brutality. He started running towards Sally's inert shape. Mid-stride he realised the car was bearing down on him, fast. Insanely, he changed direction to try and stop it. It missed him by a metre, its motor revving in a high pitched squeal. Police training clicked in. He tried to see the driver, then, as it disappeared into the night he tried, unsuccessfully, to get the licence plates. With its front and rear lights off, he couldn't see any part of the number.

By the time he reached Sally, he knew she was dead. Her neck lay twisted at a sickening angle to her body, but he still checked for vital signs. He pulled out his phone and dialled emergency.

"Ambulance and police! There's been a hit and run!" he yelled at the operator.

The police car arrived minutes after the ambulance, blocking the street with its lights flashing. Of the two uniformed officers doing the weekend shift, PC Walsh, disembarked first. She had drawn the Saturday nightshift and had heard Rysakov's name calling in a hit and run. She hurried over to Rysakov. Once she confirmed he was uninjured she began seeking witnesses, leaving the Senior Constable on duty with her to interview her boss.

Rysakov finished his description of what had happened and the Senior stopped writing in his notebook. "What was your impression of the car as it went past you?" he asked.

Rysakov closed his eyes. He knew how important it was to capture eye witness accounts while they were fresh. He concentrated. "A sedan, four doors, dark colour, at least not a light colour, not white or yellow," he paused. "Wait, it had Olympic rings. An Audi."

"You're sure it was deliberate?"

Rysakov nodded, "Yes."

"Probably stolen for the purpose." The Senior Constable took another long look at Rysakov and said, "Why don't you go home, sir, and rest. Nothing more you can achieve here. If we get any really hot leads I can always call you."

"I'll drive him home, sir," Ruby said.

Rysakov nodded. "My car is around the corner, you can drive that," he said.

He later remembered Ruby's gentle queries getting him to go through the whole episode again. By the time they reached his terrace-house he felt exhausted. Ruby came inside with him and poured several stiff drinks of bourbon. She stayed, dozing on the couch. He got up several times in the night and saw her, asleep. By dawn he had had maybe an hour or two's sleep, the rest of the time he spent thinking. He was showered and dressed with coffee on when Ruby woke. He had developed several possible motives, and, more importantly, at least two potential candidates for Sally's murder.

35

Although he expected it, Rysakov could not help arguing the point. Sally was *his* friend so he had the strongest motive to track down the slime bag who'd killed her.

"That's the point," the superintendent said. "Solving a crime needs a mind capable of dispassionate assessment. As a result the hit-and-run has been assigned to uniform. If, as you say, the post-mortem and other evidence indicate a deliberate hit-and-run, then it becomes a murder enquiry and Homicide will take over the investigation."

Rysakov nodded. He felt flat, without energy. As he walked down the corridor to his desk, he decided that the bastard who killed Sally would see justice, in one form or another, when he caught him. He had no trouble focusing. Cold anger helped.

He pulled out the Alice Martin file. He didn't believe in coincidence. Three deaths, all of the victims knew, worked with or were married to Alice. Alice Martin, no matter where he looked, there was no sign of her. Sometimes he had to remind himself: *she* does *actually exist*. So the question remained: Where is she?

"Very sorry to hear about Sally, Nic," said Tom O'Leary. Rysakov had not heard him come in. "They said you were there and saw it happen?"

Rysakov nodded.

"Mate, I can't imagine how awful that must have been," O'Leary said. "The usual platitudes don't really help, but if you want someone to have a beer with..."

"Thanks, Tom. The funeral will be next week."

"Mike Smith was making man-power enquiries earlier. Looking for help on the hit-and-run, among other cases. He agrees with you, looks deliberate. That makes it a murder enquiry. Anyway, the search for Alice Martin's slowing down so I volunteered. Apart from anything else, I thought you might like some eyes on the ground. DS Smith said if it's OK with you he'll arrange the secondment," said O'Leary.

"You'll either love or hate Homicide, Tom. Thanks for letting me know. Give me a call if you make any progress finding the bastard."

He returned to the Alice file. Schmidt, Kay, Nestor, and the divorcee, Ann Stratton, were the four main remaining links to Alice. Her other friends and casual acquaintances he dismissed, they had all been interviewed and none had any useful information. What connection did any of these four have to Sally? She had told him of her meeting with Schmidt. How were they connected? What was Sally's relationship with Alice? These questions seemed even starker in the aftermath of Sally's murder.

He sat there for some time evaluating possibilities from the reasonable to the bizarre before reaching a decision. Any connection between the Alice case and Sally McIntosh's death he would pursue himself. Once he'd chased it down, then he might pass on the information to Homicide. That was not how the system was supposed to work, *but fuck it*.

Nestor felt annoyed when Callaghan sat down in his office, arriving precisely on time. He could never get enough intelligence to make up his mind if the investment banker was back in the game or simply acting on behalf of investors. He decided to opt for the latter. It made him feel superior.

"Seen any good deals lately?" Nestor asked with a slight smirk.

"The deal flow never stops, Clive. Good deals on the other hand, are a little harder to find."

"I hope you got your REI applications in on time, demand's been incredible." Nestor made no attempt to hide his excitement. "Even after we expanded the size of the issue we're going to be sending a lot of share applications and cheques back. We've had to push out the stock exchange listing date as a result."

"Not knocking back any of your shareholder's applications, I hope." Callaghan smiled to soften the query.

"Of course not."

To his surprise Callaghan got the distinct impression that, had he not asked, he may indeed have been cut back. "I'm pleased to hear it, which brings me to the other reason I asked to meet you today. I've heard rumours that you owe one particular shareholder a substantial amount of money, and that the debt is secured by a charge over your control of the business. We may be able to help."

"It's all under control. Once the REI issue is completed we'll be able to repay it out in full."

There was something wrong with Nestor's smile, but Callaghan could not put his finger on it. For some reason the phrase "be able to" stuck out. Maybe it was the way Nestor said it, or maybe he was being over-sensitive. He wondered whether Nestor did actually intend repaying the loan.

"I hope you know what you're doing," Callaghan said.

"Forgive me if I don't offer you coffee, but I'm extremely busy as I'm sure you can appreciate."

Nestor ushered Callaghan to the door, shook his hand and turned back to pick up his phone.

By the time Callaghan walked out of the office tower and wandered around the corner onto Macquarie Street he had made up his mind. Either he wrote off the investment in Nestor, Nankervis & Co., or he put up the money to repay Kay and took control of the firm himself. In a billion dollar portfolio the amount of money involved was not significant. Callaghan simply did not like making losses.

Yet Nestor's attitude to the repayment of the loan to Kay concerned him. He had some familiarity with the legal tactics that could be used to delay repayment. When he had got into trouble several years ago he briefly considered the tactic, before rapidly deciding not to. It did two things. It delayed, not avoided, the day of reckoning; and it really pissed off the funder. Generally not a very sensible course of action with any lender, unless you had no intention of repaying the debt, then of course it didn't matter.

I wonder? he thought.

Clive Nestor really did have a busy schedule. REI was almost certain to be the outstanding new issue on the stock market this year. Judging by press comments the issue would list on the Australian Stock Exchange at a premium. The only discussion was how big a premium. He instructed his PA early in the day to transfer all calls for shares in REI to his executive team. Let them decide who got shares and who missed out. They had decided last week on a pro rata reduction of all public share allocations. This tactic would ensure strong demand once REI listed on the ASX, which, after all, was one of his objectives. Nestor had other reasons to be pleased, however, and these were far more important to him.

"Clive, my boy, the stars are aligning in your favour," he said to himself. He punched a URL internet address into one of the two laptops on his desk. Live graphs of cobalt metal prices on the London and the Shanghai Metal Exchanges, the Rotterdam market, and Wall Street displayed in a quartered screen. Not much had changed, for months. After an initial spike in the price two years ago, prices had stagnated. That was about to change.

Over the past months Nestor had quietly acquired forward delivery contracts for cobalt, in small quantities each time, using different entities, from producers and metal traders, including some contracts on the London Metal Exchange. He had now accumulated sufficient metal, he believed, to influence the market price. All of the cobalt was ultimately owned by a company in the Bahamas. By withholding it from the market, the price of cobalt would rapidly rise. Particularly when ICI announced the latest test results for its revolutionary solar and storage batteries, and the market finally realised that the process relied on cobalt to operate. Without cobalt the technology didn't work.

Clive Nestor was going to clean up, tax free. Within a few months, six at the outside, he was going to be a very wealthy man. High stakes, high risk, high return. If his undisclosed involvement was uncovered, a prison sentence for insider trading faced him. The risk. He put that thought out of his head and concentrated on the second laptop showing live trading on the ASX and an

Excel spreadsheet automatically updating the value of his holdings, worldwide, a value that would increase exponentially over the next few months. So explosive was this data that it existed only on an encrypted USB flash drive hanging on a cord around his neck, 24/7. In his more rational moments he recognised the danger if anyone saw the spreadsheet. Yet, he needed that reassurance, that adrenalin rush when he saw the current figures, then alongside them the result he actually anticipated. The return.

The market expected REI to double in price when it listed. He clicked on the spreadsheet, typed in the doubled price and watched the large shareholding, ostensibly owned by a Bahamas based hedge fund, calculate out a nine digit value. He knew the number by heart and still couldn't stop a smug smile. After closing Excel he disconnected the USB drive and hung it back around his neck.

Whenever he reviewed his plan for REI the problem of Warren Kay arose. Retaining Kay's funds had enabled him to secure contracts for the large quantity of cobalt metal he had his foot on. Without that money he could not have achieved the position. The timing was nearly right to begin the short term squeeze on cobalt. It only needed the quotation of REI shares on the stock exchange, the final trigger. Withholding this quantity of metal from the market would drive the price up in the short term, long enough for him to sell out. The balance of funds for the cobalt play he had diverted from the business. It would take months before the auditors noticed it missing. By that time he would be long gone.

Kay's loan presented a more immediate problem. He had to keep the funds until the cobalt contracts were closed out. To enable Nestor, Nankervis & Co. to repay on time would require premature selling of a key portion of the cobalt. It would mean the price squeeze he had carefully set up would fail.

"By the time the lawyers get involved, I won't be here," he said out loud, as if the sound of his own voice made it more certain. He unlocked the drawer in his desk and took out his passport. A business class air ticket to Bangkok protruded from both ends, paid for in cash. Once in Thailand he would disappear, using a false passport he had arranged to collect. His own passport, and the ticket to Bangkok, he slipped into his pocket. As he relocked the drawer his phone rang. Ignoring it vibrating on the desk, he left his office.

Warren Kay kept the phone to his ear until it disconnected. He had made the next move. The outcome now rested in Nestor's hands.

36

That night Callaghan spoke with his chief analyst in London and the resident Australian analyst by video link in the local office.

"What money are we talking?" London asked. He told her. "Is the upside worth it?"

"The real attraction is their position in REI. The day-to-day business could probably be on sold to another investment bank," Callaghan said.

"I agree. If the technology works," a pause, "yes, agree. As for the rest, whatever. Will, I have to go." The screen went blank. Callaghan smiled. An investment this small would struggle to get any attention at his head office staff in London, unless spectacular returns appeared likely. Even though he had decided to go ahead, he spent the next hour testing the concept on his local analyst.

The westerly wind blew hot all night, only abating at dawn. Callaghan woke early and peered out the window to check the Narrabeen surf. Barely a ripple disturbed the water surface after twenty-four hours of onshore wind. *Too bad*, he thought, *I'll swim to the club*. The surf club stood half a kilometre south across the bay and members would already be enjoying a coffee.

He changed into Speedos, jumped off the veranda and ran across the sand to the ocean. By the time he reached the surf club he felt refreshed. He spoke to several of the other early swimmers and headed to the coffee machine. Half an hour later he left for a scheduled workout with his grappling trainer at the Brazilian Jiu-Jitsu centre in Manly, although they were so evenly matched it was debatable who was really training who.

Mid-morning Callaghan rang the Nataliya Trust's Australian bankers and explained what he wanted and what he aimed to achieve. They assured him they would not only meet his wishes, but also the likely timetable. Finally, he explained what he proposed to the Fund's long-term lawyers. The partner wished him good luck, adding, "Watch your back. I say that advisedly."

Nestor caught a cab to a suburban internet café, one he found in the Yellow Pages. He paid the driver in cash, went in and opened an account in the name of Lleyton Federer. He paid cash in advance for five hours use, far more than he expected to need.

The teenager at the counter barely lifted his head from the portable DVD player. Nestor knew the emails on this account could be accessed, but who would think of looking here? Even if the intelligence services scanned his emails for key words and phrases, the wording of his emails was so boringly normal they could have been sent by any one of thousands of businesses. That they were signed by a number and not a name, so what? The sender was a privacy geek. But the number was his only possible concern. It was his account identifier. What were the chances of the emails being linked to him? So remote he dismissed the thought.

Instructions sent, Nestor left the café and set off to walk to the main road to hail a cab. Although confident his plan would follow through, he had a niggling doubt. From the start, he had not, at any time, received confirmation his instructions had ever been carried out. This initially caused him to express concern, only to be asked by the banker managing his account to which email address should they respond? Point taken. He simply couldn't take the risk of any connection to him or Australia. Thereafter, because he had no reason to think otherwise, he assumed everything had been set up as he instructed. No one else knew about the account.

37

"Were you able to get any more information on Honey French or her movements on the twenty eighth of November from the escort service?" Rysakov asked PC Ruby Walsh. "I'd like to have another go at Kay."

"Her real name is Angela Stratton. Looks like she was a niece of that friend of Alice Martin, Ann Stratton, though I haven't rung her to confirm yet. If so, she may also have known Alice," Ruby said.

Rysakov raised an eyebrow. "Worth a phone call, but don't waste much time on it."

Ruby nodded. "Apart from that, nothing new."

"Would you also find out if Kay, Schmidt, Nestor, and Stratton own an Audi?"

"Wouldn't the killer be more likely to have used a stolen car, sir?" said Ruby.

"It's a long shot, I know, but sometimes criminals overlook the obvious."

Rysakov rubbed his eyes. They felt gritty. What sleep he had managed over the last few days did not leave him rested. Confused, and sometimes horrible, dreams woke him last night. He had lain on his bed, covered in sweat, unable to get back to sleep. His superior officer suggested, as a matter of course, that he see a counsellor. Then the police union rep recommended a counsellor.

"It took a long time to get the Department to fund counselling for our members," the union rep said. "You won't be Robinson Crusoe in taking advantage of it. Most members who've used it say they get some benefit. Even if you don't, you're no worse off."

So Rysakov made an appointment to see the counsellor.

The timing could not have been better. Two days after Nestor's visit to the internet cafe, ICI announced it had signed an agreement granting

REI the world-wide licence to commercialise its revolutionary solar power generating and storage technology. Demand for shares in REI, already high in anticipation of the grant of a licence, soared on this confirmation, well in excess of market expectations.

Nestor could barely hide his elation. He made one more visit to the suburban internet café before bringing his departure date forward. The executive staff and the firm's external lawyers had years of experience between them in ensuring the stock exchange listing was completed smoothly and on time. Nestor's absence would not affect the process. He was due for some annual leave anyway.

The Nataliya Trust controlled a hedge fund as well as a variety of other investment entities, all based in the Channel Island of Guernsey. Callaghan held the sole controlling interest in The Nataliya Trust. He made certain the Trust subscribed early, before any announcements, for the maximum possible number of REI shares. Once the ICI licence was made public, any unallocated shares became severely rationed. Once they listed on the stock exchange, Callaghan intended to sell sufficient shares to get his money back. His hedge fund would then keep half the balance to see if the technology worked, commercially. If it did, it would be a bonanza.

Within twenty-four hours, professional investors, traders and the large international hedge funds, stimulated by surging interest in REI, took a closer look at the company and its product. The message was clear: "The technology will revolutionise renewable energy sources, but will not work without cobalt. The demand for cobalt will be huge."

Both the trading price and quantity of cobalt surged overnight. Suddenly, cobalt was the hottest item in financial markets.

The day before the cobalt spike, Warren Kay arranged to meet Clive Nestor.

"Rysakov," he said, answering the phone at his desk.

"Nic, Mike Smith. You mix with some dangerous characters."

"Part of the job, I'm afraid."

"Maybe, but just to let you know it'll be in tomorrow's papers, and probably on the TV news tonight. Your banker, Clive Nestor, has been murdered."

"Damn, you sure it's murder?"

"Bit hard to cut your own throat, mate," said Smith. "Happened yesterday evening at his home. Seems Nestor parked his car in the garage and came out to use the front entrance instead of the internal door which remained locked. He apparently checked the mailbox then walked up the driveway. The body wasn't discovered until around midday today when the cleaners came. There are a lot of shrubs along the drive, they hid the body."

"Wasn't a random attack?"

"Nope, far from it. In fact, it looks a lot like another attack on a banker a couple of years ago," said Mike Smith. "That guy had the good luck to live next door to a surgeon, saved his life. Nestor wasn't so lucky. Same MO. My guess is it's the same guy."

"No one was charged on the first attack, were they?"

"No. We had a couple of suspects, but we couldn't tie any of them to the scene."

"Thanks for the call, Mike. I'm starting to think there might be something in conspiracy theories. This is the fourth death of a person who knew Alice Martin. How, or if, she's involved, I don't know. What's worrying me now is: who's next?"

"I'll send you a list of the suspects in that earlier attack, but leave them to us at this stage," said Mike Smith. "One name on the list you've already met, though we never had any hard evidence linking him to the scene two years ago."

Rysakov hung up. He frowned. Something important was on the edge of his consciousness, but he couldn't quite nail it.

"Sir, I've got the information on the motor vehicles," said PC Ruby Walsh. Only when she spoke did he realise she had been standing at his desk, waiting.

"Sorry, Ruby."

"No one owns an Audi," she said, adding, "but a burnt out old

Audi has been found in bushland west of Campbelltown. A local contactor saw the smoke and called the District Fire Service, the day after the hit and run. It's taken this long to get through to Homicide. It was reported stolen a week ago," she paused. "They said they had reason to believe it was the vehicle used."

"OK. No real surprise there."

"However," Ruby said, "Schmidt and Kay both owned an Audi in the last three years."

At the mention of Schmidt's name Rysakov remembered what had been eluding him. Sally had said Schmidt tried to get confidential company data from her, and she refused. Schmidt needed to explain why someone his age would threaten a young PA for such information. The CEO had been confident of his internal security systems, that no classified data had been leaked. So why had Sally told him she was concerned for her safety?

He needed to talk again to Heinrich Schmidt.

38

The day before Nestor's body was discovered a lawyer entered the cool lobby on Castlereagh Street, grateful to escape the rising humidity outside. He walked across to the directory board, although he knew the floor for Nestor, Nankervis & Co. A few extra minutes for his shirt to cool and dry in the air-conditioned surrounds, then he would be ready to go up. He put on his suit coat, straightened his tie and pressed the elevator button.

The lawyer had read the front page article on REI in the financial press so was not surprised to see about twenty people in the reception area, some brandishing share application forms, others demanding their application be accepted in full. The firm had wisely set up a special desk, staffed by two women who looked like lawyers, specifically to handle REI queries. The large man in a security guard uniform only added to the drama. The lawyer caught the receptionist's eye.

"Mr Nestor, please. My name's Tom English. I'm a solicitor from Baker, Snell & English. He's expecting me," he said.

"I'm sorry, Mr Nestor is not here, sir," she said. "I'm not sure when he'll be returning."

Obviously he was not the first person that morning to ask for Nestor.

"Then perhaps I can see your financial controller."

Ten minutes later the receptionist ushered him into the board room where he introduced himself to the controller.

"Sue Hope," said the controller, "and this is Jo Amis, our in-house counsel. Mr Nestor is not here, can we help?"

"As I explained to Mr Nestor yesterday, I have instructions to advance you sufficient funds to repay a loan from interests associated with Mr Warren Kay, with half of the funds converting to equity in your firm in two years, on a formula related to profits,"

English said, before explaining in detail the terms and the way the formula worked. The financial controller used an iPad to do some calculations.

"I expect you are aware that conversion of the loan will give your client control of the firm when that happens," she said.

"That is correct," said English, "unless a new arrangement is negotiated."

"Are you aware the Kay loan was due last week and Mr Kay served notice on Monday stating he has taken possession of the security for the loan, and that as a consequence he now controls the business?" said Jo Amis.

"I wasn't aware of that," said English. After a pause, he added, "Clive Nestor sent me copy of the loan security documents last week. The clause relating to default or non-repayment does allow the lender to take the security. However, the clause following provides you, the borrower, with a one week period of grace to make good the repayment, at a higher rate of interest. I have with me a bank cheque for the full amount at the higher interest rate, once the documents are signed."

"Mr Nestor advised the Board after your discussion yesterday and the Directors have authorised us to sign," said Jo Amis. "Once the funds are cleared we will immediately repay Mr Kay. As you say, we have until the end of this week."

"Good, once the documents are executed I'll serve notice on Mr Kay's solicitors to release the security to me."

By late afternoon the documents had been signed and the funds banked. Tom English returned to his office to prepare the security release for Kay's solicitors, Garand & Co. It was served, together with a bank cheque for the loan repayment, by courier close to six o'clock that evening. Reading the name of Joe Garand, the staff member who had received the envelope placed it on his desk. When Garand read the letter first thing the next morning, he immediately checked the loan documents. He then rang Warren Kay.

"It's too late," said Kay, "I've got the security for the debt. I now control Nestor Nankervis. They can't do it. Tell 'em to get stuffed."

"'Fraid they can, Warren. I checked the documents. There is provision for a week's grace before you can exercise your rights on the security. If they repay the loan by the end of this week, we must hand back the shares. Of course, you could refuse to. But that would lead to court and you'd lose. It'd take a couple of years because of the court backlog, and your money would be retained by Nestor until then."

"Where did they get the funds? Nestor told me it would take a month or more," Kay asked.

"A shareholder, Callaghan Investments Ltd. One of Will Callaghan's companies I gather. He's an experienced investment banker."

"I know who he is," Kay cut in. "Fuck! Who the fuck does he think he is? WHO THE FUCK!." The fury in Kay's voice caught Garand off-guard, so he stayed silent. Finally, Kay calmed down, though Garand could still feel the undercurrent of fury in his voice.

"Alright, do as they ask," Kay said and hung up, figuring if Garand could not see a way out of this mess there was little point in arguing. He knew where Callaghan lived and he had no intention of letting matters stay as they were.

The Bang & Olufsen hi-fi system emitted superb sound in every room. Speaker size and location had been carefully selected to suit each room, large and small. *Beethoven's Fifth* followed Kay as he stalked through the penthouse, volume close to maximum. Each room switched on and off as he passed, the controls hidden in his palm. Music calmed him. It did not lessen his rage, simply made it more rational, as he methodically thought through the alternatives.

The morning after discovery of the Nestor's body, the details were released to the media. Callaghan was listening to News 24 on the car radio when he heard the report.

Well known bachelor banker, Clive Nestor, was found yesterday with his throat cut. A police spokes-person said the assailant had allegedly ambushed Mr Nestor next to the path. Any member of the public who saw anyone entering the property on the day of the murder or any unusual activity in the vicinity is asked to contact Crime Stoppers.

The news of Nestor's murder rapidly swept through financial markets. The directors of REI released a statement deploring the murder, but pointing out that Clive Nestor was not a director and assuring the market the issue would proceed as planned. At Nestor Nankervis & Co, the crush of applicants spilled into the lift lobby. In-house counsel, Jo Amis, figured the late surge in people at the offices could in part be accounted for by vicarious interest, curiosity to see where the murdered man worked.

Callaghan immediately thought of a similar attack over three years ago. Another banker, his throat cut. The very banker he, Callaghan, had been negotiating with to fund his business deal. In the aftermath of that attack, he and Zoe were stalked by an unknown party in a failed extortion attempt. The threat so unnerved his girlfriend her motor vehicle crashed at high speed, killing her.

That had been the time he had discovered his inheritance, The Nataliya Trust. One of the first decisions he made after taking official control of the Trust was to appoint a Chief Analyst, Dr Sarah Longhurst, on the advice of his lawyer. She had since become his CEO and he spoke to her almost every day, wherever he happened to be in the world. Notwithstanding her undoubted ability, if he didn't speak to her his day did not feel complete.

He turned the Jaguar XFR into the driveway of his beach-front home in Narrabeen as the twilight darkened into night. He turned the ignition off and sat motionless for a while, wondering if there really could be a connection between the murders of the two bankers. He shrugged and got out of the car, slamming the door.

Leaving the supercharged Jag in the driveway, he stepped onto the wide veranda that swept around three sides of the house. He stood at the top of the steps and looked towards the sea expecting, well, he didn't know quite what. Listening to the rhythmical sound of the surf hitting the beach, he turned into the ocean-facing section of the veranda. With twilight nearly gone he could barely see the far end draped in shadow.

The instant it registered he turned back. His peripheral vision had picked up a nonconformity, a shadow that should not have been there. It moved towards him. Every muscle in his body tensed. He rose lightly onto the balls of his feet, ready.

"You work long hours William Callaghan," said a deep but disembodied voice. The shadow stopped moving, just far enough away that Callaghan could see no detail. A tall shadow, too far away to get a hold.

If he has a gun I'm dead, he thought. "What do you want?" asked Callaghan.

"To find out why you stopped me taking control of Nestor's business."

Callaghan considered his reply, now he knew the identity of the shadow. "It's simply business, Mr Kay. Clive Nestor told me he had a short term cash flow issue. I offered to fix it. My assessment is that it's a good investment. Nothing personal."

"Clive Nestor is no more. Do you still intend to go ahead? Or do you think you might be better off taking your funds and doing deals elsewhere?" said Kay.

Callaghan knew he had just been threatened. Nothing concrete, nothing he could report to police. He decided to make it clear to Kay his scheme would not work. "Nestor's murder doesn't alter my view on the merits of the investment. Today we advised Nestor Nankervis we are proceeding as planned."

There was silence before Kay spoke again. "Am I correct in my recollection that about two years ago your girlfriend died in a motor vehicle accident?"

Taken aback by the question Callaghan did not reply. What relevance did Zoe's death have to Nestor Nankervis?

"A sad and no doubt avoidable tragedy. Was it speed?"

The shadow began moving toward him. He braced for an assault. Tension rippled through his body. Then, nothing happened.

Kay moved smoothly between Callaghan and the veranda rail, just out of reach. All Callaghan saw was a tall silhouette momentarily outlined against the white of the surf. He sensed, rather than saw, a sneer on Kay's face.

As the sound of footsteps retreated to the street Callaghan gathered his wits. It was totally unexpected, the mention of Zoe's death and how she died. How did he know? It had happened in the UK. He felt bile rising in his throat.

Later that night, Callaghan decided that whatever Kay said should not be taken at face value. There were far more sinister overtones. Kay must have been secretly watching him to note his habits. That was worrying enough, but it was more than just the stalking. The man's actions bore the mark of experience, of a professional.

Perhaps he is *as dangerous as he appears*, Callaghan thought.

Tomorrow morning, he decided, he would report the incident to the police. In his desk he located the card of the officer who had spoken to him on his return from the UK after Zoe's death. DS Mike Smith. Unlikely they could do anything about his visitor. No crime had been committed, yet. They should just be aware and know it was Kay.

39

The minute he made a firm commitment to go through with it, Rysakov rang the counsellor and made an appointment before he changed his mind. He rationalised that a psychologist was not a psychiatrist. The latter implied mental impairments not automatically associated with the former. *Sophistry*, he thought, but felt better about it nevertheless. He had sufficient common sense to know talking to an experienced specialist might help, particularly with the dreams.

"Were you in love with Sally?" asked the counsellor after Rysakov had described in detail what happened the night she died, commencing with their arrival at the restaurant.

"I thought I might be falling for her," he said.

"But you weren't sure? You hadn't begun to think about marriage?"

"No. I figured that would be a long way down the track."

"When you saw the vehicle hit Sally, what went through your mind?"

"That it couldn't be happening, and that it was deliberate."

Anticipating the next question he explained why he thought the vehicle had hit Sally deliberately. The counsellor nodded. He did not tell her his suspicions as to the driver's motive.

"I thought if only I had insisted on going with her it wouldn't have happened."

"Didn't you say that she frequently bought coffee at this café?"

Nic nodded. The counsellor then asked him to describe his dreams.

"From discussions with hundreds of officers, the dreams will fade over time. How long? It varies, but they will go. In my experience, talking about the events has helped most of those officers. One final word of advice, don't let anger at what happened colour your judgement. Let Homicide handle the investigation."

Rysakov promised to make another appointment if the dreams persisted. One detail he had not mentioned because he couldn't make sense of it. It was a woman's face that appeared at the periphery of his dreams, not only the dream about Sally's murder. It appeared in all his dreams over the last month. It never changed. In every dream it remained the same. As he walked onto the street he finally knew, without doubt, whose face it was.

The face belonged to Alice Martin. A woman he had never met. He didn't even know whether she was alive or dead. Chances were, he would never see her, ever. Yet in the process of looking for Alice he had met four people, each connected to Alice, and all of them were now dead.

He had to find her, simple as that. With Sally's death it had become personal, no longer just another case. Homicide may have official carriage of the investigations into the murder, but, while the search for Alice remained under his control, there were still avenues he could legitimately pursue. He intended to get to Sally's killer first. Tom O'Leary had now been at Homicide long enough to know where they were at. They had no leads in Sally's case. No doubt they were doing their best. But Rysakov had a hunch and he intended to follow it.

It was the least he could do for Sally.

PC Ruby Walsh drove the unmarked vehicle through heavy city traffic and over the Harbour Bridge. While they drove, Rysakov ran through what they knew about Alice Martin, asking Ruby to confirm or deny each fact as he went. He then examined the assumptions he had made about the connections between Alice and each of the four dead, asking Ruby to suggest other possibilities.

Thirty minutes later, Ruby brought the vehicle to a stop against the curb.

"What did you tell Schmidt when you rang him?" Rysakov asked, before pressing the doorbell.

"That we would like to ask a few questions about Alice's time at ICI," said Ruby.

The door opened and Schmidt said, "You're early," before turning his back and walking into the living room. He was wearing a light jacket despite the heat outside. He sat in what was obviously his favourite chair, with his back to the window. A lone settee lay against the wall behind the door to the hallway. The only other seats were two straight-backs, with no cushions, facing the window.

Soviet-style interrogation technique, Rysakov thought. *He must be worried.* Neither Nic nor Ruby sat on the upright chairs, both stood in front of them less than two metres from Schmidt. He detected no cordiality, instead he sensed anger. Rysakov had not come armed, and he began to wonder if that had been wise.

"Can you tell us the nature of the relationship between Alice Martin and Sally McIntosh? ICI confirmed both women worked there until Alice's disappearance," Rysakov said.

"I do not know this Sally McIntosh," said Schmidt.

"That is not true, is it? You met with her several times."

"Rubbish," scoffed Schmidt, making it clear, in case there had been any doubt, he had no intention of cooperating.

"Sally told me before she was murdered that you arranged the meetings."

"You have proof of this?" said Schmidt.

Rysakov now believed his hunch was correct. "Not only did you meet her," he said, his voice harsh and rising, "you threatened her, unless she gave you confidential data and information on ICI product tests and formulae. Is that what Alice did, industrial espionage?"

"You know nothing," said Schmidt. He had not moved since he sat down, hands crossed in his lap, right hand on top.

Rysakov let the tension in the room grow, never taking his gaze away from Schmidt. The stakes had just been raised.

"Where were you last Saturday night?" he said, breaking the silence.

"Here, in my home, reading," said Schmidt. "I read Suskin's novel, *Perfume: The Story of a Murderer*. In the original German," he added with a sneer.

He's baiting me, Rysakov thought, astonished.

He watched as Schmidt turned to his right and pointed to the middle shelves of a bookcase before turning back to face them. It was time to change tack."Do you own an Audi?"

"No."

"You did own one, though, didn't you? It was the same model that the killer used to murder Sally. We found the car used in the murder. Even though it had been burnt out forensics were still able to get a surprising amount of information from the remains."

They hadn't got much at all in fact, but Schmidt didn't know that. Schmidt sat, silent.

"It was your Audi that was used, wasn't it?" said Rysakov to see what reaction he got.

Ruby now added, "The numbers on the engine block matched up and even though it had been burnt out the damage to the vehicle's bodywork is consistent with eye witness accounts of the murder."

Rysakov did not let the surprise show on his face. He hoped Ruby was right, but why hadn't she told him? "You knew where it was garaged so you took it and used it to kill Sally McIntosh," he said, pressing the line with confidence. "What was it, tidying up loose ends?"

As he said it Rysakov saw a tightening of Schmidt's eyes and lips. A slight movement by his right side and, as if magically, a gun appeared in Schmidt's hand. It had been hidden under the light jacket Schmidt was wearing. It looked like a nine millimetre Beretta, very effective at close range. Schmidt held the weapon like a professional, rock solid.

"There are two of us. One is bound to get to you. Put the gun down," Rysakov said.

"Do not waste your time Mr Rysakov, I cannot be persuaded. I am dying of cancer," Schmidt said, now standing. "Threats of prison or worse do not concern me. I am determined my record will be clear before I die. So, you have a choice, a quick clean death if you obey my instructions. Or, I will shoot you in the stomach, the woman first. Believe me, it is a most painful death. Now, put your hands behind your head."

Rysakov did not doubt Schmidt would carry out his threat and slowly lifted his arms. In his peripheral vision he saw Ruby change stance as she also lifted her arms to comply. Sensing that the momentum was slipping away from them and they may not get another chance, Rysakov threw himself hard, forward and to the left. In the confined space the percussion of the Beretta sounded impossibly loud. The bullet hit his upper right arm, pushing it back. He hit the ground with his left shoulder absorbing the impact. He swung his right leg around Schmidt's legs unbalancing him and kicked. The instant he moved he sensed Ruby, airborne. Her left leg forced the Beretta's barrel vertical as her right leg landed a vicious kick to Schmidt's head. Rysakov scrambled to his feet, Ruby not far behind him. Schmidt lay on his back on the floor, semi-conscious, still gripping the Beretta.

Without stopping to think, Rysakov grabbed Schmidt's right hand, twisted it around and pulled the trigger. This time they were both prepared for the sound.

"Ruby, are you alright?" Rysakov called.

Ruby stared at the neat round hole in the centre of Schmidt's forehead. The Beretta, still clasped in his hand, lay on his chest. Blood spilled from under his head in a steadily widening pool.

"Ruby!" he said again, this time louder.

"Is he dead?" she said, looking at him, eyes wide.

"Yes. It was him or us. He was the bastard who killed Sally. When he turned to the bookcase... it was the same profile... he drove the car... I saw him," Rysakov said, trying to catch his breath. He shook his head in disgust.

Ruby tore her gaze away from the pooling blood and turned to Rysakov. As the adrenaline rapidly wore off pain spiked through his arm and he groaned.

"Your arm. You've been shot," said Ruby. Blood, already soaking his shirt sleeve, now ran down the fingers of his right arm, dripping onto the carpet.

"If you hadn't kicked him his next bullet would have been in my stomach," Rysakov said. He sat down, shaken. Fingers all move, wrist OK. He lifted his arm. "No broken bones, but God it hurts." With his left hand, he pulled out his phone and turned to Ruby.

"Schmidt got shot in the struggle for the gun. He was a killer. He'd already killed Sally. Maybe he also killed Alice. It was going to be him or us. Are you OK with that?" Nic asked. It was the truth anyway.

"Absolutely," said Ruby.

He could read in her face that the thought of a bullet in the stomach terrified her as well. There were no doubts about Schmidt's intent. Rysakov was satisfied. He nodded and dialled for an ambulance. Next he called for an incident team.

"Nature of incident?" asked the police switch-board.

"Officer wounded, assailant shot dead," he replied. He could hear instant action in the station background. Ruby turned the other straight-backed chair away from Schmidt and sat down, her face pale.

"Thanks Ruby, things could've got awkward if you hadn't been there," Rysakov said while they waited. Ruby smiled weakly and passed him a cushion to support his arm.

The ambulance took Rysakov to hospital where they confirmed a flesh wound to his right deltoid muscle, no serious damage. Cleaned and stitched he returned to the Redfern station with his right arm in a sling. Ruby had already been debriefed, now it was his turn. By the time he had finished he felt exhausted. There would be more interviews, particularly for him. Since they both told the same story, self-defence, it would be routine, and it could wait. The police doctor told both to take the rest of the week off to recover from the trauma, and in his case, the wound.

Ruby declined the offer of a squad car lift home. "I've got my car down the road, can't leave it there till next week. I'll drop DS Rysakov off on the way."

Rysakov made no move to get out of the car when they arrived at his Paddington terrace. Finally, he said, "Would you like to come in for a coffee or a glass of wine?"

"That would be nice," she said.

It fell to Ruby to do most of the making. Rysakov used his good arm only to get the cups and glasses. They chatted about the case, the noise made by a handgun in a confined space, and the smell of blood.

"I regret you were placed in such a dangerous situation, Ruby, though you handled it superbly."

They sat opposite each other, silent. Rysakov noticed tears running down Ruby's cheeks. Before he could think what to do she began to cry. It rapidly became uncontrollable sobbing. Emotion and reaction, they had both come close to death. He got up and sat next to her, putting his good arm around her shoulder. Ruby lay her head on his chest and put her arms around him. He could feel the depth of the sobs through the rise and fall of her breasts against his chest. He desperately needed the warmth of someone to hold, and to be held, and he hugged her closer.

Over the next five days he saw Ruby on four of them. He enjoyed her company more as he got to know her, and, he had to admit, being one-armed had its limitations. Having two-handed help made life a lot easier.

40

Will Callaghan knew the time had come to act. The first week after REI listed on the stock exchange it had quadrupled in value. The financial markets had learned that interests associated with the company had secured a short term controlling position, a corner, in the cobalt metal market. The cobalt metal price soared and REI shares peaked at ten times the issue price. The number of shares traded over two weeks exceeded by several times the total number issued. Even the press became caught up in the euphoria. It extolled the benefits of the new technology for the environment and the emergence of "A new paradigm". One journalist headed his article SANTA'S BIGGEST PRESENT. The market had never seen a Christmas like it.

When Callaghan read these stories he acted swiftly. He sold all his REI shares. The profit enabled him to recoup his entire investment in Nestor, Nankervis & Co. plus a tidy margin. The shares continued to rise on huge turnover. Callaghan watched bemused, content with the profit he had realised. In addition, the value of Nestor's firm, now controlled by Callaghan's group, had trebled.

He figured it could take several years of hard work to translate the technology into a commercial product. He would monitor progress over that time. The market would lose interest as the development work progressed, always chasing quick results. Once REI was ready to go to production they would need more money. That is when Callaghan would be pleased to oblige, at a far more realistic price than current levels.

John Martin had decided to take up Callaghan's suggestion and go to Prague, where a lawyer had been briefed to assist the eighteen year-old in the search for his identity. They had both agreed there would be no advantage to leave before Christmas. John decided to spend the festive season with friends, including regular visits to Callaghan. With the public holidays now over and the new year well under way, it was time for Prague.

The flight left early so Callaghan drove John Martin to Sydney International Airport himself rather than rely on a cab. He made sure they had more than adequate time and took him to the business class lounge for a bon voyage glass of champagne. Callaghan could feel the young lad's excitement.

"To a new year, new discoveries and the trip of a lifetime," said Callaghan, raising his glass. John returned the gesture. "Someone from the law firm in Prague will meet you at the airport and take you to your hotel. The next day they'll take you to their offices and help in the search for your biological parents. There is a real possibility the records lead nowhere. The names on the birth certificate may not be traceable, so keep your expectations low. It may even be difficult to track information on Alice Braun, assuming that is her real name. Finding her also may not lead anywhere," said Callaghan. "But most importantly, enjoy yourself."

They shook hands. Callaghan smiled, turned and left the lounge. He had mixed feelings about the possibility of John Martin finding descendants of his grand-father's sister. After so many years of being certain he was the sole living relative of his great-grandmother's lineage, the possibility of family was both exciting and unsettling.

In his penthouse looking across the harbour towards the city skyline, Warren Kay followed trading in REI on his screen. He sold one fifth of his shares, recouping his total outlay in REI, letting the remainder, his profit, run. The satisfied smile on his face only faded when he realised the rise in REI share price meant Nestor's firm had also increased substantially in value. A business now controlled by Callaghan. His mood blackened.

One day there will be a reckoning with Callaghan, he promised himself.

A week later, an enterprising financial journalist compared the top twenty shareholders at the time of listing on the Australian Stock

Exchange with the present top twenty shareholders. Callaghan was not surprised with what he discovered. The original large holders had all disposed of most of their shares. In particular, a hedge fund in Bahamas, with the curious name A.V. Ago Inc., once the largest single holder, no longer appeared on the list. Every one of its shares had been sold.

"Yet another secretive hedge fund generating hundreds of millions of dollars in profits for its wealthy investors," said the article. "REI is likely to be the most successful new listing of a company on the Australian Stock Exchange in the last two years. Millions of dollars in profit have been, and remain to be, made."

Callaghan spent some time thinking about this information before scanning the article into his computer and filing it. The identity of the investors behind the hedge fund interested him.

Kay skimmed the article before putting it aside and later rereading it.

"I bet Nestor, that scheming bastard, had something to do with the hedge fund. If he was going to do a runner, he'd follow the money," he muttered to himself. The more he thought about it the more it seemed to fit. It would explain Nestor's cockiness and his total lack of concern when it came to repaying the loan. He thought of the risk he had taken despatching Nestor. All totally unnecessary, if only he had known. Cold anger rose from his stomach.

"The stupid, greedy bastard."

Throwing the newspaper away in disgust he walked out onto the balcony. Thick humidity lay still and oppressive over the city.

"We could have struck a deal. I would have taken the lot and Nestor could have lived. A fair deal."

Kay uttered a cynical laugh. A major missed opportunity.

"He must have covered his tracks well," he said with grudging admiration.

Then it hit him. Nestor was dead. So someone else knows, because all the hedge fund shares have still been sold.

Whoever it is, they've just made a shit load of money, and all offshore. Has to be that bastard Callaghan. He probably did a deal with Nestor. Now he'll keep the lot.

Suddenly, Kay felt depressed.

41

If Nic Rysakov had not pointed out that five of the key individuals on the list of Alice Martin's friends and relations were dead, Mike Smith would not have thought about it. The way Rysakov put it, over a drink at the Imperial Hotel in Paddington, it sounded like an epidemic. Neither of them believed in conspiracy theories, but Mike laughingly agreed, after the third beer, that Alice was definitely manipulating events from a secret location.

"If she's still alive she has to be working for Spectre," said Smith. "James Bond never did finish 'em off completely."

Rysakov laughed, careful not to jar his arm which was healing well. The stitches came out in a few days but the enforced inactivity had begun to bore him.

"Back to reality for a moment, I had a visit from Will Callaghan the other day. He had an encounter with Warren Kay," Smith said, and outlined what he had been told.

"Kay was one of the persons of interest for the attack on that banker a couple of years ago, wasn't he?" asked Rysakov.

"Yeah. That bloke also had his throat sliced. Similar MO as the Nestor murder. But we found no evidence linking Kay, then or now. Just a feeling. Whoever it was, they were very careful, very professional."

Rysakov drained his beer and placed the glass on the bar. Neither spoke for a moment.

"By the way, I hear you're being well looked after by a certain PC. If it were me, that bullet wound would take months to heal," said Smith innocently as he ordered another round.

"Yeah, sure," said Rysakov, and left it at that.

PC Ruby Walsh had been back at work several days when she told Rysakov she would come around and cook dinner, a celebration before he returned to the job. He had steadily gained more use of his injured arm and didn't actually need the help, but he liked Ruby. A lot. The violence they had experienced with Schmidt had brought them closer, though he could equally imagine it having the opposite effect. It gave him an insight into why soldiers didn't talk about battle time, or police about shooting or being shot. If you weren't there you couldn't really understand. There was another reason. You got fed-up answering inane questions such as, "What's it like to get shot?" The real answer, "It bloody hurts," never satisfied the questioner.

The dinner at Rysakov's house was over by around nine that evening and the wine drunk. The conversation drifted to an end. Ruby raised her eyes. Rysakov was looking at her and smiled. She smiled back and gathered her bag. At the door she stopped and turned. She was about to say goodnight when Rysakov took her hand in his, pulling them closer together. He bent down and kissed her tentatively on the lips. Ruby put her free hand around his neck and returned the kiss.

"It was a lovely night, Nic. I'd like to do it again, soon," she said, taking her hand off his neck.

Rysakov sensed it was too soon after Sally McIntosh's murder for her to feel comfortable about spending the night with him. As for his own feelings, he liked Ruby, but whether he was ready to get serious yet he didn't know. As she stepped through the front door, she turned again, kissed him lightly on the lips, and walked onto the street to hail a cab. He stood there for a moment after she had gone, before closing the door.

A few days back at his desk, Rysakov took his arm out of the sling. He felt sensitive whenever anyone came close. Light duties for another week gave him the opportunity and time to review the Alice file with a fresh mind. He watched the CCTV from the State Art Gallery once again. It took half a day. First he watched the tape from the commencement of the function to the closing of the Gallery. In addition to trying to spot Alice and to imagine himself there, he constantly checked the time code. By the end, he had eliminated the remote possibility that a short section of tape might be missing. He then replayed three different sequences before admitting the section on the stairs with the unknown female wearing the beret was still the best bet. He could not realistically identify any other segment that might show Alice.

On a hunch he pulled out Jack Martin's statement. According to that he and Alice arrived about fifteen minutes after the official commencement time. He checked the time code on the CCTV. The woman in the beret came up the stairs thirty minutes later. Just enough time to have a drink on arrival, go down to the toilets, reverse the jacket, add the waist tie, apply different make-up, and then to leave the gallery before anyone would think of looking for her. He knew he could not be certain, but it would explain how Alice disappeared. To his mind it offered the most feasible lead so far.

Rysakov thought it an outside chance she was still alive. If she was, where was she and why did she vanish? And why was it that wherever he looked she wasn't there? He pushed his chair back from the desk and considered the matrix he had constructed on her disappearance. One sheet set out the queries on one axis, known answers or most likely outcomes and why. The second sheet laid out a third dimension, most likely perpetrators for each of the queries, and why. With no new leads the already scaled down search for Alice Martin ran a very real risk of being relegated to cold case at the next case load review. The deaths and murders were being handled elsewhere and were not part of the Alice Martin case so far as Homicide was concerned. He needed to rethink his approach. At the back of his mind sat a nagging feeling he was missing something. Something important. It happened in nearly every unsolved case he'd been associated with, the feeling that maybe he had missed one little thing, a small clue perhaps, some little item that could unlock the mystery. That, maybe he could have done better.

He decided to interview Ann Stratton again, taking Ruby with him.

Rysakov thought of cattle at the saleyards as Ann Stratton inspected the two of them from head to toe when she opened the door.

"Do you have a niece who works under the name Honey French?" asked Rysakov.

"Ah, yes I do, or did," said Ann Stratton. "My sister rang me several days ago to tell me Angela was dead, murdered." She paused. "To say my sister was relieved would give the wrong impression, but I know she was. She had given up Angela years ago. She tried for years to get her daughter to stick with drug rehabilitation, without success. They finally had an almighty row and Angela walked out."

"Were you aware how Honey French earned her living?" asked Rysakov.

"Angela worked as a call girl, and, from what she told me, earned a lot of money. She knew the risks and talked about having a family and getting out." She shrugged her shoulders.

"You spoke to her?" queried Rysakov, surprised.

"Yes, she knew she could come and talk to me and that I would not be judgemental. She would often just knock on my door at all hours."

"Any ideas on who might have killed her?"

"None."

"Did your niece know Alice Martin?" Rysakov asked, not expecting much.

"Yes. I don't know how, but Alice happened to be here when Angela called one day. They discussed a man they both knew. I think his name was Warren something. I asked Angela how she knew Alice. She said they knew some of the same people."

As the unmarked car drove back to the police building, apart from the odd monosyllabic answer, Rysakov remained silent. The Warren could only be Kay. It was possible another Warren existed in Alice's life, it just wasn't probable. Honey French brought to six the number of dead bodies with a connection to Alice.

The case was getting to him. He even found himself talking

sharply to Ruby for no reason. He could tell by the hurt expression on her face. By the time this had sunk in, the moment had passed. He intended to go and apologise. Instead he procrastinated, seeking the appropriate opportunity. Then it became too late.

Part of the problem, he now realised, related to Sally. Although her murder occurred barely a month ago he increasingly thought of her as a case, not as a person close to him. Now her killer, Schmidt, was dead and the case closed, at least in his mind. The internal investigation had concluded: "Death by accidental shooting during a violent struggle with an officer." Ruby had corroborated the sequence of events. Schmidt still had the weapon in his hand, no other fingerprints were found on it. Then there was the practical fact that Schmidt had no relatives in Australia and none that could be identified in Germany. No one in this country knew whether Schmidt was his real name or not. So the matter was closed. Rysakov knew he had executed the bastard, knowledge which gave him considerable satisfaction. This was one cold-blooded killer that was not going to waste taxpayer's money or anyone's time with appeals. Sally had been avenged. Now *that* was case closed.

And don't forget, he reminded himself, *the bastard intended to first shoot Ruby in the stomach, then me.* It truly was self-defence.

He poured himself a cup of coffee, coffee brewed long enough to develop the bitter burnt taste of the public service. If only for distraction, he opened the morning newspaper lying half read on his desk and turned to the sport. The paper opened a page early, in Arts and Entertainment, and he noticed a minor heading near the bottom of the page: GALLERY DISPUTE TO COURT. It read:

> *The NSW State Art Gallery is suing the builder of the recently completed new wing claiming the work is not to specifications.*

Rysakov got to the end of the opening paragraph, thinking, *what an industry to be in*, and flicked the page over to the rugby.

42

One city, one photo, one woman, seven bodies, and no evidence as to the woman's whereabouts or whether she had anything to do with any of the deaths. Each dead body had a connection to Alice. *Six degrees of separation*, Rysakov thought. No guarantee for survival. Will there be more?

Will Callaghan woke early after a disrupted night's sleep. He checked the surf from the living room window, grabbed an eight foot long-board from the garage and jogged over the low dunes to join the riders already out there. The lazy three-foot breaks rolled intermittently in from the southeast giving Callaghan time to think. No Blackberry, no iPhone, no Excel, only the wind, waves and other surfers waiting for a ride.

An hour after he paddled out Callaghan saw against the horizon the outline of a big wave forming. He immediately began paddling as fast as he could. Four other long-boarders saw the same outline. Callaghan and two others timed it perfectly. He jumped to his feet as the lip on the heavy ten footer curled, guiding the board in a perfect trajectory towards the shore. Waving to another surfer who also made it to the beach, Callaghan picked up his board and called it a day. He had decided on a course of action and wanted to get on with it.

Callaghan now held a majority shareholding in Nestor Nankervis. He decided to contact the beneficiary of Clive's estate and offer to purchase his equity as a first step towards buying one hundred percent. Next, he wanted to know the parties behind the Bahamas hedge fund. Several days ago he had undertaken a detailed examination of the situation with his staff. Out beyond the wave break, he had run through all the angles again, realising he would not be the only party interested in the hedge fund. One party who might also be interested could be more dangerous than any of his normal adversaries.

He finished a post-surf coffee and flicked over the Arts and Entertainment section of the newspaper. An unusual headline caught his eye as the page turned: X-RAY FOR GALLERY.

Bizarre, he thought, *why would the State Art Gallery spend money on an x-ray machine?*

He closed the newspaper and picked up his phone.

Warren Kay kept fit at the gym, honing his kick-boxing in sparring matches several times a week. He winced as his sparring partner, an ex-State champion, landed a shin kick to his ribs. The attack happened so fast Kay barely had time to get his arm in a partial block. That absorbed some of the impact, but not enough. As he stumbled to his left from the hit, the sparring partner moved in to make a punishing left chop to Kay's trapezius muscle. Kay feinted and now delivered a wickedly painful left-cross that went straight past his opponent's defences hitting his sternum, just below his heart.

Both men were breathing heavily and covered in sweat. They touched gloves and called it a day. Kay, invigorated by the physical action and on a high from the pain, had several problems he needed to resolve. The most pressing involved Will Callaghan. It still infuriated him that Callaghan had been able to move so fast, putting an end to his own well-conceived plan to gain control of Nestor, Nankervis & Co. The man had used what Kay considered a drafting flaw in the documents. Just the sort of opening he would have used himself, given the opportunity.

Another, much larger prize required his immediate attention. Whether it was wild thinking on his part, or something else, he didn't know. At the moment he could not figure it out. The Bahamas hedge fund had sold its REI shares. Maybe it was what it appeared, and had nothing at all to do with Nestor or Callaghan.

Somehow he didn't think so. If not, what the hell was going on?

"Where's Ruby? She call in ill?" Rysakov asked the other officers in the station. An early training session had left his muscles sore, the result lack of exercise while his wound healed over the last two weeks. Even so he couldn't help favouring his right arm. That Ruby was not at her desk surprised him.

"She said something about secondment, and leaving the paperwork on your desk," said one of the detectives before returning to the file on his desk.

"The Boss figured if you can't find one missing person, you wouldn't notice another one," the detective said.

Rysakov smiled at the joke and sat down. The transfer form was on top of the pile: *Short term deployment due to general personnel shortage.* She had been moved to Family Law due to an unexpected increase in the number of cases and larger than normal absences of female officers on sick leave. She would be released back to normal duty as soon as numbers were back to operational complement.

Beneath lay a folded sheet of paper with NIC hand-written on it.

Nic, sorry I didn't have a chance to tell you, but you have been distracted by other things recently. The notification came through several days ago, and I did try a couple of times. I hope it's a short term deployment. Hope to see you for a drink soon. Ruby.

He folded the note in half again. If he needed it he could call on any of the other detectives or uniform officers on the floor. That wasn't an issue. Crime didn't wait for staffing to be properly allocated. No progress in the disappearance of Alice Martin meant resources, including his time, were being deployed to other cases. Trouble was, as his aunt insisted on singing at family gatherings, *I've grown accustomed to her face.* He missed Ruby's presence already. The note hit home: he had been distant. *But, hell, a few things have happened.*

He resolved to call her before the end of the week. The phone rang and his day began.

Late Friday rolled around before he realised he had not rung Ruby. By the time he tracked her down she had gone for the day. He left a message and prepared to leave. The ritual Friday drinks didn't have much appeal today. He got as far as the door when the phone rang.

"Rysakov."

"DS Rysakov? This is the State Art Gallery curator. I apologise for the late hour, but I think you should come straight over. We may have found your missing person."

43

The curator explained he had called Rysakov because of his earlier involvement with the Gallery.

"I'll come immediately, don't call anyone else until I get there," Rysakov said, and hung up. "Maybe I've found you at last, Alice, and then I can be rid of you," he said as he rushed to the lift.

He did not waste any time. He commandeered a car from the police garage in the basement, switched on the flashing blue lights, one behind the front grill, one on the rear shelf, and pressed the siren button.

The car screeched to a dramatic halt at the steps to the State Art Gallery, siren wailing. As he stepped out of the car, turning the siren off, Rysakov saw the curator waiting at the top of the entrance stairs. Just in front of his car stood a heavy duty truck-mounted boom crane with a long lifting arm. Taking the stairs two at a time he was nearly at the top when he saw, at the entrance to the Gallery foyer, what looked like a Crown lift truck.

"It's an electric lifter," said the curator, greeting him at the entrance. "They used it to bring the x-ray machine in. Our architect and several of our maintenance staff are concerned the load-bearing capacity of the reinforced wall at the rear of the old Gallery did not meet specifications. If that section failed at least half of the extensions could be at risk."

"Yes, I recall seeing it under construction."

"Well, it got to the stage where our engineers could see slight depressions under one of the main steel support columns. The contractor contends this is quite normal. Our people don't agree, so we withheld payment."

"And that led to the court case?"

The curator nodded. "To try to get a resolution we agreed to x-ray or gamma-ray the support wall to see if the internal reinforcing meets the specifications. If they do, then I suspect the Trustees may sue the consulting engineers for specifying inadequate reinforcing, meaning the wall may not support the load. We can't run the risk of damage to any of our exhibits."

They had been walking as they spoke and were now where the Pissaro exhibition had been held.

"Imagine our surprise when, after they took the first images using 3-D technology, they found a foreign object that should definitely not be there. The imaging company subsequently took a series of sequential adjacent shots until the mystery object disappeared."

They arrived at the site. Arc lights made it as bright as day. Three men in iridescent vests turned around from their discussion. An array of equipment lay on the ground, most of it linked by one or more cables.

"This is Detective Sergeant Rysakov who is investigating the disappearance of a woman from a function here in November last year. Could you please show him the images?" said the curator.

An hour later Nic Rysakov agreed, there could be little doubt a human-shaped entity lay inside the dual skin concrete wall. Any conclusion beyond that would be complete speculation. It could be Alice Martin. In fact, he couldn't think who else it might be. Not yet anyway.

"I'm afraid I'll have to declare this a crime scene. I'll get our people down here as soon as possible so they can decide what the next step will be. In the meantime, can you cordon this area?" he asked the curator.

"Certainly. It's been off limits due to the dispute anyway."

"And I'd like a copy of the full image and its exact location marked on the wall."

"OK, will do," said one of the technicians.

On an impulse Rysakov asked them to measure the length of the image, which they confirmed would be the real-life size. Satisfied the site was as secure as it could be, he walked out with the curator.

Back in the car he pulled out his phone and rang Ruby. Then he called in an incident report and asked for a technical team.

44

Will Callaghan could hear the excitement bubbling over the phone when John Martin rang him from Prague.

"We've found the records of when Anna Macek became a Czech citizen," John said. "It says she was the wife of a hero, Charles Macek, and had four surviving children. Her address, which is several hours out of Prague, is still in a farming area according to Mr Wendt, the lawyer. It could even be still owned by her descendants."

"Great," said Will cautiously. He had told his young cousin before he left Sydney what little he knew about his great aunt, Anna Macek, so the search could proceed from both ends. "Anything on your natural parents?"

"Not yet," John said. "Mr Wendt says names of one or both the parents were sometimes altered in adoptions of that period. They're still checking records using the names on my birth certificate, but so far there's nothing that cross checks."

"How about Alice Martin, or Alicia Nemec? Wasn't that the name on the birth certificate you found? Did you ever find a certificate for Alice Braun?"

"No, only the one for Nemec," confirmed John, "Apparently there are a lot of women with that name. They say Nemec originated as a Czech name for a German. When I showed Mr Wendt the birth certificate he was not optimistic. It could be a forgery, he said."

"What made him think that?" asked Will.

"Well, he checked the parents listed and he said they appeared to be people who died before Alice was born. He said that if she was the age shown, she would have grown up after the Soviet invasion and the hard line Cold War communist government. Her identity could have been created as a cover for some purpose. He got very vague then, especially after I told him we always thought her maiden name was Braun."

John paused, confused. Then he said, "He asked me if we had any photos of her. When I said we only really had one, he nodded his head as though he wasn't at all surprised. I don't understand it. Does he mean she was some sort of secret agent?" He paused again. "I guess that could be kind of cool."

It also means we'll never find her true identity, thought Will. "If you can track down some blood relatives, and it sounds like you just might, I don't think it matters whether Alice was a foreign agent or not."

"Mr Wendt said the next step would be to find out who owned the farm over the last eighty years. He said it may take some time dealing with the bureaucracy, and will be expensive to get it right. Is it OK if I stay here to help?"

Will could hear the anticipation in the boy's voice. "Sure, stay as long as you like. Tell Mr Wendt I'll send some funds on account. Also, ask him to follow every possible lead to try and track down Alicia Nemec."

Next, Callaghan called the Sydney legal firm he used for investigatory work, this time to find the family or beneficiaries of Clive Nestor. They told him to expect the answers in a few days.

When they finally reported back the result held no surprises. Both parents were single children themselves and both were deceased. They had two children. Clive Nestor was not married, and they found no evidence of any de facto relations for either. No offspring.

He wrote down the sibling's address and filed it as a matter the lawyers could follow up in due course. There appeared to be only one beneficiary. He sent an email to the lawyers asking them to track down Nestor's will, if any.

Exciting though the discovery of family had been for Will Callaghan, The Nataliya Trust was still a large multi-national business requiring careful strategic planning, daily decisions and the implementation of those decisions. While his worldwide staff had the competence to implement, he still had to make the decisions. With a smartphone and top of the range computer tablet and the internet, he received all the information he required wherever in the world he happened to be. However, spending time with John Martin brought into focus a more personal issue.

Sarah Longhurst, his first executive appointment, was the Group Chief Analyst and de facto CEO. The nature of the business ensured they spent more time together than apart. They got on well, enjoyed each other's company and, as they were both single, often dined together. The events in Sydney over the last month meant Callaghan had ended up staying a lot longer than planned and he found he missed Sarah a lot more than on previous trips to Australia.

It wasn't a eureka moment as such. He couldn't actually put his finger on when it happened, but he now knew, without any doubt, that he had fallen in love with Sarah Longhurst. He had always liked her. Over the last year he found himself thinking about her more and more. Suddenly, he was anxious to be back in London.

A distant low rumbling of thunder provided nothing more than background noise to the silence inside the penthouse. Occasional flashes of lightning forewarned of the storm to come. That the music had stopped barely registered with Warren Kay.

No matter how he wrestled with the problem, the only plausible explanation always ended with Callaghan. He had the opportunity, he was a foundation shareholder. He had the ability, the money and an intimate knowledge of how markets worked. And he had the motive. As a deal-maker he liked a successful deal, and without question he enjoyed making money.

Finally, Warren Kay smiled a cold humourless smile. *I should have thought of it before. Alice has a son.*

Two days later a phone call gave him the last piece of information he needed. It was perfect, almost as if he had organised it himself. When John Martin returned to Sydney he would have his pressure point with Callaghan.

45

Night brought no relief from the building thunderstorm. In the oppressive humid air, even the open window offered Rysakov little respite from the heat. His mind had just slipped into the comfortable nether region before sleep when a sudden shrill ring startled him awake. Instinctively he reached for the phone. Wrong tone. The front door. One o'clock in the morning, he saw on the radio alarm as he swung out of bed. He assumed it was bad news. Rysakov pulled on a pair of boxers as the bell buzzed again. He opened the door with his shoulder braced against it.

"Ruby!" His surprise turned to amusement as she stumbled through the doorway.

"Hello, Nic," she slurred.

"You'd better come in," he said, grabbing her by the arm as she tripped over the doorstep. He half carried her into the TV room, where she flopped onto the settee.

"Sho you waited till I wash gone, then found Alish?" she said.

Rysakov told her about the events at the State Art Gallery, wondering how much she would actually remember the next morning. "It could be Alice. We'll have to wait on DNA tests. If it's not her, then who is it?"

"I'm pleashed you called me."

"Where were you? Sounds like a party."

Ruby ignored the question and stood up, kicking her shoes off in the process. She began to overbalance, steadying only when Rysakov put an arm around her shoulders. "I need to go to the bathroom," she said, slurring the words.

He steered her down the hallway and through the right door. As he turned to go she grabbed hold of his arm tightly.

"Stay here or I'll fall."

She pulled down her knickers and stepped out of them, still

gripping his arm. When she had peed, she stood up, released his arm, and put both her hands around his neck. Resting her chin on his bare chest she looked him in the eye and smiled. He would not forget that first kiss for a long time. Even the mixture of vodka and beer on her breath tasted sweet.

After a late Saturday morning brunch at Fiveways, they strolled hand-in-hand back to Rysakov's house. As they were about to go in, Ruby asked, "Do you think of Sally much?"

Rysakov considered the consequences of the question for a moment, before deciding to answer it honestly. "Not really. I liked her a lot, but I'm beginning to doubt it would have worked out between us. She had her sights fixed on getting rich. That would have guided her decisions into areas I wouldn't have been comfortable with." He looked out the window wondering how to summarise his feelings for Sally. "I feel there's been closure with Sally. The cowardly bastard who killed her is dead."

He started to justify Schmidt's death as an accident, when she put her fingers on his lips to stop him.

"Nic, I would have done the same thing. He deserved it. What's more, I think he was almost expecting something to happen," she said, and pulled his face down to kiss him. They had faced death together and survived. It was an indissoluble part of their relationship no one else could replace, or understand.

The following week Rysakov had all but forgotten about Alice Martin, with new priorities, new cases, and new demands. A forensic team and construction experts had been instructed to sort out the State Art Gallery discovery. Little input would be required from him.

When Will Callaghan called, to say he had information on Alice Martin and would come in later in the day, Rysakov pulled out the file. A loose sheet of paper, torn from a technical pad, lay in the front: *1.4 Alice?* it said in his handwriting. The imaging technician at the Gallery had telephoned the approximate length of the body in the wall, in metres. He had forgotten to check.

After a few minutes searching he found Alice Martin's height – 1.65 metres. Even allowing for the approximation of image measurement of the body, it was not Alice. The body would not shrink to that degree. DNA would put it beyond doubt, but it wasn't necessary: there was no chance it was Alice. He jotted a note to the file and sent a short email on the police intranet to DS Smith advising him.

"DS Smith mentioned your name recently," Rysakov said to Callaghan in an interview room later the same day. "Something to do with Warren Kay."

"That's right. He made an unannounced visit one evening. He's not a man I'd want to be associated with."

"I agree. It turns out Warren Kay also knew Alice Martin well."

"I didn't know that," said Callaghan. "He's a shareholder in Nestor Nankervis & Co. Clive Nestor, the founder, was recently murdered." Rysakov nodded. "Kay had loaned them money, which could have given him control of the business. As a foundation shareholder I wasn't prepared to see that happen, so I repaid Kay's loan. End result, I now control the business, though Kay is still a minority shareholder."

"I don't imagine Kay accepted that gracefully."

"I think you could say he was not impressed."

"Clive didn't talk about his family, at least not to me," Callaghan continued. "So after his death I decided to find them to ask if they wanted to sell or were happy to hold Clive's shares. I've got my agents continuing to search, especially for his will. So far it looks like there is only one beneficiary, a brother. I expect to know for certain within the week."

"Could you send me a copy of the information, including the will when you get it?"

"Sure. Now, the reason I asked to see you," said Callaghan, "was to pass on some information about Alice, in case it might be useful."

He explained that John Martin, while principally in Prague to trace his biological parents, was also making enquiries about Alice, in case the answers had a bearing on his main search.

"I'm funding John because it happens we share a common ancestor, so I have a vested interest in any discovery he makes. I understand Alice's family thought her maiden name was Braun."

"That's correct," said Rysakov.

"Before he left for Prague, John found a birth certificate which we assume is Alice's. The name on it is Alicia Nemec. It's not an unusual family name in the Czech Republic I'm told. However, the Prague lawyers believe that certificate may be a forgery. They have even suggested the possibility Alice may have been sent here for some other purpose, industrial espionage, spying, who knows. Perhaps her controllers, wherever they are located, had some hold over her. They are of the opinion that she is not Czech, but is possibly from East Germany. How they come to that conclusion I don't fully understand, but I guess it doesn't really matter.

"Then it occurred to me that, if they're correct, perhaps whoever she worked for arranged her disappearance, maybe back to Eastern Europe, or, had her killed." He shrugged. "Anyway I'd be pleased to send you copies of the documents the lawyers send out if they'd be of interest. Maybe she also had a passport in the name of Alicia Nemec."

"Thanks. I'd appreciate copies of anything you find," said Rysakov. "We're not ruling out any possibility at present. If she has come in from the cold, it'll no doubt remain an open case, particularly if the missing person is not who we thought it was. Can I buy you a coffee? I'd recommend against the coffee here if you value your stomach lining."

As they left the building and headed in the direction of a well-patronised café, Rysakov said, "Thanks for the information on Nestor's family; it'll save us some time."

"No problem," said Callaghan. He remained silent until they were ushered to a table in the café. "Nestor's sibling is a brother, called Charles. It took us some time to track him down."

"Have you spoken to him?"

"Not yet. They'd have to get probate granted on the will before disposal of any assets, assuming they want to sell. So we haven't been in a hurry."

"If they haven't already, Homicide will want to talk to him," said Rysakov, sipping his coffee.

"Sure. Just tell me if he wants to sell his shares."

Once Callaghan had gone, Rysakov returned to the station and reopened the Alice file. What he had heard made sense, although it didn't bring him any closer to finding Alice.

Once out of earshot, Callaghan called Nestor Nankervis & Co. "Is Clive's PA in?" he asked the receptionist.

"No, Mr Callaghan, she's still on stress leave."

"You may be able to help instead," he said to the receptionist. "Did you know Mr Clive had a brother?"

"Yes," she said. "But he didn't come in very often."

"Do you know if anyone has contacted him about Clive?"

"We haven't. We thought the police would," she said.

"Do you have his address and phone? I'll arrange to go see him."

"Yes, just a moment."

After failing to get Charles Nestor on the phone, Callaghan departed early the next day for the drive north, assuming the brother would be at home. The supercharged Jaguar chewed up the freeway and he arrived with twenty minutes to spare. After several false leads he found the correct road in the small country town. Charles lived in what looked like a magazine feature house designed to be as ecologically efficient as possible. He could see solar panels covering most of the north facing portion of the roof, timber shingles, overlapped cedar planking walls, and what he assumed was a vegetable garden, though it showed signs of neglect.

After the third attempt knocking on the front door, each time louder, he peered through a window. Light curtains restricted vision, but he could see no evidence of movement inside. An old model Toyota Land Cruiser sat parked at the side of the house. He tried the door, locked. As he walked to his car he noticed the mailbox half full of mail. Callaghan pulled a couple of letters out. The name and address confirmed he was at the right place. He put the letters back and returned to the Jaguar.

"What're you lookin' for fella?" demanded a deep voice.

Will turned to see a tall knock-about type coming towards him from the neighbouring property. A sign at the street said FENCING CONTRACTOR.

"My name's Callaghan, from Sydney. I'm looking for Charles Nestor."

"He's not here."

"Do you know when he'll be back?" Will asked. "His brother, Clive, is dead. I wanted to tell him personally. I knew Clive."

"Didn't know he had a brother," said the contractor.

Twenty minutes later he climbed into his car, but not before the neighbour had explained Charles was a music composer and a computer game developer who often travelled interstate and abroad. Will gave the man his phone number and email address, asking him to ring when Charles returned.

As he drove back to the city he thought about what he'd discovered. Nothing really changed the explanation that had been going through his mind, far-fetched as it was. The truth usually turned out to be rather dull, exotic explanations usually remained the purview of fiction. Occasionally, however, real life outdid the writer's imagination.

He rang the receptionist and asked her to extract some very specific information for him. He would collect it tomorrow.

While Callaghan tracked down Nestor's brother, Kay tackled an immediate problem. Since his only contacts with the police were those he could not avoid, Kay had no sources in the force. In Immigration by contrast, for a reasonable contribution to the private school fees for the son of one well-placed official, he could obtain any information he required. He also knew which travel firm Nestor used, since he had used it in the past to get a corporate discount. By the end of the week he received two perplexing pieces of information. So far as the Immigration records showed, Nestor had never travelled to the Bahamas. Nor had he travelled to the USA, the usual departure point for the Caribbean, in the last two years.

Maybe Nestor did not have anything to do with the hedge fund in Bahamas. Maybe it *was* always Callaghan, as he originally suspected. He decided to keep track of the investor. Pretending to be a Tax Office official reviewing travel claims, he rang Callaghan's local office. It required minimal effort to extract the name of the travel agent. Using the same cover, he would now be able to find out when his target booked to travel overseas.

46

The police vehicle pulled up outside Charles Nestor's house. As the constable got out, the heat and humidity hit him like a blast furnace. When DS Mike Smith had requested a member of the local force call in at Charles Nestor's house to advise him of the death of his brother, the local police sergeant asked him to chase up several speeding tickets while visiting Nestor.

The constable surveyed the house. No sign of life. The Toyota Land Cruiser in the driveway suggested he was home. He slammed the car door to keep the air-conditioned vehicle cool and walked to the letterbox, empty.

"He's not home," said a familiar voice.

"Gidday Col. Bloody hot," the constable said to the fencing contractor. "Know where he is?"

"Nah, been gone a week or so," said the contractor. "Some bloke from Sydney was asking the other day. I've got his details if you're interested."

The constable wrote up his report and faxed it to the Sydney detective before he closed the station that evening. Nic Rysakov read a copy, courtesy of Tom O'Leary, next morning. He found it curious that Callaghan had moved so fast to track Charles Nestor. He thought about his meeting with him the other day. It appeared his instinct had been correct. For whatever reason, the man was acting swiftly.

It would be useful to know why, he thought. He should keep in close contact with him.

Will Callaghan had just hung up from a lengthy conversation with Sarah Longhurst in London when the phone at his Narrabeen home rang again. He glanced at his watch: nine p.m. After the usual courtesies, Herr Dr Wendt in Prague said, "We have visited the current owners of the Macek farm. They claim no knowledge of the former owners. They referred us to neighbours who have lived in the area for generations. We had a clerk for one day investigating at the Public Records Archive and the Land Registry Office in Prague. It has been found that Macek sold in 1947. The neighbours recall being told of Macek emigrating to Canada or England, they did not know which. They believe one daughter stayed in Prague to marry. A visiting relative of the farmer said a son also stayed. It is possible Mr John is descended from one of them. We do not have the names for these people. So we are having difficulties in tracing them. I do not think it is good to continue to spend money in that search without more information."

"Very well," said Callaghan, "I'll take your advice on that. Can we assume that Macek left Prague to avoid the Communists?"

"That is most likely. The woman known as Alicia Nemec may be worth more expenditure," Wendt continued. "I have been in contact with a legal firm in Berlin with whom we have dealings. They say it is possible a person of that name is on the Stasi files. It may even be the name is in Kremlin files, but that is not possible to know."

"I would like to proceed in Germany, Herr Doktor," said Callaghan. "From what you say it seems possible Nemec may be a creation of one of the Eastern European or Russian intelligence agencies."

"From what we have discovered so far, that is what we believe."

"Thank you," said Callaghan, and disconnected.

Wendt may have identified the correct Alice, or Alicia, or not. They would have to work on the balance of probabilities. If so, she would be about the right age. East Germany collapsed in 1989, the Soviet Union in 1991, about twenty years ago. Alice was said to be about forty, so she could have been trained before coming to Australia. Like all foreign agents she probably had a handler, someone local and older most likely. He wondered how John was coping and decided to contact one of the international agencies specialising in tracing lost relatives. Lawyers were not always imaginative thinkers when it came to problem solving.

Next morning he called in to the Nestor Nankervis office. The receptionist had done a thorough and timely job extracting the information Callaghan requested. He made a mental note to speak to the new CEO about a more productive role for her. My new CEO, he reminded himself.

He opened the file the girl handed him. "Are you certain this is it, you couldn't have missed anything?" he asked.

"Yes, Mr Callaghan, I asked our financial controller to double check. She couldn't find anything else," she said.

Callaghan was beginning to suspect his suspicions were wrong. The file had three sheets in it. Clive Nestor, according to the company records, had never been to the Caribbean let alone the Bahamas. His only contact with the Bahamas had been to speak to the hedge fund, A.V. Ago Inc., on a number of occasions. Since they were the largest shareholder in REI at the time, there was nothing unusual there. Each time, Nestor had called the same number in the Bahamas. Someone had written on the top sheet: *Chester Saunders, A.V. Ago*. That was it, no other information. It appeared boringly normal, and it probably was. Yet something didn't feel right, he just couldn't figure out what.

Callaghan was happy that progress had been made since yesterday. Now he had a name, a phone number and a location. He strolled on to his veranda at Narrabeen later that afternoon. The roar of the surf on the beach always acted as a reality check. Wave after wave reared up to a crest before crashing onto the water below. White foam surged into the beach, forced by the weight of water behind.

"What am I trying to do?" he asked himself.

It was not about Nestor Nankervis & Co., the business would run itself, and was a relatively small investment in any event.

"It's the mystery of Alice Martin, or whatever her real name is."

He watched a set of waves break, one after the other.

"No," he corrected himself. "It's really about John. My cousin and sole living relative"

He closed the door and sat down at his desk. The serendipity of meeting a direct descendent from his mother's side, the only such relative alive he had so far identified, could not be ignored. Finding the true identity of Alice, John's putative mother, became important only as part of the puzzle to uncover John's full identity, and how he came to be in Sydney.

47

When the head of the Family Division suggested there could be a permanent position, PC Ruby Walsh had to make her mind up before the secondment ended. She knew instinctively what her answer would be. Rysakov would expect her to go back to her old position. Two problems. The prospects for promotion were better in Family, or Domestic, as the older hands still called it. And she'd really like to make detective on her merits. Until another alternative presented itself, Ruby intended to build a career in the police force.

Over the last two nights she spent a lot of time thinking, trying to make a rational decision. On the weekend Rysakov had asked her to move in with him. Hence, problem number two. If she went to live with Rysakov, working with him might be overdoing it. She did not want anything to jeopardise their relationship.

"There are some substandard humans in family law," Rysakov said when she told him later that night. "Females on a mission, blokes out to right an injustice."

"You're jealous," she said, kissing him on the cheek.

"Never. Well, maybe a little."

He smiled and put his arms around her.

Light snow fell across Prague and the surrounding countryside. Sitting warm inside the *pension*, John Martin wondered what to do next. Wendt had failed to uncover any definitive answers. They had identified half a dozen possible candidates who could be Alice, or, more likely, were not. Wendt, for reasons John did not entirely understand, continued to be suspicious of the Nemec birth certificate. When he received comments on it from his colleagues in Germany, Wendt pronounced it a definite forgery. If true, it left John with no leads to find Alice, the woman who, for all his life, had been his mother, albeit his adoptive mother. On the other hand, because of the DNA test, he knew he and Callaghan had a common female ancestor. What he needed to do now was establish a direct link, through the bureaucracy, between Anna Macek and one of the parties on his birth certificate. Why was that taking so long?

He looked at the paper in his hand. For the third time since leaving Sydney he wondered what it meant. Now, with other leads drying up, the number written on it assumed some importance. This snippet of information he did not intend to share with anyone, at least until he could figure out its significance.

Before he'd left Sydney John had done a number of things, most of which he had not mentioned to anyone, even Will Callaghan. First, he convinced his parent's bank to issue him with a credit card. Fortuitously, he had just turned eighteen. Second, he drew out every bit of cash he could. In addition, Will Callaghan had given him a debit card with a one hundred thousand dollar limit, to use as required. Finally, he undertook a thorough search of his parents' belongings, inside drawers, underneath possible hiding places, everywhere he had seen used on unlikely TV crime shows.

He found three items, the Nemec certificate, which had to be disclosed for it to be of possible use, and two others he did not disclose. One, a large amount of cash, he paid onto his own credit card together with the cash he had withdrawn from other accounts. The second item was the scrap of paper in his hand. It had what looked to be an international telephone number handwritten on it. He discovered the paper because he pulled his mother's drawer completely out of the chest, as he had with all the drawers. The paper had been pressed hard against the back.

The only way to find out what it meant, if anything, was to call the number. He picked up his phone and dialled.

"First Bahamas Trust, good morning," said the voice at the other end.

"Sorry, who is this?" John asked, surprised.

"This is Bermuda's leading bank, in Nassau, sir. Who were you calling?"

John disconnected. What on Earth did this mean? It raised a whole new series of questions. He felt confused. He needed to think. Maybe be it meant nothing. For the first time since arriving in Prague he felt alone, and unsure who to trust. Finally, he came to the conclusion there were only two people he could contemplate telling about this development. Callaghan, who he suspected would have contacts even in Nassau. He seemed to be able to find out just about anything, with ease. There was no doubt he deserved to be in the loop.

The other person had, he figured, a real advantage. As a cop Nic Rysakov could do things civilians could not. He also believed the police could be relied upon to keep a matter confidential. *And you never knew when you might need friends in the force*, he thought. So he rang DS Rysakov.

In a decision he hoped he would not come to regret, he did not tell Will Callaghan.

That evening Rysakov put down his phone and sat thinking, the sound of Ruby cleaning dishes in the kitchen filling the background. After rolling this new information around in his mind, he still wasn't sure whether or not it meant Alice Martin was alive or dead. Could it explain why and where she disappeared to? It warranted some enquiry.

The next day Rysakov called the number John Martin had given him and, explaining he was a member of the Australian Police Force, asked if the Bermudan bank held any accounts in the names of Alice Martin or Alicia Nemec. The male voice at the other end declined to give any information. "It is against our policy," he said.

That didn't surprise Rysakov, police or no police. "In fact it's the proper response," he told Ruby that evening, "I wouldn't like my banking details given to someone on the phone who claims to be a cop. I could have been anyone, a divorcee, a business rival."

"So what did you do?" asked Ruby.

"I contacted the Royal Bahamas Police Force. The Deputy

Commissioner handles requests from international police," he said. "I explained we're seeking a missing person and what we wanted from the local bank. He said he'd get back to me."

"What, no trip to the Caribbean?" Ruby laughed.

"If it turns out Alice has a bank account in the Bahamas we might be able to track her down. If not, back to square one."

Rysakov briefly considered calling Will Callaghan before deciding not to.

What could he add? he thought.

As the Qantas Boeing 747-8 levelled out to cruising altitude and the sun finally dropped below the horizon, Callaghan left his seat to stroll the length of the aisle in the first class cabin. Surprised, he returned to his seat, eased it back to a more comfortable position and switched on his laptop. With the cabin only half full the service would be even more attentive than usual. He intended working for several hours before a light meal. After years of experienced commuting he would make sure to sleep for the rest of the journey. When he landed in London he'd be ready for a day's work. Even with the high quality staff in his main office he would have a pile of paperwork to process.

The stay in Sydney had stretched to more than double his original plan, but for very good reason, the discovery of family. Briefly he considered the possibility of John Martin becoming his heir, before dismissing it. That could always be addressed at some time in the future. Instead, Callaghan made certain John would be financially secure for the rest of his life.

That left him with the unresolved issue of an heir. With its rich history and multibillions, it was essential The Nataliya Trust had continuity of the blood line. *No doubt this is stating the bleedin' obvious,* he thought. Sitting in the quiet of the first class cabin he realised that meant he had to ask someone in particular to marry him, and damn soon.

"Hell, Callaghan," he said under his breath. What if Sarah had interests elsewhere? He tried turning his mind to other matters, with limited success.

Before embarking in Sydney he had initiated two lines of enquiry to satisfy his curiosity about the ultimate ownership of the Bahamas hedge fund, A.V. Ago Inc. A germ of suspicion had begun to take root since the listing of REI. One enquiry, via London, dealt with the information he had requested from Nestor Nankervis on First Bahamas Trust. Those queries were to find out if Alice Martin currently had any, or had had any, accounts with that bank. Callaghan based the questions on the action he would have taken if he wanted to vanish. The other enquiry he initiated out of North America, through Canadian and New York banks, was to find out if Alice had flipped funds out of First Bahamas into any of the hundred or so other banks in the Bahamas. Whatever the answers, he would have them by the end of the week.

48

When he sold the balance of his shares in REI, Warren Kay crystallised a substantial profit. *Not as large an amount as the hedge funds, or that bastard Callaghan*, he thought as he totalled all the proceeds he held in other names. He looked at the grand total again on the computer screen. He couldn't remain outraged for long. The gain on this one deal far exceeded the profit made on all his property deals combined. And he had made it faster, with less hassles. A smile of genuine pleasure softened his face.

"This share trading business could get addictive," he said to computer screen.

No word from his contact in Immigration meant John Martin had not yet retuned from overseas. At his age the boy could be away for years. He cradled a whiskey, watching ferries ply to and from the city across the harbour. He had been so focused on gaining control he had lost sight of the alternatives. What did he want with young hotshot investment bankers anyway? One of the many things Kay was good at was making his presence unwanted. Now he could exploit his unpopularity to get top price from Callaghan. The more he thought about it the more he became convinced he could get close to the same profit he had just made on REI.

I'll give him a very good reason. I can be very unpleasant. I might cut off his balls. A small mirthless laugh tickled his throat. "I'll make the bastard an offer he can't refuse."

Kay spent the next half an hour considering a number of scenarios. Once completed, he stood up to refill his glass and promptly sat down again. There was one more set to be played in this game. He had to go to the Bahamas, to see what he could extract from the hedge fund Nestor had made some arrangement with.

Pleased with himself, he picked up his phone and called the same Madam who supplied Honey French. He felt he'd earned some fun, though he knew not everyone would agree with his idea of fun. In fact, most of the callgirl services in Sydney had him on their blacklist. What he required of the girls scared them. And sometimes he did get carried away, with disastrous results.

As he waited, his thoughts turned to the one person, who, in his own mind at least, he considered a sexual soul mate. Alice. They knew instinctively what turned the other on, their tastes were similar. If he was honest with himself, and he generally was, he suspected she didn't even like him as a person. It was only the raw physical need that required satisfying. They were not friends. She talked little about herself, only the occasional brief conversation about a business related subject. When he heard she had disappeared he was not surprised. In fact, he had half expected it to happen.

Alice would not be seen again. Of that he felt certain. Even if she'd arranged her own disappearance it didn't surprise him that she had left the kid. It wasn't that he was a bad kid. She simply wasn't the motherly type.

It's quite possible that she's dead, he thought.

Two shrill rings on the entry security bell interrupted his reverie. The girl had arrived.

The first snowfalls were a novelty for John Martin. Draped in a soft white mantel, Prague looked like a fairyland. When it kept falling with little let up it became an inconvenience, and a cold one.

"The snow, it can go on for many months," explained the barmaid in broken English. Martin went to the tavern next to his *pension* for a beer and a meal most nights since arriving.

"Doesn't it stop till summer?" he asked.

"Of course, some days are no clouds in the sky. Then maybe rain. But snow is better."

All of a sudden he wanted to feel the hot sun on his back, to walk along the beach at Bondi, to dive into the surf. After a month and a half in the middle of an ancient and historic European capital, he had had enough. Even the attitudes of the people seemed bound by some arcane traditions, most of which he could only guess at. John knew that was unfair because many of the people, particularly the younger ones, were very friendly. They tried to be helpful. Those around Dr Wendt's age all told him what a great city Prague was to live in. How cultured, how historic, how good the food, provided you knew where to look, and how privileged they were to live in a city that was largely original. Then how come, Martin thought, most of the young people were so eager to leave?

"You are not staying for your dinner, Mr John?" the barmaid asked as John put his empty tankard on the bar and turned to leave.

"Not tonight, Heidi, maybe see you tomorrow."

"You will need recommendation for restaurant."

He pretended not to hear and continued out the door. Even the heavy overcoat he had bought soon after his arrival needed the extra warmth of the thick woollen scarf he tucked in as he walked down the street. The icy breeze made him pleased he had outlaid the extra funds on top-of-the-range skiing gloves.

After one block he turned into a café. He made a pretence of reading the menu. Some of the items had enough English beneath to make an informed guess. He replaced the menu on the stack and pointed to the bar. The waitress nodded. He would go to the bar before coming to the table. "Beer," he said to the barman.

He turned to face the door as a male, probably in his early twenties, entered. The man was heavily rugged against the cold, as though he expected to spend some time outdoors. Martin watched as the man did a rapid scan of the room stopping a second too long on him. Now he was certain he had a tail, not just tonight, but every night. When he had told Wendt and asked if he should go to the police, Wendt had smiled politely.

"I'm sure you are mistaken. Perhaps they mistake you for a footballer," he said. "Have any of them ever approached you?"

"No, they just follow me wherever I go."

"Well, please do not worry. If any of these people approach you let me know and I will take you to the police."

That conversation had been over a month ago and John was sick of the attention. *What would Callaghan do?* he wondered.

He stared at the man, put money on the bar for his half-finished beer, stood, and strode past the tail out into the street. Turning right he quickened his pace until he reached the corner. Martin turned the corner as the man at the bar came out of the café.

Martin stood with a shoulder ready for impact. Immediately the tail appeared around the corner he stepped directly into the man's path. The tail jerked back, tangling his feet and falling onto the icy pavement. Realising he was bigger than the stalker, he offered his hand to help the man up.

"Why are you following me?" he said.

"No hit," said the man, obviously aware he was at a size and strength disadvantage.

"No, of course not," said John. He had no intention of getting into a fight. "I just want to know why you're following me."

Martin ended up buying the hapless tail a beer and, although the man's English was not much better than his Czech, he got part of the story. By the time he returned to his hotel later that night he had come to the conclusion he could be in danger. He rang Callaghan and, after a long conversation explaining what had occurred, went to bed. The next day he phoned Callaghan again. "I spoke to Dr Wendt this morning as we agreed and he told me the full story. Apparently my great-great-grandfather came back from Russia with a lot of gold. Some was used to buy a farm and some went into setting up a soldier's bank. He said there are people in places of influence who believe a lot of this gold is still hidden and they thought I might have information as to its whereabouts."

"So, Wendt assumed you were descended from Macek," said Callaghan picking the story Wendt had told him overnight, "based solely on our DNA match. He strung out the search for your forebears to allow enough time to see if you had any information that would lead them to this fictional gold. Everyone in Prague knows the story of the Czech Legion who came back from Russia at the end of the First World War with part of the Tsar's gold. But to imagine any of it remains hidden." He paused. "Wendt probably also believes in the pot of gold at the end of the rainbow."

"He told me he will have copies of all the paperwork they have found in the next two days," Martin said. "There are some gaps, like the identity of my biological father. He didn't think these gaps would ever be filled. He still believes Alice, or whatever her real name is, came from East Germany or Russia. I think I'll leave once I get the papers. Doesn't seem any point in hanging around and its damn cold."

Callaghan noticed how the schoolboy had matured, no longer asking what he should do. "What will you do?"

"I might travel a bit while I'm here," Martin said.

Callaghan hesitated before asking if he had sufficient funds. He chided himself. Such an obvious question did not deserve an answer. John Martin had to make his own mistakes and find his own solutions. Time to spread his wings.

"Good idea," said Callaghan. "Keep in touch. Let me know where you are from time to time."

49

Alice Martin remained an enigma for Rysakov. A woman who had disappeared in full view of one hundred and fifty people. A woman who remained the common denominator between six people, all of whom are now dead. With the exception of Sophia Hamil, Alice had a direct, personal relationship with each of them. With Sophia the nature of the connection could well be construed as a motive for murder, although they had no evidence that had occurred.

"That's not to say she had anything to do with any of the deaths," Rysakov explained to Ruby that night. "There's no evidence whatsoever to support that. But based on what's happened so far, it could be argued that the longer Alice's disappearance remains unsolved, the more people will die. When I put this to Mike Smith at Homicide he scoffed until I went through each of the deaths. He reckons there are often common factors between multiple homicides if you look hard enough. It doesn't mean they're real. On the other hand, he's not dismissing it out of hand now."

"Surely you don't believe there's any correlation?" said Ruby. "It sounds a bit farfetched, almost like some supernatural show on television."

"Of course not," said Rysakov. "Yet I have problems treating it as one large and expanding coincidence. I'll just be a lot happier when I find out what happened to Alice."

Two large investment proposals awaited Callaghan when he returned to London. Sarah Longhurst had attached a one-page summary to the front of each report. Each summary began with a very brief recommendation: do it or don't do it. Callaghan read each report in full. She got it right most of the time, but occasionally Callaghan ignored her recommendation and did the opposite. Over the last two years he had an eighty-five percent success rate. His one failure caused by a sudden deterioration in international economic conditions, not by the deal. Sarah had warned of the downside if this happened. She had been right.

At the end of his first week back in London, Callaghan received the answers to the queries he had sent about Alice Martin and First Bahamas Trust. Because the investment deals presented by his staff were large, complex and potentially highly profitable, he spent the next week giving all his attention to the normal business of the Nataliya Trust. The Bahamas responses sat on his desk until he had time for a proper consideration.

The answers came in an email in Q & A format, each query followed by the bank's answer. In these cases the banks were a Canadian, USA or Bahaman institutions. He asked one of his analysts to consolidate the answers to cut the repetitions and answers without comment. That evening he read through the single sheet result:

> *Q. Did First Bahamas Trust (FBT) have a current account in the names of Clive Nestor, Alice Martin or Alicia Nemec? Had any of these persons ever had accounts with FBT?*
> *A. No and No.*
> *Q. Had Nestor Nankervis & Co. ever had an account with FBT?*
> *A. No.*
> *Q. Had any of the above flipped money from a source other than FBT through FBT into another bank in Bahamas or elsewhere?*
> *A. Not applicable and no, not through FBT.*

Callaghan paused. It looked like Nestor had been calling First Bahamas Trust for normal business reasons. Like any CEO he had been concerned to ensure the success of a major transaction, the new issue by REI. Nothing out of the ordinary there. Then he read the final question:

*Q. Does A.V. Ago Inc. have a current account with FBT? Has
A.V. Ago Inc. ever had an account with FBT?
A. Yes and yes.*

He read the last Q & A again. The query was slightly differently
expressed yet the answer used the same phraseology as the first
query. He shrugged. *Don't try to be too clever*, he thought. The hedge
fund had accounts in a tax haven. So what? After one final look he
put the paper aside to be filed in the morning. From the information
he had seen, Alice had had no contact with the Bahamas. Nestor
had no bank account with FBT; he simply conducted business with
FBT. There was nothing to pursue. Or so he thought.

Next morning he unexpectedly had to refocus on Nestor
Nankervis & Co.

"Morning, Will," Sarah greeted him. "That little investment bank
you invested in in a moment of weakness in Sydney seems to have a
problem. One of the shareholders has lodged a false and misleading
information allegation through their lawyers. It revolves around the
REI new issue and how good REI really was. They allege that had
they been told how good the technology really was, they would
have invested substantially more funds, and of course made a much
greater profit."

"Which shareholder?"

"A Warren Kay. He's threatening to ask for a public enquiry, an
investigation by the corporate watchdog, damages, and so forth."

He asked Sarah to close his office door before telling her the
background on Kay that DS Rysakov had given him. When he told
her of his own direct encounter with the disgruntled shareholder he
felt pleased when he saw concern in her eyes.

"He could have assaulted you, Will."

"Perhaps he was wise not to have tried," Callaghan said bluntly.

Sarah thought for a moment before smiling. "I think you're
right," she said.

Later, in Sydney the same day, Rysakov opened the attachment to

Callaghan's email and scanned through the one-page Q & A. In a very succinct format it gave him more information than the Deputy Commissioner in Nassau whose reply had also arrived. "FBT advise they have no accounts in the names of Alice Martin or Alicia Nemec, or Alice Braun. I trust this is of assistance," he had said.

Rysakov had mentioned Alice Braun in passing and had, correctly, not expected it worth pursuing. That the DC had thought fit to include the name made the result more complete. The Bahamas looked like a dead-end. He was about to delete Callaghan's one-pager, but before pressing the DELETE button he quickly reread it. Maybe they had both missed some angle. Callaghan clearly thought there might be more in it than the police. He reached over to pick up his phone to call Callaghan. He figured he knew what Callaghan was doing. Like a good financier, he was following the money. As he was about to punch the number, the phone rang in his hand.

"DS Rysakov, it's Deputy Commissioner O'Ryan, Nassau," said a voice with a crisp British accent. "I trust you don't mind my ringing you direct. We have a rather curious situation here. Not sure it has any connection to your matter, but thought it worth a phone call."

"I'm pleased you rang, sir, so I can thank you personally for your help."

"We have a man here who is becoming a public nuisance. He claims to be Australian. He also claims that substantial funds have been stolen from a bank account he says is his. He claims to be the signatory. For some time he lived at one of the better hotels in Nassau. About ten days ago they asked him to leave when his credit card bounced. The manager had already asked for our assistance on several occasions. The man has become a drunk and started worrying other guests," O'Ryan said.

"Do you know his name?"

"His passport, which took an effort to obtain, says his name is Brown, James Brown."

"Like the American blues singer. Is he white?"

"Yes. However, some weeks ago he started to insist he had killed a family member. Not long after, human remains were found on a remote and isolated beach. The state of decomposition and the sex, a female, pretty well put Mr Brown out of consideration for that death. He would not have been in the Bahamas at the likely time of death and he has only ever talked of killing a male family member."

"How can we help?" asked Rysakov. If James Brown had anything to do with Alice, it could present unexpected complications.

"His passport appears legitimate, but," O'Ryan let the doubt hang, "perhaps he could be someone you are looking for, maybe under a different name."

"Would it help if we brought him back to Australia?"

"Immeasurably."

"Can you send me a copy of his passport, a current photo and any other information?"

"You'll have it today."

"I can't give any guarantee, but if we identify Mr Brown as a person of interest would you have an officer to accompany him?"

"That's possible, isn't there a cricket match in Australia soon?" O'Ryan chuckled. "You would have to pay the cost of course."

"The test series will be over, but the one day matches run on into February," Rysakov said. He thought he heard a grunt of approval at the other end.

Rysakov sat thinking for some time after he had hung up. He opened the Alice file in which he kept details of every related crime, or alleged crime. Time slipped by before he remembered Ruby would be waiting. He called and arranged to meet at the Imperial, hoping some of his local drinking buddies would also be there this evening. There was something he needed to ask one of them.

Ruby had not arrived when he walked into the bar, so he booked a table, bought a beer and joined Rob King, his stockbroker. The group standing around the table were deep in a discussion on future trends in interest rates. Rysakov pulled King to one side.

"Rob, I'm glad you're here. You know about hedge funds, don't you? What do you know about a guy called Will Callaghan?"

"The mysterious Mr Callaghan," said King. "Until a couple of years ago his appearance as a company's shareholder would strike fear into the hearts of the directors. Then he overstretched and lost the lot. Within a year he was back doing deals. No one knows where he gets the funds. It's all very private. His operation's based in the UK with representatives in various countries, like here."

"What's his reputation like?"

"He's always been good for his word in my experience," said King.

In London Will Callaghan received the first report from his enquiries to several Canadian bank groups he knew well. He immediately asked for clarification on several items, though he knew it was not strictly necessary. What the report revealed was entirely unexpected.

50

Following a short and direct phone call from a very annoyed Callaghan, Herr Dr Wendt quickly accepted that John Martin knew nothing about any missing Russian gold. Wendt immediately produced copies of the only surviving paperwork concerning Martin's biological mother. To John's disappointment, no mention was made of his biological father on the real birth certificate: FATHER UNKNOWN it said. On the other hand, a clear paper trail from his mother put beyond any doubt he descended from Anna and Charles Macek, confirming him a blood relative of Will Callaghan. They were second cousins. Wendt finally produced a death certificate showing his biological mother had died before he reached his second birthday. Influenza.

The search suddenly ended within twenty-four hours after weeks of investigation and waiting, a real sense of anti-climax. *What an arsehole Wendt is*, John thought. Then he smiled at the thought of Wendt receiving his final hotel bill. *Don't get mad, get even.* He'd read it somewhere, and put it into practice on his last night in Prague, ordering the most expensive wines and shouting the bar drinks.

On Callaghan's recommendation he decided to go to Germany to visit Wolfgang Spit, Dr Wendt's counterpart in that country. After several conversations with Spit he caught a flight to Berlin. From his window seat he could see below villages, roads, snow-covered hills, and rivers, possibly even the Danube. The ambient hum of the aircraft engines blocked out nonessential sounds and made it easier to think. No distractions. The films were crap anyway.

The airhostess eventually came with a choice of beers. He pointed to a Carlsberg, and lay back. He hadn't given up on finding out the true identity of Alice, or Alicia, whatever her real name. *After all,* he thought, *she started the whole thing. She was my mother until she disappeared. I'd like to at least know who she really is.* He picked up the

Carlsberg and took a mouthful. In spite of himself he felt his eyes getting moist. Why was his mother not his real mother? He quickly wiped an errant tear from his cheek. He didn't cry, though he did feel sorry for himself.

By contrast with Wendt, the attorney in Berlin was a model of helpful efficiency. Wolfgang Spit met him with a car at the airport. He had a pile of papers already laid out ready on a desk in his office. By mid-afternoon Martin had a clear appreciation of where he stood in his quest to find out the identity of his adoptive mother.

"We have found a large number of women named Alice or Alicia Nemec, and we have eliminated all but two based on age, too old or young, marital status, or provable residence in Germany for many years," Spit said.

"That must have taken some time," said Martin.

"Not so long. The data is all digital so it is a matter of applying the right filters. The two possibilities are being checked, but I am not optimistic. As I told Dr Wendt, we suspect the papers you have are forgeries. They do not match either of the two women."

Spit did not waste any time. Two days later Martin met him in his small austere office. The filters they had agreed to apply to the available data had drawn a blank. "We have now exhausted all avenues of enquiry available to us and I can report to you that Alice Martin, the name you best know her by, is not a citizen of Germany, the Czech or Slovak Republics, any of the Scandinavian countries, France, Belgium, Holland, UK, or Italy. At least under the names we know her by.

"My own opinion after reviewing the data is that it is likely she is from Russia or another Eastern Bloc country. If her real identity is hidden you will not find it." He looked at the young man and said gently, "My advice is to treasure your good memories and follow your own destiny."

Spit's efforts convinced him beyond doubt – he could learn no more in Europe. Spit gave him one more piece of advice. "While you are here, spend a few days seeing Berlin." The attorney recommended several museums, art galleries as well as the remnant of the Berlin Wall, Checkpoint Charlie and the Brandenburg Gate. As a result the eighteen year-old could now say he had seen places that had previously been only names on the page of a history book.

As January came to an end he lay back in Business Class in the long distance Boeing direct to Nassau, the Bahamas. His most pressing problem now was deciding which main course to order from the menu the air-hostess had just handed him. *Bahamas and heat here I come*, he thought. Maybe Alice had gone there to live. The only evidence he had of a Caribbean connection, the piece of paper with a bank's phone number, he suspected would not justify the NSW police making the trip. Besides, the Bahamas sounded exciting.

As the hostess offered a plate of hors d'oeuvres he had a disturbing thought. What if Alice *had* been murdered as the police suspected? Maybe no one would ever know. The phone number represented his only remaining lead. He had to follow it to the end. Then he could be satisfied he had taken every action possible to find Alice. *My mother.* Try as he did to think of her as Alice, a woman he knew, the habit of a lifetime was not easily changed.

Once he had checked everything out he would ring Will Callaghan and tell him what he had discovered. And DS Rysakov.

The response Kay received from his threat to seek an independent investigation into Nestor Nankervis surprised him. An immediate rollover by Callaghan he did not expect. Neither did he expect the unequivocal response he received from the firm's lawyers:

> *Go ahead and seek an enquiry, initiate any legal action you wish. However, be certain you know the result before you begin. Costs and damages will be sought against you in the event your legal action fails. We remain confident no grounds exist for an action.*

Callaghan was tougher than he expected. The counter threat was clear and real. They would pursue him, for monetary penalties. Kay briefly considered a late night visit to Callaghan and dismissed it immediately. A bad idea. *He's not going to be intimidated and I'd be the obvious suspect.* He had to change tactics.

At the end of the week, on the advice of his solicitor, he sent Nestor Nankervis & Co. an offer to buy a controlling equity by either subscribing for a new issue of shares that would increase his shareholding to over fifty percent, buying Callaghan's shares, or selling his own shares, all transactions to be conducted at the same price. Garand called it a 'Savoy Clause'.

"Basically, Warren, when you strip all the legal crap out, a Savoy Clause says that when shareholders recognise they are in an untenable position, as you appear to be, then you offer to buy the other shareholder out, Callaghan in this instance, at a nominated price. If he doesn't want to sell, then you agree to sell your shares to him at the same price," Garand said.

"Does he have to sell?"

"No," said Garand. "If he point blank refuses to consider the offer, you could apply to the courts for an order forcing him to buy. No guarantee you'd get it but chances would be good on a sale happening, just to get rid of you as a nuisance, or you would get rid of Callaghan."

"I like it."

Five days after delivering the offer, Garand received a firm offer to buy Kay's share. The price: ten percent less than Kay's offer. Kay accepted promptly; Callaghan had read his adversary well.

He poured two glasses of Veuve Cliquot and proposed a toast. "To the Savoy Clause."

The girl, from the same agency as Honey French, smiled uncomprehendingly and drank the champagne. Kay refilled the glasses. Ten minutes later he paid her and sent her home. He didn't feel like sex tonight. The thought of all that money sitting in his bank account was far better than sweaty flesh.

For the next hour he sat looking over the harbour, barely registering it or any of the vessels moving to and from Circular Quay. Instead he focused his attention on potential investments for his newly acquired wealth. For the first time his net worth approached one hundred million dollars.

Finally he got up, poured the last of the champagne, considering if there was any point in going to Nassau. Could there be more money to be made? So far he had made a small fortune out of Clive Nestor, and no one even suspected him of the murder. He was on a roll. He would fly over, check out the hedge fund, have a holiday, and maybe try out some of those Caribbean women.

Two days later, on the day he was due to board a Qantas aircraft bound for the USA en route to the Bahamas, Joe Garand called him. "I've got to see you before you go Warren. It's important."

51

Nic Rysakov had a totally unexpected and eventful day. Information from unrelated sources landed on his desk in a coordinated assault. By the time he received the last report, he knew the investigation into Alice Martin's disappearance had just become much larger. In the space of twenty-four hours, matters had escalated dramatically.

By ten past eight in the morning he was at his desk, by quarter past he was dialling London. The email he received from Will Callaghan said: *Important new information. Ring my mobile as soon as you get this regardless of time.*

The phone answered after the third ring. "Nic Rysakov, Will. Hope it's not too late in the day."

"Not at all, Nic. I flew in to Sydney yesterday. I've got a couple of meetings then back on the plane." Callaghan's reply was crisp and business-like. "When we last met I gave you the results of my enquiries about accounts in Alice's name. What I didn't mention was that I had also initiated more detailed queries through my Canadian and US banking contacts. The results of their enquiries came in via London overnight."

"Have they found Alice?" Rysakov had no idea where this was going, only that it must be worthwhile or Callaghan wouldn't waste his time on it.

"No, and the chances are you never will, if she's still alive," Callaghan said. "You recall the hedge fund, A.V. Ago Inc., the one Nestor had been in contact with?"

"Yeah."

"It seems that a large sum of money has recently flowed through their hands. Money that was almost certainly not theirs," Callaghan said. "Historically, Canadian banks have had probably the largest presence in the Bahamas, usually through local subsidiaries. The

American and European banks are also reasonably represented. I put the same queries to four banks, in case some of them were unable to get the answers. As it turned out they all got much the same results.

"A.V. Ago was set up as a wholly owned subsidiary of an established international hedge fund, North American International Fund, or NorAm as it is usually referred to. NorAm has had indifferent management for the last few years and, unless they produce a better than average result for investors this year, it's very likely they'll be replaced. NorAm are also long term customers of First Bahamas Trust."

So far Rysakov could follow the story. He hoped it wouldn't get any more complex.

"How they achieved it no one has been able to find out, but A.V. Ago appears to have held a large forward delivery position in cobalt, and to have been the largest shareholder in REI. At the time of the REI stock exchange listing A.V. Ago closed out its position in cobalt at a huge profit and sold its entire holding in REI for a substantially larger profit."

"How much?"

"It came into the fund's bank account progressively over a period of ten days. A total of just over three hundred million." He paused briefly, as if to dramatise the size of the profit.

"When we first heard of the Bahamas I wondered whether all the international intrigue would be worth the trouble. However, with that amount of money as the prize, a couple of murders could easily fit the bill," said Rysakov.

"That's the motivation, or as you say, the prize. What is more interesting is the method. Within forty-eight hours of the transfer, once all clearances on the funds had been secured, it was transferred immediately to clearing accounts in tax havens used to shuffling money, no questions asked. The money was traced to the Maldives, then to the Cook Islands and Cyprus where it vanished. All the banks lost track of the funds by this stage. Names of accounts were changed, the transfers were broken down into multiple small amounts and sent to God knows where. It was clearly carried out by someone who could write the computer program to manage the dispersal or had access to such technology. My guess is that the money would be re-aggregated into two or three amounts in different countries where it would be available to whoever the signatory really is."

"NorAm isn't the real owner then."

"This is where it gets really interesting," said Callaghan. "A transfer of ten million US dollars was made to a main NorAm account at this time. I think that was their fee for assisting in this whole charade. That, and the fact that A.V. Ago Inc. was set up less than six months ago with only five hundred dollars sitting in its bank account until these transactions. One of my contacts says a secretary at FBT told them they had instructions to liquidate A.V. Ago Inc. by the end of the month."

"So you think A.V. Ago was a special purpose company?"

"I'd bet on it," said Callaghan. "One other thing, and this information is a little confused, the instructions for the whole transaction were given mostly by phone, confirmed by email, with the password and access code verified by the Canadian bank that's a shareholder in FBT. FBT said the voice on the phone could have been a woman's, but they couldn't be certain."

"I thought Clive Nestor handled all the dealings with FBT and A.V. Ago," said Rysakov, his mind racing ahead.

"So did I."

"If this all checks out, then someone got in before Nestor, because he was dead before the date of these transfer of funds."

Callaghan remained silent.

"Am I right in thinking that the ability to transfer money has to be put in place at the time the account is set up?" asked Rysakov.

"Yes, it's exactly the same as the signatories, although with the right authorisations they can be changed."

Neither man spoke until Rysakov broke the silence.

"So someone knew what was going to happen and set this all up."

"Yep, I reckon that's what happened."

For a long time after he had finished speaking to Callaghan, Rysakov stared at the notes of the conversation on his desk. Was it possible Alice had set it all up, and then disappeared with three hundred million? It was motive enough for anyone. She had high level computer skills, he recalled John Martin saying. "Awesome," her son had said. Did she have the financial knowledge of banking? If the controller of the account really was a woman it pointed to Alice, which meant she was still alive.

It had to have been Alice or Nestor, he decided. It didn't make sense otherwise, all the evidence pointed to one of them. He corrected himself. *What evidence?* What hard evidence did he have that would enable the Director of Public Prosecutions to make a decision to prosecute. There wasn't much, certainly not enough to get a conviction, in his opinion. *Who would we charge? Nestor's dead, Alice is dead or location unknown. Charge her with what? Insider trading, maybe. Wasting my time?*

If the party remained outside Australian jurisdiction he could not pursue it. He needed to clear his head. As he stood, ready to leave the office to walk around the park opposite the building, his phone rang.

"Good morning, Detective Sergeant, it's O'Ryan, Nassau."

"Afternoon, Deputy Commissioner, it must be getting late in paradise."

"Another hour and I'll be at the Yacht Club. How is your planning going to repatriate my drunk problem?"

"I expect to have approval for the airfares and three days accommodation by the end of the week," Rysakov replied.

"Good. Yesterday your man, James Brown, started the day drunk as a skunk. Where he gets his liquor from we can only guess, probably stolen. By mid-morning he was accosting people in the street and causing a real nuisance. The men on the beat had had enough and brought him in to sober up overnight. As of two hours ago, mid-afternoon here, he was sufficiently coherent to conduct an intelligent conversation. Because he is a foreigner, and because of the claims he insisted on making, the station sergeant referred the matter to my office."

Rysakov had the feeling his day was about to get more interesting.

"I went down to the station and spent nearly an hour listening to Mr Brown. He insists that his real name is Clive Nestor. Does that ring any bells?"

"It certainly does. He was murdered outside his home here in Sydney a couple of weeks ago," Rysakov said, wondering if he could guess what the DC would say next.

"He claims to have been CEO of a bank in Sydney. He left them and came to Nassau expecting to collect a substantial sum of money, the result of several successful investments he had made. When he arrived, the funds were gone. Stolen, he says. It's a story we hear from time to time. It may be correct, or it may be an excuse to avoid paying a hotel account. So far, whenever we have investigated the claims we've not found any evidence of a crime being committed in our jurisdiction. Notice I said within our jurisdiction, what people do elsewhere is someone else's problem."

"Clive Nestor *was* CEO of a local investment bank," Rysakov said.

"Sounds like you could have a problem with a wrongly identified body. James Brown, you may recall, has been claiming to have killed his brother. We hadn't been able to make any sense of the claim. He says his brother, named Charles Nestor, lives north of Sydney, but he hasn't been able to get him on the phone or email for weeks. Apparently a man lent money to our Mr Nestor who didn't repay it and the man threatened to kill him. Does any of this make sense at your end?"

"I think so, although there're some major questions still unanswered," said Rysakov.

"Oh yes, I almost forgot. He says his brother, Charles, is an identical twin. Don't know whether that helps. I'll be at the club for the next few hours if you need to speak to me."

"PC Wal..." he stopped. Ruby of course no longer worked for

him. He picked up the phone, dialled support, and asked the PC who answered to get him Charles Nestor.

"Connecting you now, sir," said the voice when she rang back.

The phone rang until it finally went to message bank. Charles Nestor was still not home and if Rysakov's thinking was right, he wouldn't be returning. After several minutes thought, his mind working fast, he dialled Nassau.

"Hello Deputy Commissioner, its DS Rysakov in Sydney. Sorry to trouble you."

"You just caught me, I was nearly out the door," said O'Ryan.

"Some months ago Clive Nestor had contact with a man called Chester Saunders at FBT. I was wondering if he could be interviewed by the Bahamas police," Rysakov said.

"It may only be coincidence, but he went on two weeks annual leave over three weeks ago. Hasn't been seen since. If he'd been here we'd already have interviewed him. You see, he had direct contact with many of FBT's foreign customers, including those in Asia and Australia. Occasionally employees in these positions, seeing large sums of money flow through their hands, decide to divert a portion. When Mr James Brown kept insisting his money had been stolen, we called Mr Saunders, without success. He's still missing. We've since had unconfirmed reports of a man's body on a remote section of the east coast of Andros, our largest island. I think it's unlikely, however, if it turns out to be Saunders, I'll call you. I suspect it's more likely he's misappropriated some client's money and is busily trying to spend it. Most times it's their sudden ostentatious lifestyle that gives them away. Let me know when you get the funding approved," and O'Ryan hung up.

So, Rysakov mused, *Clive Nestor sends the proceeds of some insider trading to FBT, arranging the whole exercise with Chester Saunders. Once he is sure the money has been transferred, he flies out. But did he use his own passport or a false one? He certainly had the money to buy a new identity.*

He decided to get outside and take the walk he had been about to embark on. As he waited for the elevator, he tried to imagine Nestor arriving in Nassau full of expectations, going to the bank, to be told the account has no funds. His bridges are burnt, what can he do? He complains to the bank, they say the funds have been correctly withdrawn. He complains to the police. They make enquiries at the bank, only to be told there are no funds. He can't return to Sydney for fear of being charged for breaching insider trading laws, and maybe other matters. Insider trading of that magnitude alone could net him years in prison.

And where does Alice fit in, thought Rysakov, *if at all?* He didn't want to think about Charles Nestor, yet.

The *trill-trill* sound of his phone interrupted his thought process.

52

The Family Law Courts were the last repository for shattered dreams and Will Callaghan found them consistently depressing in the few instances he had ventured beyond the benign generic entrance. Today was no exception. Months ago he had promised an old family friend, as a favour, to appear as a character referee for his son in a messy divorce, now at the custody hearing for the two children. Although he caught the flight from London with almost monotonous regularity, he still felt tired.

He was about to step into the elevator when the doors closed on a single occupant, a tall man, with his finger on the buttons. Callaghan stepped back, surprised. The man had looked straight at him and kept his finger pressed down. Callaghan hit the call button and waited for the next elevator. Something didn't gel with the man who had closed the doors on him. Something looked out of place. The image played back in his mind. The man held a long narrow object like a...

"It was a rifle," Callaghan said out loud.

He checked elevator lights above the closed silver doors. It stopped on Level 2. Another elevator opened, he stepped in and pressed LEVEL 2. As the doors closed he took out his phone and dialled Emergency.

When the operator answered he told her what he had seen, his name and location. He terminated the call as the elevator doors opened. Instead of the court entrance he expected, he stepped into a waiting area with half a dozen empty chairs backing the walls and an unattended enquiry desk. Beyond that, desks and workstations with uniformed and plain clothed officers of the Family Law Division. He absorbed all this in a split second. What totally focused his attention was the back of the tall man. The man dropped the weapon's cover onto the floor before bringing the rifle up to waist height. It looked like an M-16, with the curved magazine in front of the trigger guard.

Callaghan charged towards the man who, wholly absorbed with what he was about to do, did not hear the elevator doors open. Four metres away, in a point blank killing zone, the man raised the muzzle and squeezed the trigger. The percussion in the confined space sent a shockwave like a physical force, stopping Callaghan mid-step. All activity froze. In the milliseconds of silence following the single shot, the shooter spoke in a chillingly calm voice.

"PC Walsh, tell me why I can't see my kids?"

Callaghan was a metre away when the shooter sensed his presence and spun around. In the time it took for the M-16 to complete its arc, Callaghan closed the gap and grabbed the shooter's arm and shoulder. A short burst of automatic fire tore a hole in Callaghan's suit, before he secured the shooter in a grapple hold. He twisted his leg around the shooter's right shin, pulling back as he threw his weight forward. They both fell onto the carpet tiles. Callaghan extended his other leg over the shooter, locking his legs in a scissor grip. The shooter was strong, maybe stronger than Callaghan and he strained viciously to get his rifle arm free. Callaghan couldn't hold it and the M-16 began to twist around. The shooter sensed he was winning the fight. Callaghan knew he had one last chance. He let the rifle go and slid under the taller man's back using both arms to immediately lock the shooter's left arm. Using leverage from his legs he twisted the man's arm until it snapped. The shooter screamed in agony as a door burst open and three large policemen surged into the waiting area, grabbing the rifle and the screaming man. Callaghan ceded control, unwrapping his legs and standing up, by which time the shooter had been disarmed, handcuffed and held sobbing in pain between two officers.

By the time Rysakov heard what had happened the gunman had been securely locked in a cell. He tried repeatedly to contact Ruby. The Family Courts and the police floors in the building remained in lockdown while a heavily armed SWAT team, scrambled on

Callaghan's call, confirmed it to be the action of a lone gunman, not part of a coordinated attack on the police. Ruby's phone lay unattended on the desk and the main switch took time to locate her.

"Are you OK? You're not hurt?" he asked when he finally got through, relieved to hear her voice.

"I'm fine," Ruby said, "though a bit shaken he came after me, just for doing my job. All I did was serve the AVO, so I'm the bad guy."

"You'd probably be safer in Homicide," said Rysakov, trying to lighten the conversation after she explained how the gunman had been disarmed.

"By the way I've invited Will Callaghan for dinner tonight to say thank you. His actions certainly saved lives, most definitely mine. He says he knows you," Ruby said.

An hour later, Rysakov's phone rang again.

"I thought you might be interested in the Gallery body in the wall," the Chief Pathologist said. "It's female. Judging from the fracture of the skull, she was murdered. She was thrown into the wall head first, if that helps? But there's a problem."

Rysakov waited, saying nothing.

"The problem is, she's been dead for over two thousand years. Reckon she'd have made a better exhibit if they'd left her in the wall," the pathologist said. They talked for a few more minutes before Rysakov thanked him and hung up.

Rysakov closed the Alice file on his desk. "I *will* find you," he said and left the office.

53

Compared to the airports John Martin had experienced so far on this trip, Nassau had a great holiday feeling about it. The warm breeze, tropical palms, locals in shorts and short sleeve shirts, the initial impression was of a vacation paradise.

This sure beats Europe in winter, he thought.

Once outside the terminal, he took a cab to the budget hotel he had booked over the internet. That evening he took a stroll downtown. He had an idea, which he knew to be wishful and silly, that he might see Alice. Of course he didn't. Instead, he returned to the hotel tired and a little drunk. It hadn't taken long to prove Jamaican rum really was as strong he'd heard back home. As he searched for a cab he passed a low but impressive building: ROYAL BAHAMAS POLICE FORCE. Tomorrow he would go to the bank. Maybe after a swim, the beaches looked divine.

Joe Garand sat in his office in Sydney endeavouring to hide his agitation from the man on the other side of the desk. Warren Kay made no attempt to hide his own impatience.

"I'm going overseas this afternoon. What's so damn important?"

Garand didn't ask Kay why and where he was going in case people, say the police, decided to enquire. Garand could truthfully plead ignorance. "You remember my younger sister, Mary?" he said.

"The one who married the prick?"

"That's the one. Well, he's still hitting her. When he began threatening the kid she took out an AVO and the court got the police to serve it to remind the arsehole it's now serious. So what does he do? He shoots up the police office with an M-16. Now he's locked up and will be for some time."

"So why are you telling me?"

"The courts are so fucking weak with serious crimes he'll be out in a few years and then the M-16 will be used on Mary and the kid. Even if she moves he'll find her. I'd like to find a way to make sure he never comes out."

For a minute Kay said nothing, his cold eyes bored into the lawyer.

"Accidents happen, maybe he'll catch a fever," Kay shrugged, "I suggest you pray. I'll be back in a few weeks."

Several blocks away from the lawyer he made a call.

"Joe Garand might have a cleaning contract... what? Yeah, the lawyer. It's over to you. Call him if you're interested." In Garand's position, Kay would never have let the matter get to this stage. The solution would have been on Kay's terms.

He hailed a cab and headed for the airport and the Bahamas.

At Rysakov's terrace-house in Paddington, Will Callaghan and Nic Rysakov finished their BBQ steaks. Will reached over and topped up their glasses with an aged Barossa Valley shiraz he'd brought for the occasion.

"The way you took down the guy with the rifle looked like Jiu-Jitsu," said Ruby. "Where did you learn that?"

"It's Brazilian Jiu Jitsu. Years ago I thought I knew enough to compete in mixed martial arts comps. After some very painful experiences I discovered some fighters don't play fair. These days I keep it up just to stay fit."

"I checked him out," Rysakov said to Ruby. "He won a couple of titles."

"I'm impressed," Ruby said, raising her glass in salute.

The meal finished, they continued talking over their wine. The cut sandstone flagging, flanked on two sides by thick conifer hedges, kept the air pleasant for a hot night.

"Some years ago I met a British lawyer whose firm, it transpired, had acted for my family for over a hundred years," Will said. "Amazingly his family had passed down the story, some of it documented, some verbally, from generation to generation. From what you've mentioned about your family, Rysakov, I believe our great-great-grandfathers could have known each other."

215

Will Callaghan told how his ancestor, Mikhail Morozov, become friends with a policeman, Maksim Rysakov. How Mikhail saved Maksim's life, and Maksim helped the Morozovs escape Moscow after the Revolution.

"I'd heard pieces of this from my father, but had no idea about the rest of it," Rysakov said.

"Now the two of you are continuing the story," said Ruby.

54

On arriving at Lynden Pindling International Airport at Nassau, Warren Kay showed little interest in all the trappings of a tropical paradise. From habit he scanned the crowds. Calypso music set the mood for incoming holidaymakers, mainly Americans escaping the cold and snow of February back home. Brightly coloured, loose-fitting short sleeved shirts combined in a kaleidoscope of vacation fun. Through it all, American accents, loud and excited, overpowered the laid back Caribbean drawl.

Kay collected his bag from the carousel and made for the exit and taxis. A woman walking towards him, trailing a carry-on bag on wheels, suddenly veered away at ninety degrees, her face averted. Kay stopped dead, not sure what he had seen. Was it the sudden change in direction? Something about her seemed familiar. He remained stationary and followed her with his eyes. The woman stopped, as if she felt him looking at her. She turned and for several seconds they locked eye-to-eye, then she looked away. His heartbeat returned to normal. It was not Alice. For one incredible moment he could have sworn he had seen his missing ex-lover. Since her disappearance only that one, old, image of her face had been broadcast in the media. As a result, it had become the image in his mind. As he watched, the woman embraced a man also trailing a carry-on bag. The two walked, smiling, to the departure gates.

The right height, similar hair length, even the face on a casual glace looked right. But it was not Alice. Yet he wasn't here for her. Chasing money, not ghosts, brought him to the Caribbean. Such a totally unexpected encounter, however, left him feeling off-balance.

As airport taxis weaved through the afternoon traffic en route to homes and hotels, John Martin caught a taxi from his hotel to an appointment with the manager of First Bahamas Trust. As the taxi accelerated, he thought about the call he had made from Prague. He tried to work out the best way to approach FBT. When he had finally told Will Callaghan about the strange phone number Alice had written down, Callaghan had surprised him. He already seemed to know about FBT.

Martin did his own research on the internet and had asked banking questions in Berlin before he left. Whichever way he approached it, there seemed only one basis on which to visit FBT. The taxi completed the short journey. He paid the fare, got out, took a deep breath, and pushed open the glass door to the FBT offices. *Looks more like an accountant's office*, he thought. It did not feel anything like a bank.

"I have an appointment with Mr Hamilton," he told the receptionist.

John established his identity using his passport and certified copies of his birth certificate and parent's marriage certificate that he had obtained from the Australian Embassy in Berlin.

"So, Mr Martin, I'm not sure we can help you. We have no accounts here in the name of Alice, or Alicia, Martin," said Hamilton. "I can also tell you that we have never held accounts in those names, or in the name of your parent's company. I can say that with some certainty, as you are not the first to enquire, and we have checked."

Although James Hamilton spoke with a very English voice, the attractive Caribbean rhythm of his speech, not to say his dark complexion, left no doubt he was born in the islands. John liked him. He felt he was being treated as an equal.

"If we could assist in your search for your parent's assets we would be delighted to help. If there is any other way we can assist we'd be pleased to do so. On an obligation free basis, of course."

"Who else has been enquiring?" John asked.

"The Deputy Commissioner of Police, on behalf of the Australian police I understand, and two private parties. Of course we can't disclose names," said Hamilton. "Why don't I take you to an early dinner at my club? Nassau is not all business, you know, and I do not want you to leave with a poor impression of FBT. You may become a successful businessman in future years, and remember our bank in the Bahamas."

John decided to walk back. He had two hours to fill before Hamilton picked him up at the hotel. He suspected he could have obtained the answers to his queries by telephone and saved the journey. What the phone would not have achieved was the clear message, that this was all the information he was going to get from FBT.

So I'm going to enjoy dinner, order whatever's most expensive on the menu, he decided.

Some overweight American and English tourists were complaining within earshot about the late afternoon heat as they hurried between air-conditioned shops. A tour company window caught his eye, offering air and boat tours of the islands. Maybe he'd do one. The helicopter tour looked fun, and he had the money.

Several blocks from his hotel he passed one of the prestige resorts. A taxi pulled up next to the curb and a guy in long trousers got out. *Straight off the plane,* he figured. The man paid the driver and turned to enter the foyer. As he did, Martin saw his face clearly. He stopped, surprised. *That's Warren Kay,* he thought. *What's he doing here?*

Kay had been an acquaintance of his mother, Alice. He had met him once, so briefly he didn't expect Kay had noticed his presence. He would not have remembered the encounter had Alice not told him to stay away from "that dangerous man." How curious he turns up in Nassau.

For some reason he could not explain, he decided not to make contact. Maybe it was the warning from his mother. Instead, he waited until Kay disappeared into the lift before going into the hotel coffee shop and ordering a cold fruit juice. When the reception clerk wasn't occupied attending the needs of a patron, he crossed the foyer.

"Excuse me, is a Mr Warren Kay staying here?"

She checked her computer screen. "Yes, he's just arrived. The house phones are near the lifts."

Fifty metres along from the resort a loud Australian voice caused

Martin to look across the road at an unkempt, overweight man, almost certainly drunk, haranguing an embarrassed, middle-aged couple. The man's clothes were dirty and crumpled, as if he had been sleeping rough. Martin ignored him when the drunk shouted at him too, continuing on back to his hotel.

An hour after arriving, Kay stepped out of the resort hotel for a walk in the short tropical twilight to stretch his legs after the long flight. He turned left and strolled towards several restaurants at the end of the block. Light but steady traffic moved at a leisurely pace in both directions. Halfway along, he heard several horns beeping in annoyance as a drunk staggered across the road ahead of him. Kay paid little attention.

As he drew level, the drunk suddenly launched himself off a light pole that had propped him upright. He staggered directly into Kay, swivelling around to see who or what he had collided with.

"Shhhorry," he said. He regained his balance, his eyes unfocused, and weaved on his way.

All colour drained out of Kay's face. Cold sweat trickled down his spine. He had just come face to face with a ghost. Clive Nestor, the man whose throat he cut in Sydney, had just spoken to him.

55

"Tom, Nic Rysakov, still only solving the easy ones?" Rysakov said into the phone.

"G'day Nic, what's new?"

"In the last twenty-four hours I've received information that makes it pretty well certain the body of Clive Nestor is in fact that of his identical twin brother, Charles."

"You sure? The brother was a twin?"

"Ninety percent. Once I get the real Clive back here there'll be no doubts."

"Shit, you better get over here straight away. I'll tell the Boss, he'll want to hear this. Hell, wrong body and still no suspects."

"Doesn't get any better than that."

He was going to enjoy the next half hour. He had no doubts they would want in on getting Clive Nestor back from the Bahamas. It would cost them though, half the airfare and accommodation for the DC onto their budget. Rysakov smiled; he would try to offload the full cost. It was a murder after all. It wouldn't matter if they had first go at Clive, his MP wasn't going anywhere.

Will Callaghan completed yet another London conference call and had just poured a black coffee when his phone rang again. Since waking at five a.m. he'd had over a dozen calls, mostly from his head office, all requiring decisions. Wearily he picked it up.

"Will, it's John Martin."

"Hi, John. Are you still in Europe? Don't forget my head office will look after you in London." Callaghan had not heard from Martin for five days.

"I'm in Nassau, the Bahamas," said John.

Callaghan's mind went on alert. "That's a bit of a surprise. Got any new leads?"

"No, none really. I went to see First Bahamas Trust, but they couldn't help. Then on the way back to my hotel I saw this guy from Sydney that mum, ah... Alice, used to know. She pointed him out to me a few times. His name is Warren Kay, and I remember her saying he's dangerous and that I should stay away from him. That's probably why I remember him," said Martin. "I thought I'd ask him if he knows where Alice is. Maybe she's here, in Nassau. I thought I'd just bounce it off you first."

Callaghan was silent for a moment. "Would he recognise you?"

"No, I don't think so."

"OK. The police suspect he's responsible for a number of violent attacks in Sydney, maybe even attempted murder, so stay away as Alice said. I think the best thing to do is ring Nic Rysakov and tell him. They might even be looking for him," said Callaghan, adding the last for effect. "When you've heard enough reggae and realise the sunburn in Nassau is the same as on Bondi Beach, come back via the States, New York in particular. When you're back you might give some thought about getting some financial training," Callaghan suggested.

If he showed promise and received sufficient training in the city, then maybe he could bring him into his world, the world of money management. A lot rested on the boy's character.

That's all a long way into the future, if ever, Callaghan thought.

When he'd hung up he walked down to the beach, to clear his head, to feel the sand between his toes. While he had the money to do as fancy took him, the work ethic had been strongly imbued in him by his father. And he enjoyed what he did. Making a successful investment in any company, especially a new business, provided considerable satisfaction. The motivation was not money, he didn't need it. As a wealthy investor said many years ago, "Money is just a means of keeping score." When one of the businesses increased profits, employed more staff, or gained greater recognition in the marketplace, he knew his money had contributed to that achievement. The knowledge his decisions helped build successful enterprises was a source of considerable pride to him. It made life rewarding. Or so he thought in his more philosophical moments. With the discovery of John Martin he now had the added enrichment of family.

Although finding Alice only interested him for John's sake, several aspects of the money flow remained unexplained and that intrigued him. Callaghan thought he had the answers. One phone call should resolve the matter. He could then file it with the Nestor Nankervis & Co. investment. Nothing depended on it, knowing would not affect John. It was simply intellectual tidiness.

"Did John ring you?" Callaghan asked Rysakov over the phone.

"Yes. I told him to stay well clear of Kay. I gather you said much the same thing," said Rysakov. "Warren Kay will be there for a good reason. I don't believe in coincidences with people like him. I rang the DC in Nassau to warn him. But, until Kay breaks the law all we can do is wait."

"Good, I'm sure John will take notice of your advice. While it's probably irrelevant to your search for Alice, you might be interested in a conversation I had with the general manager of FBT, a James Hamilton. Nearly a month ago a man with an Australian accent presented himself as the signatory on the account in the name of A.V. Ago. When the account manager, Chester Saunders, checked he found that the man on the other side of his desk was indeed mentioned in correspondence. That was all. He had never been confirmed as an authorised signatory by the account's controllers. Consequently, he had no access to the account. FBT had no obligation to give him any information or allow him to withdraw any funds. It's almost certain it was Clive Nestor using a false passport and identity.

"I tried to get Hamilton to tell me the name of the person who operated the account. Not surprisingly he refused, citing bank confidentiality. Anyway, I don't think the name would be much help. It's bound to have been fake and any attempt to trace it would hit a blank wall.

"After a bit of cajoling he told me that funds transferred into the account were immediately forwarded to other banks. The client had been very specific about that, and, he told me, had paid a generous fee to FBT to guarantee performance.

"Saunders left the bank two days after the funds transfers. He didn't formally resign, but hinted he intended to. They assume he got a better offer from the client, as he hasn't been seen since. Hamilton also told me FBT had received by email, with all the correct codes and access numbers, instructions to close the account, and apply the remaining funds to costs. I've confirmed independently that NorAm LLP, the large hedge fund based in the US, still has operating accounts with FBT. They seem to have rented out their name for a fee for a few months. Nothing improper about it, just not how I do business," Callaghan concluded.

An hour after being accosted by the ghost of Clive Nestor, Kay started coming to his senses. He had no clear recollection of returning to the hotel. Once in his room he became aware of rumblings in his stomach. Without any further consideration he called room service for food and coffee, two pots. Again he went over what must have happened, resisting the temptation to write it down on the hotel pad.

There had been one terrible moment as Nestor lurched away from him and disappeared among the pedestrians on the sidewalk, when his heart stopped and he felt sanity slipping away. If a car had not honked its horn when he staggered close to the curb, he could have fallen over the edge and lost his grip on reality.

He emptied one coffee pot into his cup. By the time he had emptied the second pot an explanation started to take shape. It took an hour on the telephone, getting Joe Garand to work out of hours and expressing sympathy to several staff at Nestor Nankervis before asking if Clive's brother had been informed. Eventually he sat back in the hotel chair, piecing together what had occurred.

Obviously, he had slit the throat of Nestor's identical twin. He'd heard of a brother, but how was he to know they were identical? And what was he doing in Nestor's house? He must have had an arrangement with Clive to stay with him when he came to the city.

Pity, he had nothing against him. It had been needless exertion and risk.

That left him with a problem, Clive. It had to be dealt with. He could not afford to have Clive alive, stirring up trouble and seeking revenge for his brother. At some time Clive would be bound to point the finger at him. A rudimentary plan began to take shape in his mind. Immediately, he felt more like himself again. Picking up the phone he ordered a *Lonely Planet Guide to The Bahamas*, and any other tourist guides the hotel had, to be sent to his room.

Next morning Kay discussed with the concierge which of the ship's chandlers and fishing supply shops carried the biggest range of goods. The cab driver assured him, as soon as he saw the addresses, that the second place on the list had the biggest range of equipment in Nassau.

"This's were Ah'd shop if Ah wanted a partic'lar rod, sar," the driver said.

It looked distinctly unprepossessing from outside, a hotchpotch of corrugated iron sheeting, timber and aluminium cladding. As soon as the door closed behind him, Kay saw the accuracy of the driver's assessment. They had everything all laid out logically in clear displays. The timber floor looked in good condition and recently swept. Despite outside appearances, the whole enterprise had a professional feel about it.

"I want a good bonefish rod, middle of the range price, and some tackle to go with it. I'll also be after some fish we can eat. I'd like to be able to change tackle and use the same rod," he told one of the men behind the counter.

After a lengthy discussion between several of the staff he purchased three rods and a variety of tackle for fish he never knew existed, let alone had any intention of catching.

"When I catch them are they best cooked whole or filleted? Not the bonefish, of course. The more edible fish," he said, anticipating the answer.

"Most fish are better filleted. Do you have a filleting knife?" his main man said.

"I've got a nice one back home, but they won't let you carry them on aircraft these days," he said and smiled. "What have you got?"

This was what Kay had come to buy and he bought quality, German stainless steel. This knife he knew from experience would hold its edge. The shape of the handle enabled the person doing the filleting to retain a firm grip even if water, juices or blood ran down it. The narrow blade itself had a point with which to pierce the skin of the fish. The blade had a flowing curve to part flesh from the bone. It came with a leather scabbard that could be fitted to a belt. Perfect.

Kay half-heartedly bargained for a package price, as the store keeper clearly expected he would. If ever asked, the store keeper would barely remember what he purchased; just another tourist buying fishing gear, which provided Kay the benefit of a cover story. He left well satisfied. The next phase of his plan could prove a little more difficult. Once the gear had been locked in his room he left the hotel and hailed a cab on the street, several blocks away.

"I've got half an hour to fill, show me the sights," he said.

In the ensuing conversation he explained how he had a friend he wanted to surprise with a trip to Andros, the largest island. *And the least populated*, he thought. The guide books proved very useful, extolling benefits such as deserted beaches, which he planned to put to a use never considered by the authors. After a little prompting and mention of a fee, the cab driver remembered a cousin who he was certain could persuade Kay's friend to come on the trip, without mentioning the birthday surprise. By the time Kay parted company with the driver the details had been agreed. Kay insisted on paying a deposit as an indication of good faith.

"It'll take a day or two to get everyone organised. Then I'll call you," said Kay.

The driver gave Kay his phone number. As the cab drove away Kay entered a seafood restaurant. That way the cabbie didn't know his hotel. He had seen Kay's face on the other hand and might be able to provide the link to Nestor.

Never leave a loose end, he thought as he picked up the menu, the final piece of the plan now slotted in.

John saw Kay exit the cab and enter The Haven Seafood Restaurant. Having nothing better to do he ordered a long cool drink at a small café-bar opposite and waited. Forty-five minutes later he saw Kay leave, and followed on his side of the road. Kay stopped and faced the road searching for a cab, hailing one several minutes later. John went in the opposite direction confident he had not been recognised.

56

Towards the end of January, Ruby Walsh received news that so annoyed her that by the time Rysakov finally walked in late from work that evening, she was hopping mad.

"I came damn near top of the course and they gave it to a jerk who is nothing more than a yes man. Doesn't say much about the man in charge of the Family Division does it? What a creep. And you said you know him. Fat lot of good that did," she railed before he had time to shut the door behind him.

"I did call him and said your promotion was well overdue. I told him I'd have you back in a heartbeat if he couldn't keep you. But I told you I knew him, not that I liked him or thought he was any good," Rysakov said in as reasonable a voice as he could muster.

"The next promotion list is not for another three months at least. With this jerk in charge there's no guarantee that if I actually do get promoted I won't just stay in uniform. He promised me detective by now," Ruby said. She stood in the middle of the room, looking rather forlorn. "Do you know what he said when I complained? That I had too high a profile! Because that psycho came gunning for me. Can you believe that? What a prick."

Rysakov put his arms around her and pulled her against his chest. "You would make a good detective," he said. "Why won't you let me get you transferred back? You'd be a detective within a month."

"No, it has to be on my own merit."

This was old ground, a squabble they had had many times. Rysakov put his hands up in surrender. Tiredness made his legs ache, he needed a workout. Instead, he went to the wine rack, pulled out bottle of red wine and held it up. Ruby nodded. He put two glasses on the table, filled them and passed one to her.

"To a better day tomorrow," he said, raising his glass.

Two days ago Rysakov had emailed the DC in Nassau asking him to take Nestor into protective custody. Before he left the office he received a reply asking if he had funding approval for Nestor's escorted trip home. Rysakov smiled. The quid pro quo couldn't be any clearer. He made a mental note to hurry the accounts department along tomorrow. When the Deputy Commissioner rang the following morning, Nic guiltily remembered he had yet to chase up the funding request.

"Sorry, sir. No word yet of the funding."

"Well give 'em a rocket, Nic, I don't want to miss all the cricket. However, that was not the reason for my call," DC O'Ryan said in his clipped British accent. "We've found a body. While the case in no way impinges on your jurisdiction, it might have some relevance to your missing person."

"You mean Alice Martin?"

"Yes. The body is Chester Saunders, the missing accounts manager from First Bahamas Trust. A bonefisherman on Andros, searching for a secluded spot, found it. You recall FBT assumed he had left for a better offer with a client. When they didn't hear from him they crossed him off their staff list, though they thought it appallingly bad manners."

"How did he die?" asked Nic.

"A nine millimetre bullet to the back of the head. Whoever pulled the trigger knew what they were doing. Only one shot, a Winchester. The nine shot magazine was empty."

"I'm impressed."

"Don't be," O'Ryan said followed by a brief chuckle, "we found the bullet. We also have the murder weapon, a Lady Hawk. The killer left it at the scene. Didn't want to risk being caught with it, no doubt. I'm told this is a quality weapon, expensive, slim, dependable, easily concealed and accurate over twenty metres. A gun often favoured by small statured shooters, such as women."

O'Ryan let the pause hang in the air.

"Where was the body found?"

"Off the road to Stafford Creek, south of San Andros airport.

229

It's a lonely stretch through pine forests. The killer and Saunders pulled off onto one of the old logging tracks, out of sight of the main track south. One can only postulate they knew each other, whatever the ostensible reason they had for not being seen together. Lovers? No corroborating evidence so far. Drug dealing? Possible, large quantities of drugs are trans-shipped through the Caribbean to the US coast. Though I must say there's never been the slightest suggestion FBT has any involvement in financing drugs. Perhaps Saunders refused a transaction after agreeing to fund it. We'll never know."

"It sounds like an execution."

"There are wild boars on Andros, dangerous beasts. There were signs several had been attracted by the smell of decomposition. As a result it's not possible to reconstruct Sander's position at the time he died. Some parts of the body had been separated. We know his identity from a distinctive cygnet ring Saunders always wore. We're also getting dental records checked to be certain," O'Ryan explained.

"It sounds like your people have been very thorough, sir." He could tell immediately the compliment pleased the DC. "Thank you for keeping me informed. Every piece of the jigsaw helps."

Could Alice be the killer? If so it casts her in a completely new light. So far there has been no suggestion she had weapon skills, or a capacity for cold blooded murder. *Mind you, we haven't looked*, he thought. *Then there's Uncle Henry. Until he tried to kill me and Ruby we had no inkling of his capability. And, he reminded himself, three hundred million bucks is a lot of motivation. It's possible. What we need is evidence.*

When he chased up the Accounts Department he actually spoke to a voice that had authority. "The funds should be approved tomorrow, DS Rysakov. I'll ring you when I get authorisation," the clerk said.

57

Six fishermen and scuba divers ate a hurried early breakfast with Warren Kay, all determined not to miss the eight a.m. Andros ferry from Potters Cay. Kay spotted Clive Nestor well before they reached the ferry gangplank and turned his head as he boarded, aware of the banker's anxious scanning for the face of his anonymous benefactor. The cabdriver's cousin had done a good job. Kay went below and stowed his gear before finding a seat where he could remain undiscovered until they were well underway. When he booked his ticket, paying in cash at the ferry office, he also left several hundred dollars in an envelope with the young woman behind the counter.

"This is a surprise for an old friend, Clive Nestor. Could you please make sure he gets it once the ferry is underway," he said.

Kay surmised Nestor had very limited access to cash.

John Martin decided to follow Kay, notwithstanding the warnings from Alice and more recently from Rysakov. After waiting outside Kay's hotel and tracking his taxi, Martin saw him board the Andros ferry carrying fishing gear. Once Kay disappeared to find a seat Martin purchased a ticket for the same trip and boarded immediately. He found himself a window seat on the upper level and settled back to enjoy the trip. For the next few hours no one was going anywhere.

Kay waited half an hour after leaving the wharf before heading for the coffee bar. He arrived just as Nestor, carrying a sandwich pack, pastry and coffee balanced on a tray, left the counter and searched for a seat. Kay waited until Nestor was comfortably seated and eating one of the sandwiches.

"This is incredible. I go halfway around the world for a holiday and I see someone I know from Sydney," Kay exclaimed as Nestor was about to take another bite. "Are you going to Andros for the bonefishing, Clive?"

"Warren, what are you doing in the Bahamas?" Nestor said, his expression changing from pleasure to apprehension to bewilderment in rapid succession.

"It's good to see a friendly face. Are you with a group?"

Warren Kay became his most charming, chatting amiably with the sole aim of putting Nestor at ease. By the time they arrived on Andros he needed Nestor to be happy to join him. Together they would search for a suitable location, though not necessarily for bonefishing.

"I'm meeting some friends for the day trip. They said they had a surprise for me on Andros. No idea what it is."

"OK," said Kay. "If you change your mind I'm hiring a vehicle with plenty of room. It'd be much more enjoyable with someone I know, and I've got plenty of gear. I think I got conned at the fishing shop and bought more than I really needed. I guess they figured I could afford it."

He stared to walk away before turning to Nestor.

"I'm not sure how up to date you are, Clive, being on holidays, but I've sold out of your company. Will Callaghan bought my shares and repaid the loan. So I reckoned a holiday to an exotic location was in order. See you later," he said, before buying a coffee and returning to his own seat.

John Martin followed the signs to the restrooms adjacent to the coffee bar. Glancing into the cafeteria, he saw Warren Kay in a friendly conversation with an unshaven, dishevelled looking man. He'd seen that man before, drunk, near his hotel. He only realised he had been staring when the dishevelled man stared back. John turned away just as Kay turned around.

Kay returned to his seat near the stern, picked up a magazine and waited for Nestor to find him. Midway through the trip the ex-banker found the putative fisherman and accepted his offer. He had not recognised another soul on board.

"My friends must have missed the ferry," he said, not looking Kay in the eye.

Martin made sure he was amongst the first onto the jetty while Kay and the drunk he'd been talking to collected their fishing gear. He did not want Kay to see him in case he was wrong about not being recognised. He found a small food store closed for the offseason and slipped inside. Opposite his hiding place, two faded VEHICLE HIRE signs advertised their vehicles side-by-side.

Finally, Kay and his companion walked off the jetty and down the crushed coral street. They stopped outside what looked to be the larger hire firm and, after a brief conversation with the dishevelled man, Kay went inside. The man, carrying a tackle box and rod, walked on toward the general store. Ten minutes later Kay came out, climbed into a well-used 4WD Ford and drove to the store. Once the gear and bait were stowed they drove off and John lost sight of the vehicle. He thought it turned north where he could see a giant plastic crab the size of a two-storey building.

He hired a bonefishing rod and joined the last guided group out. "This is the best fishing experience in the world," the guide said. "Excitement and thrills you'll never forget."

The next day, an hour before the ferry's departure, Martin and his group were downing cold drinks and discussing the early morning catch, when Kay's 4WD Ford drove past. Excusing himself, he hurried to the corner in time to see Kay alight, unload his gear and enter the rental office, alone. Even at the short distance he was certain the vehicle was empty. He began to feel very uneasy. For the first time, he realised that following Warren Kay might not have been such a good idea. On the return voyage he stayed in a remote corner with his face in a book in case, by chance, Kay wandered past.

As the ferry docked back at Potter's Cay, Martin decided to disembark quickly. By shear bad luck, Kay went down the gangplank within seconds behind him. This time John Martin had no illusions.

Kay had recognised him.

With no gear to slow him down, Martin hurried on, grabbing the first cab. Kay, with his gear, was forced to stand in the queue. Kay stared after the Martin kid, Alice's kid. He remembered exactly who he was. Warren Kay rarely forgot a face.

Suddenly, he had a new, and potentially serious, problem. He now recalled seeing the kid on several occasions without it registering in his conscious thought before the ferry trip; across the road from the restaurant, outside his hotel and at the ferry coffee bar. The inescapable conclusion: John Martin was following him.

He would have to assume Martin had seen him with Nestor. Kay needed to think through this development. The boy was now the only person who could make a credible direct link between him and Nestor. Loose ends could not be ignored. Judging by the look he saw on the boy's face as they came down the gangplank, the boy knew Kay had seen him.

He'll be expecting something, Kay thought, *he just won't know what, or when.*

The more John Martin thought about what had happened, the more scared he became. He considered going to the local police. He nearly stopped the cab as it sped past the Royal Bahamas Police Force HQ. But he only had suspicions, no crime, no body. So he rang Nic Rysakov.

Rysakov did not hesitate. "Check out of your hotel immediately, go to the airport and take the first flight to anywhere in the USA and keep moving until you're back in Sydney," he said. "Get away from him. Your life is in danger if you stay. When you're back in Sydney, come and see me."

58

Rysakov eyed the clock on the wall. The Bahamas were sixteen hours behind Sydney. He put the phone down and did his sums. Ten minutes to nine in the morning here made it ten to five the previous evening in Nassau. He picked up the phone and dialled DC O'Ryan. The DC answered immediately.

"Good news, sir, approval for the funding came through overnight," Rysakov said, hoping to put him in a cooperative mood.

"Excellent news, Nic. I'll get my office to make the necessary arrangements tomorrow."

"Unfortunately it's not all good news."

He relayed what John Martin had told him, adding the Australian Police's assessment and suspicions of Warren Kay. When he had finished, O'Ryan remained silent. Finally, he spoke.

"Am I correct in saying that no crime has been committed unless we find the body of Mr Nestor, or establish he has disappeared in suspicious circumstances?"

"That would be the case in Sydney, sir."

"So it is in the Bahamas. Well, we'd better find Mr Nestor soon, and alive. Drunks frequently turn up, sometimes in unlikely places, and after days of absence. I'll organise an immediate search around his usual haunts in Nassau. No luck in twenty-four hours and I'll send two dogs and their handlers to Andros. As soon as we find him alive I'll make the flight bookings and put him in protective custody. Why do I get the feeling my trip might be slipping away?" asked O'Ryan. "I assume you would not require me to accompany a corpse?"

"Unlikely, sir."

Kay sat in his air-conditioned hotel room and reviewed what had happened. He was under no misconception. John Martin, by making allegations about him and Nestor, could cause him real trouble. *At best the evidence is circumstantial. My word against his. It'd never be beyond reasonable doubt, even if they find the body.*

Nevertheless, no purpose could be served by staying in the Bahamas. Allegations by Martin would lead to an investigation. Money and time would be wasted defending the proceedings. He made an appointment to see FBT first thing in the morning. After seeing Nestor's parlous condition, he held little hope of securing any money from the bank. Once he had confirmed there were no funds to be had, he would catch a late morning flight to Miami. He had one final evening in Nassau, and one last loose end to attend to. He changed his clothes and strolled downtown to find a payphone to ring the taxi driver. Martin would, in due course, return to Sydney where he could be dealt with at leisure.

Immediately after he had spoken to Rysakov, John rang reception and arranged an express checkout, agreeing to pay for an extra day.

Within fifteen minutes he had packed, vacated the room, and stood waiting for the elevator. He caught the last American Airlines flight to Fort Lauderdale. Two days later his Qantas plane cruised past the Harbour Bridge on descent to Sydney Airport. Safe.

Forty-eight hours after Rysakov phoned DC O'Ryan, he received a return call. He sensed from the tone of voice the news was uniformly bad, and he wasn't wrong.

"Unfortunately, we were too late. Your instincts were correct. When no trace of Mr Nestor could be found in the first eight hours, I ordered the dogs to Andros. Better to err on the side of caution. They were ready to give up searching when, halfway through the second day, they found the body. High probability it's Nestor," O'Ryan said. "No papers on it, but the clothing matched what he was reported to be wearing. We've sent samples to Florida for DNA analysis. I asked them to email you a copy of the results."

"Thank you. Any idea how he died?"

"Preliminary findings only, but our local doctor is firmly of the view the deceased had his throat cut, with a very sharp knife wielded by someone who knew what they were doing. The body has also been interfered with by local wild boar, but the examining pathologists will make appropriate allowances."

"Anyone see anything?"

"No. So far we've found no person who remembers seeing a man answering Nestor's description. Several of the ferry passengers recall a dishevelled man on the vessel. No one had any interest in him. They were all talking about the fishing or diving. One couple said they thought a man spoke briefly to a dishevelled chap at the coffee shop. So far as they could recall it could have been a polite conversation about the weather. None could remember him on the island. Our team spoke to each of the vehicle rental businesses. None had a rental to Warren Kay, so we're endeavouring to trace each of the rental names for up to two days before the date of the murder.

"Your Mr Martin appears to be the only witness linking Nestor with Kay. Without forensic evidence we don't have a case against Mr Kay," said the DC. "In any event, he's left the Bahamas for the US, so he's no longer under my jurisdiction."

"If you find the evidence I'd be more than pleased to bring Warren Kay to Nassau. By the way, sir, if you are able to get to Sydney in time for any of the cricket matches, my house is within walking distance of the Sydney Cricket Ground. And I've a spare room you'd be welcome to use."

"Thank you Nic, I'll let you know," said O'Ryan. "Incidentally, the discovery of Saunders' body gave me more leverage on FBT. While it hasn't yet yielded much useful information, you might be interested to know that Mr Nestor had no proper authority to operate any account at FBT. As you know, he insisted he did. He'd sent instructions, but the person who set the account up never approved his signature. Nestor was never authorised to operate on the account in any way. He just didn't know it. Mr Nestor came to Nassau under the misapprehension that he had opened the account. Whoever the real controller is, he or she got in first. I can only assume Saunders was paid a substantial fee by this person to perpetuate the charade with Nestor. It is unquestionably corrupt behaviour, but sadly greed is the undoing of many a man. Each time Nestor sent instructions, Saunders orders were to relay them to the controller, who had the only real authority to operate it. Saunders then appears to have received instructions to reply to Nestor, acknowledging receipt of his communication, no more. Their files have all this recorded. To Nestor, it appeared to be his account, but he was nothing more than a dupe. FBT did not exactly cover itself with glory. Saunders may well have been sacked had they known. However, we saw the size of the fees that were paid. They would tempt the angel Gabriel."

"Any idea who owns the account?"

"A company based in Cyprus, I'll send you the name. The authorised operators, nominally Dimitri Namenkov and Agnes Gould, are identified by number and code with an access password. Any bet the names are fictitious?" said O'Ryan. "Talking to a chap at the yacht club, a retired banker, he says the account has more than likely served its purpose by now and probably won't be used again. The money is all gone, in other words."

This whole transaction or deal, Rysakov didn't know how best to describe it, had the hallmarks of professional planning and execution. The people behind it obviously had access to the best legal and financial advice, maybe even at governmental level. That reminded him, after Schmidt's death they had gone through his papers. One notebook in particular looked interesting, all handwritten in a form of German, according to one of the squad who spoke and read the language. He said it didn't make any sense. It appeared to be in code. He had offered, in his words, to have a go at making some sense out of it.

Rysakov did not consider it very likely any information of value to his case would be obtained from the notebook. First, he called Tom O'Leary and filled him in on the almost certain demise of Clive Nestor. Then he rang the German speaking officer.

In Nassau the following morning, Deputy Commissioner O'Ryan skimmed through a routine report on the murder of a taxi driver several days ago. The cab had been found at a quiet beach on the island. The driver's throat had been cut and his meagre takings stolen. When the man's cousin came to the morgue to formally identify the body he had been genuinely upset.

The DC initialled the file and put it in his out tray. Homicides at a holiday destination needed to be resolved quickly and quietly. He scribbled a note to this effect on the file front. He scooped up his cap and hurried out the door; the crews for the weekend yacht race had to attend a briefing today.

Homicide in Sydney tied the correct name tag on the corpse thought originally to be Clive Nestor. They referred enquiries concerning the repatriation of Clive's body from the Bahamas to DS Rysakov. The identical twins were subsequently buried together. Rysakov declined the invitation to attend the funeral in mid-March, three weeks later.

59

Warren Kay, once away from Caribbean jurisdiction, had a leisurely time arriving back in Sydney. Well satisfied with his trip to the Bahamas, he arrived to find a message from Joe Garand. Rather than ring he went around to the lawyer's office.

"That bastard won't hit my sister again. Apparently he had a fatal accident in prison," said the lawyer, smiling as he closed his office door. "Thanks for speaking to the right people."

"I have no idea what you are talking about, Joe. But you sound as if you're happy, you must be making money."

One look at Kay and Garand understood. Don't pursue the matter. "How was your trip?" he asked.

"Satisfactory, chasing bonefish was far more exciting than I expected. You should consider the Bahamas for your next vacation."

Garand could now tell anyone who enquired where his client had been, and what he had done. Kay told him some of the characteristics of bonefishing, as extra background.

Once he left the lawyer's office Kay directed all his attention to more pressing matters. His meeting with FBT on the day he left Nassau had yielded no return. They barely gave him the time of day. Just said it was someone else's account, and therefore confidential. Having successfully dealt with Nestor he decided not to push his luck. He had made more money on REI and his Nestor Nankervis sale than he had ever made before, and he intended to enjoy it. Besides, the John Martin issue still required his attention.

60

"I've finally finished translating the Schmidt notebook. Sorry it took so long," the German speaking officer said when he called Rysakov. "Not sure it'll be much use. It reads more like the outline for a novel."

When he saw the translation, Rysakov realised the translator was correct. Schmidt must have seen himself as a budding writer. On the other hand, perhaps they now had an explanation for Alice Martin's disappearance.

Following Schmidt's death a search of the man's house and belongings had been conducted. In addition to the handwritten journal several other curious items had come to light. Schmidt's actions, in particular his threat to kill Rysakov and Ruby, were in part explained by completion of the autopsy. It revealed he had at best a year to live. Prostate cancer had metastasised throughout his system. As a consequence, he was walking dead. Whatever punishment he might receive for the murder of Sally McIntosh would have had little impact on his life.

The search uncovered several substantial bank accounts. These, as well as the money, house and any other assets in Schmidt's name, would go to the State Treasury as unclaimed money unless a legitimate heir could be found. *An appropriate outcome*, Rysakov thought. Two other items caused more speculation than answers. A constable assisting in the search noticed a number of books, such as *War & Peace*, *Pride & Prejudice*, *King Solomon's Mines*, had pencil notations in the margin. No one could make any sense out of them until the same PC suggested they might represent a onetime code.

"They use them in the book I'm reading. Spies like them because they can't be broken, so long as the recipient has the same edition for decoding," she said.

The German speaking officer gave Rysakov the translation of

the notebook in a loose leaf folio for ease of examination. That night, as he finished each page, he handed them to Ruby. The more he read, the more he understood the translator's conclusion: it read like notes for a novel, a spy thriller. The notebook summarised, in chronological sequence, a series of espionage forays, theft of industrial secrets as well as other events. Scattered throughout were names, mostly foreign. The majority had a single line neatly drawn horizontally across them, followed by a date and two or three letters.

"Ruby, do you think these names could be a list of targets that Schmidt crossed off when they had been eliminated?"

"Are you serious?"

"It fits, and it could explain Alice's disappearance," Rysakov said. "The letters after the names are the initials of the killer. AN – Alicia Nemec. HWS – Heinrich Wolfgang Schmidt. I've no idea who the others are, maybe contract killers."

"You've been watching too many spy movies."

"Nevertheless, if Alice had small arms training as well as specialised training, Schmidt could have been her handler as well as another killer. At least there is no doubt about him."

"True, I agree about Schmidt. But the rest..."

"Some of the dates probably go back to before Alice married Jack Martin. Even the paper's yellowed with age. I wonder if we can take one of the dates and match it with an unexplained death."

"What about Sally McIntosh? She isn't mentioned by name, but the last entry looks about the right date."

She made the statement without any emotion, jotting the dates in her police notebook. Before Rysakov could respond, she went on. "Let's accept, for the moment, that you're right. What was their motivation?"

"Money? Schmidt didn't have the lifestyle I would expect for an international hit man. He could have saved the funds we found from his salary, no dependents, apparently no real vices."

"So not money. Hardly think it was love, certainly not between those two. And I can't imagine anyone successfully blackmailing Schmidt for twenty years because he had kinky taste."

"I agree," said Nic. "No evidence they were into drugs or gambling. The autopsy found no trace of anything other than the prescription drugs he took for his condition. That leaves acting for a foreign government. Maybe that's what all the marks in the classics were about. It could also be where the funds to buy Schmidt's house came from. If a government ever claims it they'll have some explaining to do."

Rysakov poured the last of the wine into two glasses.

"Because of the time this has been going on, my money is on a foreign government. If I had to name one I'd put my money on East Germany, and, when the Berlin Wall came down, Russia took it over. I'm going to live dangerously and send this up the line tomorrow with the qualification it might be the outline for a novel. Let someone else decide."

"Let me check the local dates against unsolved murders in Australia."

Rysakov nodded agreement. "If we're right, it's almost certainly how Alice disappeared. Either she had help to leave the country, or her usefulness had expired." He paused for a moment. "Maybe there's another, even more feasible reason for Alice's disappearance. What if she orchestrated the whole technology theft/insider trading scam? What if she set it all up? Somehow she induced Sally McIntosh to steal information. Then, when Clive Nestor decided to use the Bahamas she found out about it and stole his idea. What if she's the controller of the FBT account in the Bahamas? Maybe, even Schmidt thought it was one of his usual deals," he went on, warming to the task. "Her husband was having an affair with a student. John was about to leave school, and don't forget, he was not her biological son. She saw an opportunity to get enough money to get away from Schmidt, the Russians and her previous life. If it worked she would be rich enough to disappear, to be completely independent. She saw her chance and grabbed it."

He took a sip of wine while Ruby absorbed what he had said. Bits had been rattling around in his head for a while. Talking to Ruby helped the pieces fall into place.

"Will Callaghan's banking contacts said around three hundred million dollars passed through the account at FBT. That's one powerful motivation."

"Have we still only got one photograph of her?" Ruby asked.

"Yep, apart from the camped up passport photo. I imagine there may be others somewhere, but from what her husband told us, and John confirmed, she made a point of avoiding being photographed," said Rysakov.

"So, a change of hairstyle, maybe a bit of cosmetic surgery on the face, which she can now afford, different clothes, makeup, move overseas, change her name, and she's gone for good."

"That's how I see it," he said. "And all we have is that old, not very clear, photo. A face fixed in time."

Ruby shook her head. "I can't help feeling we're missing something. I wonder if it's really that simple. I mean, she was married for about twenty years. OK, her husband dumps her for a young spunk. That happens. I agree it could be reasonable grounds to shoot through. But that's only part of it. How does the son, John, fit in?"

"What do you mean?"

"Well, why did they adopt him?" Ruby queried.

"Probably because they couldn't have their own."

"If that was the case, Alice must surely have felt a pretty strong maternal urge. If she did it'd be unlikely she'd just walk out without a word. She'd probably take John with her, or at least arrange for him to join her later. But, he has no idea where she is or why she's gone. Unless, of course she's dead."

Rysakov gave her a quizzical look. "So? Assuming she's not deceased."

"I think you need more information on John's adoption. Maybe also talk to some of Alice's friends about her relationship with John."

Rysakov nodded his head slowly, taking the point on board. In the silence that followed they could hear the chirruping of crickets and rhythmic croaking of frogs in the heat.

"However, don't forget it's a rare criminal who doesn't make a mistake. They think they're safe and they become arrogant, or can't resist visiting a friend or relative. At some time they all do it. If we're vigilant we'll find her."

61

Icon Investment Management Ltd had been set up as the public face of Will Callaghan's empire. The head office in London did not look like the HQ of a billion dollar investment group. The four-storey Victorian town house had been built as the city residence of a wealthy landed lord, with rooms for family, staff and guests. In addition to accommodating ten highly skilled professionals, Callaghan had constructed a spacious two-bedroom apartment on the top floor. The building faced onto a private fenced garden, access to which was restricted to the houses facing it.

Since he arrived back in London, Callaghan had had dinner with Sarah several times, what he thought of as "Getting to know you dates." No work had been discussed at all. For both of them, the relationship had changed. Callaghan felt his heartbeat quicken, recalling their goodnight kiss after the second date. Tonight he had invited her to his apartment. "I'll cook dinner," he promised. From that night their relationship changed.

In the meantime, they had a business to run.

Although the letter was addressed to Callaghan and marked PERSONAL, Sarah Longhurst opened it and read the single sheet. She read it again then put it on his desk.

"Just the usual things in the mail, with the exception of that single sheet," she said pointing to the letter. "Any idea what it's about?"

Callaghan picked it up, a single sheet, with four lines typed double spaced:

> *Ask Ann Stratton about Kay and 'breathless sex'.*
> *Honey knew more than she should.*
> *Clive was unnecessary.*
> *Daily g-ems not spam.*

Four lines, nothing else. He turned the paper over, nothing. He knew what, or who, it was about. Except for the last line, which looked like nonsense. The real puzzle of the letter, why send it to him? "Can I see the envelope?"

Sarah gave it to him. Callaghan smiled: she had anticipated he would want to see it.

"Posted in London, plain cheap paper. No clues there. Why send it to me?"

"No idea," Sarah said. "We have back-to-back meetings this morning, first one in two minutes."

"OK," he said, taking a final look at the sheet of paper.

Two days later, DS Rysakov had the original sheet of paper in his hand, sent by courier from London. It didn't add anything to the scanned version Callaghan had emailed him. "Cryptic and curious," Callaghan described it in their phone conversation. "Why do think it was sent to me?"

"Probably to give you the option of trashing it and taking no action, or contacting me," answered Rysakov.

"Then I suppose the next question is: who sent it? Does this help solve your original mystery?"

"You mean Alice? Does this show she's alive? Maybe, but the letter could have been sent by someone who doesn't like Ann Stratton, for instance. It could mean the sender waited until an opportunity arose to post it in London. The last line looks to be included for no other reason than a bit of mischief."

"What will you do?" It was a trite question, but he could not resist asking.

"I'll speak to Ann Stratton, see where it leads," said Rysakov.

"Pity it's so cryptic."

"Perhaps the sender thought more specific information ran the risk of identifying them. If the reference to Clive Nestor relates to his murder, it means the sender is watching very closely, because there hasn't been any media coverage of the real Clive's death. It also suggests the sender has a more detailed knowledge of key people and events than the police. It could be an argument in support of Alice being alive," said Rysakov.

When he arrived home that day, late as usual, Ruby came to greet him still dressed in uniform. He gave her a kiss. Halfway through pouring a glass of red wine from the bottle they had opened the previous night, Rysakov stopped and put the bottle down. What had he missed? Then he smiled. She had new shoulder flashes.

"Congratulations, Senior, about time," he said, giving her a hug. "Senior Constable Walsh. Not exactly what you wanted, but almost and on the way."

The promotion had come through earlier than either expected. As he had suspected, she stayed in uniform instead of joining the ranks of the detectives. She had her heart set on making Detective and why she had been granted the extra stripe without it suggested some sort of internal compromise, an opinion Rysakov kept to himself. The equanimity with which she accepted staying in uniform surprised him.

Since the one-page note mentioned Honey French, a murder victim, Rysakov called Tom O'Leary the following day, emailing him a copy of the note. Homicide had to be involved. "Congratulations, Detective Senior, I saw your name on the list."

"The extra pay'll come in handy with the kids starting school," said O'Leary. "Interesting note you sent over. Not some kind of prank?"

"I doubt it's a prank. What it means, there's only one way to find out. I'm going to call on Ann Stratton. Like to come along?"

"Can't see any problem, there's an unsolved homicide."

Early afternoon Rysakov pressed the security buzzer to Ann Stratton's apartment. "Thank you for seeing us on short notice, Ms Stratton," said Rysakov as they followed her into the air-conditioned living room.

"Call me Ann. Miss sounds like a spinster librarian and I hope

I'm a long way from that," she said, sitting back on a two-seater lounge draping one arm along the top.

She was dressed in high heeled sandals, tight white three-quarter length slacks and a burnt-orange blouse unbuttoned to her cleavage. The draped arm pulled the blouse tight over her breasts, showing no bra outline, just two nipples hard in the cool air. The policemen exchanged a quick glance.

"Have you found Alice yet?" she asked.

"Not yet," Nic answered. "We're continuing our enquiries. Today we'd like to ask you a few questions about Honey French. However, before we start that, could I ask you about Alice Martin's relationship with her son?"

"What do you mean?"

"Were they close? Do you know if Professor Martin and Alice had difficulties starting a family? I assume they must have really wanted a child to have adopted," said Rysakov. "Then they only had the one."

"In some ways Alice was a strange person. She and Jack went overseas for a couple of years, way back. He conned his way into some research fellowship and she did some computer courses. She was always a bit vague about it. Anyway, no one cared what she studied. We were more interested in what her social life was like in an ex-Commo country. None of us even knew she was trying to have a kid. Then she arrived back with this baby boy of about two or three. Bit of a shock actually. I never imagined Alice as the maternal type," said Ann.

"Where did they live overseas?"

"In Prague. She said they also spent some time in Berlin, in bloody East Berlin, but the Wall was down by then. I didn't get the impression either of them were particularly impressed. They also travelled to Moscow a number of times, supposedly to visit a medieval historical repository. I remember this because it was just before my ill-fated marriage and I stayed with them for a week in Prague. It was only on looking back that it struck me as a bit odd.'

"What do you mean?"

"They were living in a sort of hotel or serviced apartment, and I got the impression they hadn't been there long. They didn't know where the restaurants were, or the food stores, or any of the tourist sites," said Ann. "If you were to tell me they only visited to look normal and meet with me, I'd believe it. Anyway I had a ball."

"Were you surprised Alice disappeared without any contact with John?"

Ann Stratton thought for a moment. "It may sound uncharitable but I always had the impression Alice was doing her duty with John. She was never cruel or neglectful, not at all. She just didn't seem to have the spontaneous affection mothers usually have for their kids. From what I could see, John went his own way from an early age. Jack showed more interest in him, probably being a boy. Rugby, cricket and all that."

Rysakov found the information intriguing but probably not of much help in the matter at hand. "Back to Honey French," he said. "While it may help in the search for Alice, her death remains unsolved. Tom O'Leary's now with the Homicide Squad and is running the investigation."

"When we last spoke about Honey..." O'Leary began.

"Angela was her real name," said Ann.

"My apologies, Angela, you said she knew Alice and a man called Warren, who we assume was Warren Kay."

"That's right," said Ann.

"Did you ever meet Warren Kay?"

"Not that I recall."

"You also said that Alice and Angela attended special parties. What was the nature of these parties? Were they sex parties?"

After a few seconds Ann Stratton seemed to come to a decision. She leaned back a bit further into the settee and uncrossed her legs. Somehow this seemed to pull the blouse tighter.

"There were generally no more than six people, a maximum of eight. I only went to a few. Several were plain boring, but some of the others were incredible, with experiences I'd never imagined possible. As long as both parties consented freely and there was no danger, anything was available. The only other rule, no drugs. I never saw Angela with drugs at any of the parties. She had told me she used them, so if she was on them those nights she would have taken them before arriving. Some of the parties were fun, shame they aren't on any more."

"Why is that?" asked O'Leary.

"The venue was sold, people move, change, or in Angela's case, die."

"As you say, provided both individuals ..."

"Sometimes three or more might agree," said Ann, looking to see if they were shocked.

Rysakov wasn't, and neither was O'Leary. Who did she think she was talking to, school children? "What is breathless sex?" he asked.

She barely hesitated before answering. "It's having an orgasm just before you are about to pass out from lack of oxygen. The proper medical term is anoxic orgasm. It's the most intense orgasm you can imagine. The best way is to have a plastic bag over your head while you have sex, either with someone else or by yourself. As you get closer to a climax you suck all the air out of the bag."

"Sounds dangerous. Anyone ever forget to take the bag off?" asked Tom.

"Of course not," Ann said. "We only ever used special bags fitted with a pull out valve you could rip out to let air in."

When they were back in the car O'Leary burst out laughing. "I reckon if we'd shown any interest we could have had a threesome going," he said. "Benefits they don't tell you about at the Academy."

Rysakov grinned. "How does this sound?" he said as they drove back across the Harbour Bridge. "Kay hires Angela for a bit of bondage, cuffs her, then, while he's on the job whacks the bag over her head. She can't rip it off, he gets excited watching her. He leaves it too late and she's dead. If we could find the bag it might still have her DNA on it."

"He's already admitted to hiring her at about the right time. I'll get a search warrant organised," said O'Leary. "All we'd need then would be forensics linking him to dumping the body. Soil on shoes or something similar. I'll include that on the warrant."

Will Callaghan did not mention to Rysakov, or in fact to anyone except Sarah, that he had decoded the last cryptic line in the anonymous note. "Daily g-ems not spams". It took a combined effort over several days but once cracked the solution was obvious. Icon had set up gmail accounts with Google years ago. Since those early days far more sophisticated email systems had been introduced and were now used exclusively. The gmail system had been forgotten and never used. They were, however, still sitting buried in their web site. When they looked, the same email sent from another gmail address arrived daily, beginning two weeks before the letter arrived.

So Callaghan replied. The next day the In Tray had a new unread message: *Have you discovered who he is?*

Callaghan responded: *Second cousin, related to me.* No names or additional information.

The next day – *Thank you.*

Thereafter the emails ceased.

62

It had been weeks since his return from the Caribbean but Warren Kay couldn't get rid of the feeling. The confidence he brought back with him had been steadily eroding. The unplanned and unexpected unsettled him, it always had. Now a sense of foreboding overshadowed everything he did. Had he overlooked a critical detail? Events first started getting out of his control when John Martin saw him and exited Nassau too fast. Someone had advised him. Maybe that was it. Martin told Rysakov what he saw. The cop was smart.

And that bastard Callaghan, he thought. Then it struck him. What if Callaghan had linked up with Rysakov? What if the detective, with all the resources he can muster, is behind the Martin kid? Callaghan and Rysakov together would be very dangerous. And the prospect of incarceration terrified him.

Kay spent the day carefully analysing his situation. He could not think of anything he had overlooked. He actually wrote down all the events that could be classified as crimes. In nearly all cases it was only Kay and the victim. At the end of the day he burned the papers. He even flushed the ash down the toilet. Normally such a systematic process gave him comfort, reassuring him he was OK. It didn't work this time. The feeling of vulnerability persisted and he couldn't shake it.

Finally, he reached a decision. He would leave Australia, at least until the heat died down, but maybe for longer. He still had the cash from the Nestor Nankervis & Co. transaction. It sat on deposit earning interest. He had his accountant calculate the tax payable on the transaction and set it aside in a separate account. The balance of the funds he transferred to London. Where it went from there no one would know. His properties were all owned by blind trusts located in Gibraltar, untraceable back to him, a structure he'd put in place many years ago. He would give Joe Garand instructions to manage the properties. He had total confidence the lawyer would do as instructed.

By the end of the week he would be ready to leave Australia for Spain. Maybe Cote d'Azure. Apart from the lifestyle, Spain had a major attraction: no extradition treaty with Australia. Once he made the decision he felt some of the tension ease.

"I've decided to go on extended overseas travel, Joe, and I want you to look after my properties while I'm away," he said when he met with Garand the next day.

"Bit sudden isn't it?" said the lawyer. "You've only just got back."

"By the end of the week I'll send you my instructions and where I can be contacted. Email would be best. As I'll be away for an indefinite period, you'll have full power to take any action you think appropriate in managing the properties," said Kay.

Kay could see Garand trying to evaluate what was going on.

"By the way, you might find this interesting." Kay handed Garand a flash drive. "It has audio and video. Quality is not great but it's good enough. I'll call you when I arrive."

Kay closed the office door on his way out. He knew what the lawyer would do the instant he was out of sight. It had cost him ten grand to have the digital recording made using directional microphones and a high resolution zoom lens. Money well spent. He smiled as he exited the building. Now he owned the lawyer.

Back at his penthouse he packed what he would need for winter in Spain. The laptop and iPhone went in a carry-on bag. For the next hour he systematically went through the apartment one last time, double-checking he was leaving no records of any kind, no pads or paper, no external computer drives, no bank details, and no travel information. Satisfied, he locked the door and checked in to a suburban serviced apartment till the end of the week.

Garand immediately plugged the USB flash drive into his computer. It showed him contracting the murder of his brother-in-law with the person Kay had phoned. Although it was grainy and the sound scratchy, as a lawyer experienced in criminal trials Garand could see no problem in a competent prosecutor securing a guilty verdict. The second clip showed him paying the balance of the price after the murder. Both clips had a date and time code. It helped drive another nail into a guilty coffin.

Detective Senior Constable O'Leary did not get the search warrant issued until Thursday morning. When they found the penthouse locked and empty Rysakov had a copy of the warrant sent to Garand while a police locksmith negotiated the complex deadlocks and opened the door. Four of them entered at once.

"Good, no alarm," said the locksmith and left them to it.

"No alarm, but it's safer to assume we're under surveillance of some form," Rysakov told the team, even though he couldn't see any obvious cameras. A bastard like Kay might have a pathological absence of normal human emotions, but there was one emotion all psychopaths shared: paranoia.

Kay did not have a spare minute in the days leading up to his departure, particularly since he had to be prepared for the prospect it could be permanent. He had only thirty-six hours left before his scheduled flight. Alerted by an alarm on his computer, triggered when the police locksmith opened the front door, Kay watched the police enter his penthouse. Very small cameras with fisheye lenses recorded every movement inside the penthouse, backing up to a hard disc offsite. What had initially sold Kay on the system was the facility to log in to the cameras in real time, from anywhere in the world with internet access. Black and white, live footage streamed onto his laptop as the police worked steadily from room to room, pulling his penthouse apart. One of them turned, as if responding to a noise.

"I know that face," Kay said to himself. *Rysakov!* He knew the police would come eventually, but not this soon. "They wouldn't be there without a warrant. So what are they searching for? That fucking kid must have talked to them and got them all excited. Christ, I should have dealt with him in the Bahamas."

"Sir," one of the PC's called to Rysakov. "Looks like he's gone away."

The PC pointed to empty hanging space and drawers. Rysakov nodded. If Kay was headed overseas they could not stop him without sufficient evidence for a warrant.

They were thorough. They searched the remotest corner of every cupboard and drawer, they checked for possible hidden compartments, looked behind furniture, took books out of bookcases, and tried to imagine where they might hide something private.

"Nic, in the bedroom."

Tom had a square leather case with a handle in the centre sitting on the king-sized bed. He finished taking photographs as Rysakov entered.

"Found this behind those two drawers. They seemed too short for the depth of the chest, so I reached in and there it was."

They both checked their latex gloves. While Rysakov dictated and filmed the discovery into his iPhone, O'Leary opened it. First, he pulled out several pairs of fur lined handcuffs and a leather riding crop. Next, three vibrators together with two implements the use of which he could only guess at. Finally, at the rear of the case, lay a head mould made of clear soft plastic. It had a pull tie at the neck and an oblong panel about where the mouth would be, fixed in place with an airtight tongue and groove seal. The panel had a handle on the outside to enable the wearer to open the aperture to breathe.

"Bingo," said Rysakov. "Let's hope forensics can recover some DNA."

As Kay watched, Rysakov went into the bedroom and stood beside another cop looking at a box on the bed. The other cop leaned forward to open the box.

"Shit, I'd forgotten about that, I should've trashed it. OK, get your rocks off boys," he said as they pulled out the contents. As they placed the plastic head cover in a bag, Kay sneered, "Taking it for later, boys? You pricks."

He watched the search for a further ten minutes and disconnected. He fumed all afternoon as he completed the rest of his preparations. By five o'clock he decided he would deal with the Martin kid, for good, that night. He knew where Martin lived. The boy would be alone, and he could hide the body so it wouldn't be discovered for a few days, by which time he would be in Spain. Normally he spent days planning and making sure of the details. Fortunately, this loose end was not complicated. And, he had no choice.

A pistol would be best, but purchasing an untraceable handgun was not a matter to rush. Lack of time made it too risky. Instead, he bought a German stainless steel filleting knife, very common and very similar to the knife he had used on Clive Nestor.

63

When John Martin returned from the Bahamas he headed straight to the family home in Northbridge, north of Sydney. Under the terms of his father's will the house went to him, with Alice having the right to lifetime occupancy. Once probate had been granted, his lawyer told him, the house would be transferred into his name. With Alice not there, he had it to himself.

The first night, right off the plane, he slept soundly, exhausted by the trip. The next day John called Callaghan and Rysakov and arranged to meet with each separately. He ate breakfast at a local café, stopping at the supermarket to replenish his larder. When he returned home the empty house reminded him once again, he was on his own. Neither Jack nor Alice would ever return. That thought stayed in his mind as he walked into their bedroom. For a long moment he stood unsure. Then in a single swift action he opened one door of the built-in cupboard. Men's suits, shirts and slacks. He then opened what he knew to be Alice's cupboard. Dresses, blouses and slacks hung motionless, untouched for months. With a deep breath, and every muscle tense, a single violent motion swept the dresses along the hanger rail. Through the gap created all he saw were the wooden back panels.

He sat on the bed to regain his composure, his heart still pounding in his chest. He had come to terms with his father's death. The funeral had confirmed it: Jack was dead. Alice, on the other hand, was missing. She could be dead, or she could be alive. She could even be watching him. She could manifest herself at any time, and anywhere. He had half expected her to be around their home, but he knew she wasn't.

That night he slept fitfully, reacting to every sound and creak. At two in the morning he resolved to ring the Salvation Army first thing and get them to come and take all the clothing and the furniture he did not want. Having made that decision, he realised he did not want to live in the house. He needed to rule off the past and look forward to the rest of his life.

I'll sell the house, he thought, *then there's nothing to hold me here.*

Will Callaghan noted a change in his cousin when they met later that day, a maturity not there when he left Australia for Prague.

"I'm not sure how accurate it is, but I calculate we are second cousins, twice removed. Whatever the correct description, we're blood relatives," said Callaghan after John had brought him up to date, "descended from Katya Morozov."

John still liked the reassurance he was part of such lineage.

"I have a proposal to put to you," said Callaghan. "If you like the idea we can put it in motion immediately. If it doesn't appeal, or is not what you want to do, then say so. There is absolutely no pressure to do it."

John sat with his coffee getting cold, waiting.

"Assuming you are interested in the investment management industry, which is basically what I do, this is what I propose. If you would prefer some other industry or occupation tell me when you're ready and I'll see if I can help," said Will, pausing.

"I'm interested," replied John.

"Good. I've arranged for you to join a firm of accountants in London to get your accounting qualifications, then to work for one of the main investment banks for experience and to get your own contacts in the city. After a couple of years I'll have a position waiting for you at Icon."

John started to speak and Will held his hand up.

"In addition, I own a house in Islington which will be yours, rent free, for as long as you're in London. Don't give me your answer now. Come around for a steak tonight. We can talk more."

At three in the morning following the search of his penthouse, Warren Kay edged towards the darkened Martin house. The moon was on the wane and cast little light on the ground. Kay, dressed in casual black with a black silk ski mask in his pocket, merged with the background shadows. He inched along the side of the house, his black sneakers making no noise. When he reached the rear stairs to the deck he checked the knife strapped to his leg. Once on the deck he crouched, motionless, for ten minutes looking for any movement to indicate the presence of security. He saw none. No tiny pulsing red LED, a give-away of a motion detector. After confirming the doors were locked he used a thin flexible length of metal to prise open a window. No alarm sounded as he slipped inside.

Sliding his hand under his trouser leg he pulled the tape off the hilt, freeing the knife. He located the front door and used it to identify what had to be bedrooms on either side of the main living area. The first room had a double bed, empty. He took two steps in and saw an open cupboard door with a row of dresses. Alice and the professor's room. He backed out.

The room next door had a small wardrobe and a double bed only. The guest room. He crossed to the other side of the house. Only one bedroom remained. The door creaked slightly as he pushed it. He saw posters on the wall. John's room. He pushed the door enough for him to step inside.

A large single bed, unmade. Immediately he was on full alert. Where had the boy gone? The door to the en-suite lay wide open. Empty. Had he made a noise and woken Martin? Unless he was in the wardrobe or under the bed he wasn't in this room. He had a sudden sinking feeling and strode to the bed. He bent over and placed his hand on the body indentation, cold. He'd missed John Martin, again. Furious, he brought the knife down where Martin had lain, stabbing the mattress. As he brought the knife up a thought occurred to him: *Leave a message*. Silently, he sliced a cross in the mattress, pulling the sheets off so the cuts were clearly visible. Then he exited the way he entered, leaving the window open. Another message: "I can get you whenever I choose."

He hurried back to his car several blocks away and drove off. Halfway into the city he found a quiet street and changed out of the black clothes, bundling them into a bag. He drove around until he found an industrial waste bin and threw the bag into it. Martin would have to wait.

After drinking too much wine with Will Callaghan that night, John Martin staggered into the spare room at Callaghan's insistence and slept the moment his head hit the pillow. In the morning, John confirmed his decision of the previous night. He would take up Callaghan's offer and move to London.

"It's a matter of family, after all," he said.

64

Late that Friday morning, John made his way home. The real estate agent had arranged to arrive early afternoon to assess the work that had been done and discuss a sales campaign. John hoped he would feel confident enough to leave the sale in the hands of the agent. This would enable him to immediately move to London. He made himself a ham and lettuce on rye sandwich, washed down with a cup of coffee. Replenished, he went to his room. It didn't take long to decide to leave it all. In London he would start afresh. Some of it could go to charity, the rest he would store for the time being. He flopped on his bed, and lay back for a last look at his posters.

A sharp pain shot though his right shoulder blade. John sat bolt upright and saw with horror what caused the pain. The hilt of a long narrow bladed knife had been jammed into the mattress so the point of the blade would pierce whoever lay down. If he had flopped back instead of gently laying he would now have a knife sticking out of his back. At that point he noticed the slashes opening the guts of the mattress.

In panic he spun around, expecting a murderer with a knife about to stab him in the back. Expecting Warren Kay. The instant that thought entered his head he bolted out the front door, not stopping until he reached the road. No one followed him. His hand trembled as he fumbled in his pocket for his phone.

"Rysakov."

"It's John Martin. Someone's just tried to kill me."

Half an hour later, Nic Rysakov, Tom O'Leary and a car from the local station pulled up outside the Martin house. Together, Martin and the four policemen rapidly established the house was empty.

"We'll ask the neighbours but I'd put money on this being

done last night. Obviously, whoever it was got in through the rear window," said Rysakov. "Very fortunate you were not here."

Privately, Rysakov knew it was almost certainly Kay, but he did not voice his view to the other officers. Instead, he said, "We'll get a forensic team out and see what they turn up." Then quietly to O'Leary, "They won't find anything, he's too careful, but we'll go through the motions just in case."

It came as no surprise to Rysakov when examination of the entry window, door handles, the knife, and every other likely area yielded no new or foreign finger prints. They did find several black synthetic fibres and some dirt from the would-be killer's shoes, however. When he eventually received the lab report it said the fibres were ubiquitous, they were made in China and could be found in clothing sold in all the cheaper centres, Kmart, Big W and Target. The dirt matched soil from the garden next door. No hard evidence.
Rysakov knew it had to be Kay, he just couldn't prove it.

At the time Kay figured the police would be examining the Martin house for clues, he cleared Immigration and strolled passed the duty free shops to the Business Class Lounge. An hour later, his Qantas aircraft was in the air en route for Europe.

Much to the chagrin of Deputy Commissioner O'Ryan in Nassau, rumours of a new unnamed drug syndicate making a play to control the trade between the islands and the USA appeared to be much more than rumour. Four shootings in the last week had the entire Royal Bahamas Police Force working overtime. The US DEA assisted as far as possible with intelligence, and the occasional deniable action. So when the discovery of another body came across his desk, he added it to the 'drug war' files after a cursory glance.

The badly decomposed body was discovered by a local man walking his dog. The dog dug up an arm and carried part of it to show his master. It surprised the over-worked local forensic team that a grave so shallow had not been uncovered sooner. After an initial, but superficial, examination the police pathologist wrote in his report: *Female, aged thirty to forty-five years. Cause of death: bullet in back of head, possibly 9 mm. Typical execution style. Time of death: three to five months ago.*

With a sudden spike in the number of crimes being reported, DC O'Ryan's holiday in Australia to watch the cricket now joined many other planned vacations, binned and long forgotten. No DNA samples were taken from the Jane Doe to send for analysis. He also didn't think it necessary to inform Rysakov in Sydney. Nestor's body had already been repatriated weeks ago.

65

Rysakov picked up the receiver on the third ring.

"Joe Garand, I act for Warren Kay, DS Rysakov," the lawyer said. "I am instructed that you and a team of police broke into Mr Kay's home yesterday and removed certain items."

"...and?" said Rysakov, knowing what was coming.

"Mr Kay wants to know on what grounds."

"We have a search warrant, a copy of which was sent to your office. We have reason to believe Mr Kay may have been a party to actions leading to the death of Angela Stratton, also known as Honey French. We have the right to remove for testing any items that may assist us in our enquiries. We had no difficulty in persuading the judge to issue the papers."

Ryasakov let Garand know they had real evidence. "I'm pleased you rang, you've saved me a call. Homicide is keen to have a chat with Warren Kay. Do you know where he is?"

"But you aren't Homicide, Detective."

"Not at the moment, but they will call you."

"For the record, I don't know where Mr Kay is."

Garand told the truth, he did not know Kay's destination, only that Kay would contact him.

"He is still in Australia isn't he?"

"I don't know," said Garand, no longer interested in discussing Kay's whereabouts. "Send me a receipt for all the items removed from my client's home. And, in his absence, make sure you advise me in advance if you intend entering the home again. I'd like to be present."

"I've noted your request. When Kay contacts you, as he will," he continued as the lawyer began to interrupt, "tell him he is liable to be detained if he returns."

So far as Rysakov was concerned, if Kay never came back to Sydney that would be fine. Not quite as good as putting him behind bars, but it would do. Rysakov sent a detain notice to Customs and Immigration in the event Kay tried to re-enter the country. Forensics had told him it might take several weeks to raise any residual DNA off the plastic devices from Kay's house and then compare the analysis to Honey French's DNA. If it matched, Homicide would recommend to the DPP that a warrant be issued to arrest Kay on a charge of manslaughter. Tom O'Leary assured Rysakov that as evidence accumulated the charge may be upgraded to murder and others added. Rysakov sent a return email to Tom explaining why, in his opinion, a warrant should also be issued through Interpol.

Rysakov sighed. The time had finally come, well overdue in reality, to close the file on Alice Martin. It would remain an unsolved case. Perhaps to be re-opened by a cold case team in the future. At present, with no new information, he could not justify the allocation of any further time or costs. The further one climbed the seniority ladder, the more one appreciated what every member of the police force saw in practice every day, the contest of impossible demands chasing inadequate resources.

Yet he knew the Alice case would sit in the back of his mind, an irritant to be scratched and rubbed in idle moments. Admitting defeat did not come easily to him. All police officers had examples of cases that got under the skin He was not obsessing about Alice, at least not yet. Notwithstanding the lack of a result, he did not believe he had missed anything. He tried, unsuccessfully, to explain to Ruby why he couldn't let go just yet, and why he felt there were several acts still to be played before the final curtain. Attempts to rationalise the feeling didn't really stack up. Instead it all boiled down to one thing, and one thing only – he had a hunch.

"It has to be some kind of record," he said to Ruby later that evening at home. "One missing person and seven deaths connected to that MP. And those are the ones we know about, there might be others. Do you realise that if Alice had not disappeared, six of those deaths would not have occurred. At least, I believe a case can be argued in support of that. And the MP is still missing."

"So, what are you going to say in your report?"

Rysakov pulled a manila folder out of his briefcase.

"It is my opinion," he read from the report, "after conducting the interviews mentioned and viewing the CCTV tape multiple times, that Alice Martin used a simple disguise to exit the State Art Gallery, one that changed her appearance sufficiently to go unrecognised. She left as latecomers were still arriving, thereby avoiding the risk of attendants remembering her exit. I believe that within twelve hours of that exit she had left the country. In my opinion she is still alive." He looked up. "I haven't made up my mind about including reference to the seven deaths."

"I think you should include it. It might get the case reviewed earlier," said Ruby.

His other theories about Alice, based on the German notebook, would look more at home in a crime novel than a police report. He did not include them in the report. They remained theories. The only two people to whom he could mention them without risk of being laughed at were Will Callaghan and Ruby. He closed the Alice file.

"Enough about my problems. How was your day?" he asked giving Ruby a hug and kiss.

"Pretty average. I didn't feel very well."

"How are you feeling now?"

"OK."

"Good, how about a glass of red?"

"No, thanks."

Rysakov went to the wine rack, opened a bottle and poured himself a glass. Ruby waited until he had taken a mouthful.

"Do you love me?"

Several clever retorts sprang to mind but something in her tone cautioned him, instinct telling him this was not the time. She was serious. "Of course I do, more than I thought possible."

"I'm pregnant. I'm going to have a baby," Ruby said, in a bit of a rush.

Rysakov's hand stopped midway to his mouth. A few moments of silence followed as he absorbed what Ruby had said. All his concerns about her recent moods and guardedness answered in that one sentence. "Ruby, that's wonderful news. How long have you known?"

"Coming up to two months. I know you like children. I've seen you with Tom O'Leary's, and they like you. I wasn't sure how you'd feel about having your own," Ruby said.

"It'll be great. Wow," he said, putting his arms around her.

In the space of minutes his life had changed forever. Rysakov forgot the unfinished glass of wine as they spent the evening discussing plans for the new addition to the family. At Ruby's request, they agreed no announcement until the end of the first trimester, twelve weeks.

The next day, Rysakov reopened discussions with the Superintendent. The prospects for promotion now took on a more meaningful dimension. In the past, when other fathers-to-be told him how the news changed their outlook on the future, he nodded politely, thinking it all just talk. Not so, they were right.

"Not only do I have to manage your forensic analysis with inadequate funding, I'm also expected to be a messenger boy," said the chief pathologist when Rysakov picked up the phone mid-week.

"Hullo, I'm fine, thanks for asking," he said, the sort of response he knew the pathologist expected.

"O'Leary asked me to tell you direct the results of the DNA analysis from the plastic."

"I'll get the pure science this way," said Rysakov.

"Flattery will get you everything, at least at the morgue." The pathologist laughed. "We were able to get some traces, but not enough to do exhaustive checking without more time to culture. The analysis we have been able to do provides a good match with cadaver 12HF, or Honey French to you. Without a bigger sample there is a margin for error. However, if I was a betting man, I'd put money on it being 12HF. Unfortunately, I can't provide the usual level of comfort the DPP likes, at this stage. It'll be up to you to convince them if you want to get an arrest warrant. Sorry I can't be more definite."

Rysakov hung up then called DSC O'Leary. "Thanks for getting the chief pathologist to fill me in. Are you still going to try for an arrest?"

"Yeah, we think we can get the DPP to proceed. Trouble is, if Kay gets a good lawyer overseas, extradition will be tough without more evidence. We'll keep working."

"He has shot through then?"

"Yeah, Immigration recorded him leaving a few days ago. Probably felt the heat getting too close."

When Rysakov and Ruby told their friends she was pregnant they held a BBQ at the Paddington terrace-house to celebrate. The women, most of whom had children, congregated around Ruby offering advice; the men gravitated around the bar and the BBQ.

"How did you go with Kay and the DPP?" Rysakov asked Tom.

"The best they would contemplate on the evidence was a charge of involuntary manslaughter, and we may not even get that. Same old story, budgetary constraints. The State Government sent a memo to the Director saying that because of the economic situation there will be no increase in the DPP funding. Can you believe that? Anyway, I've suggested they get Interpol to issue a Blue Notice to warn local cops. Not sure they'll do it. There's already is a 'detain for questioning' alert at all ports into Australia," Tom said before leaving the grill to replenish his beer.

It took John Martin three weeks to clear the house of furniture, arrange tradesmen to prepare the property to present well for sale, to store personal items and explain to his friends where he was going. During this time he remained at the house to save money, often having dinner with Callaghan. The local police rostered a rotation of cars to call at the house day and night, and Callaghan hired a specialised firm to monitor the security 24/7. Even though he'd been informed Kay was out of Australia, only then did Martin feel secure.

66

When Warren Kay landed in France, he changed aircraft at Charles de Gaulle Airport and flew straight to Madrid. Much as he enjoyed the Spanish capital, he immediately boarded the next AVE high speed train to Málaga on the Costa del Sol. It took him three weeks to locate the right property, in an Andalusian mountain village an hour's drive north of the coast. Originally built over a century ago by a wealthy merchant as a summer house, an English property developer had restored and refurbished it. Caught by the economic downturn, the developer was forced to sell. Kay drove a hard bargain with one overwhelming advantage: he could settle promptly and in cash. It came fully furnished and Kay kept on all the existing arrangements with maintenance of the garden, the swimming pool and cleaners. He even bought the man's vehicle, a two year-old silver Range Rover.

He immediately had the house connected to a high speed wireless internet. Kay did not intend to stay idle. He had two primary targets, two individuals who separately had interposed themselves into his plans and cost him a fortune in lost profits, not to mention increased risk exposure. The ledger needed to be redressed.

"Garand," the lawyer barked into the telephone.

"Has your man got any results?" Kay asked, following up his request of a fortnight ago.

"As you know, Warren, John Martin flew to London. It's taken the rest of the time since to find him," said Garand. "Finally, my investigator spoke to a neighbour who Martin had asked to hold some CDs for him until after the sale of the house. Martin recently requested him to post them to London. Now we have a street address, in Islington."

Garand still smarted over the evidence Kay had recorded of him ordering the prison murder of his scumbag brother-in-law. If he could figure out some way to get his hands on it, he would happily tell the police all he knew about Kay. He suspected the information would fill many gaps in police files; the DPP would have little hesitation in commencing proceedings, and for more than one capital offence.

The telephone rang. A male voice asked for Kay's domicile address so documents could be prepared for Kay to claim the residue of his family estate from pre-revolutionary Russia. The call sounded as though it originated overseas, but Garand could not be certain. The caller identified himself as a Mr Korokov, a Russian lawyer trying to restore rightful ownership of assets confiscated by the State under Communism. He had a thick Eastern European accent.

"Mr Kay must be living at the address and be able to prove his identity," he said.

After lengthy discussion, Mr Korokov agreed that so long as he knew the country where Kay now resided he would send the documents to Garand for completion and return. He left the lawyer a phone number to contact him.

Garand could see no harm in telling Korokov that Kay lived in Spain. He recalled Kay telling him his grandfather, or great grandfather, had extensive estates confiscated by the Communists. So it sounded plausible. If it was genuine, he'd get the documents and forward them. If it's not, Kay could go to hell.

"I worked Kay's Russian ancestry into a plausible story," the ex-intelligence investigator explained to his client, and then outlined the story he had told Garand. He concluded by adding, "I gained the impression that, for some reason, Mr Garand is no longer entirely sympathetic to Mr Kay. Perhaps they had a falling out." Then he said, "Warren Kay is living somewhere in Andalusia. I know that narrows the field, but it still means hundreds of haystacks to search."

The day after this conversation, Dragor Slavovic commenced a search under the alias of Korokov into newly transferred real estate in Andalusia. He did so without expecting a quick result. Lodgement of transfers did not necessarily occur promptly and Kay could have used a company to buy his house. No surprise, a nil outcome.

However, Slavovic had absolute confidence he would find Kay, eventually. Time was the only enemy, along with some irritating costs along the way, costs the client would cover, or else. He handed the matter to his small staff, most of whom were women. They had far more patience and, the good ones, a knack for extracting information. A foreigner, recently settled in the area, would stand out and his name would be known. They started contacting the Mayoral offices, the local police, tradesmen, cleaners, expanding coverage in ever widening rings

If one ignored the weather most of the time, revelling in the occasional good days, there were few better cities on Earth than London. Dr Ben Johnson said so several centuries ago and John Martin rapidly came to the same conclusion. He enjoyed the undeniable advantage of living in the fashionable end of Islington, within easy walking distance of the Underground and a host of pubs, clubs and restaurants.

The three-storey early Victorian house stood as part of a row in a quiet side street. Callaghan had renovated it extensively three years ago and used it from time to time for business associates or friends to use as a London base. A live-in housekeeper maintained the four bedrooms in a state of readiness. Martin had exclusive use of the middle floor, setup as a self-contained apartment. He could also use the ground level lounge and meeting rooms. The housekeeper had her own room at the rear.

The road in which the house stood had barely adequate street lighting. Most of the residents found this quite satisfactory; it improved privacy and discouraged restaurant parking. Break-ins did happen, as in most parts of the city, but infrequently. Martin soon felt comfortable in the environment, walking with easy familiarity across dark patches between lights. Occasionally, Callaghan joined him for a drink at the Rose & Thorn several blocks away. He wanted to be sure his cousin settled in well.

Martin soon came to the view that first year accountancy was as dull as it could get, an opinion shared by the two young women and two males comprising the annual intake to the accounting firm. Dull as it may be, he was determined to qualify as fast as possible. The five often had a drink together and before long John began playing rugby with a local club, which welcomed the inclusion of a strong Aussie forward into the team. Life could hardly get any better. So he thought.

Time slipped leisurely by in Andalusia, and Warren Kay wondered whether he had reacted prematurely. Perhaps the police did not have enough hard evidence to charge him. But, he sure as hell preferred a leisurely life in Spain over sitting in a cell in Sydney.

That brought him once again to a puzzle for which he had yet to find a satisfactory answer. How did DS Rysakov know about the plastic head cover? Obviously someone had told him, but who and why? They found it, so what? He sat pondering. He had last used it on Honey French. He had got excited watching her body twisting in spasms from the dual effect of vibrator-induced orgasms and depleting oxygen inside the plastic cover. Both hands had been handcuffed behind her to the bedhead. He should have released the tie around her neck and let air in. But he hadn't. He had waited until all movement ceased and her lips turned blue. At that moment he had spontaneously climaxed, right at the time of death, sublime timing he had never achieved before.

Forcing the image out of his mind he considered the downside. There was a high probability the pathologist could extract DNA from the head cover. He had already admitted having sex with her that night, so it was mainly circumstantial evidence. Depending on what other evidence they have, however, could be difficult to defend. He figured he could be forced to accept involuntary manslaughter with a short custodial sentence.

Had he left any DNA traces on the plastic? The more he thought about it, the more certain he became. He had not. Finger prints, yes, but it was his property. Didn't mean anything. All he had to do was convince a court that the DNA had been left by Honey French some time before the night she died. Records of the call girl agency would confirm she had been hired before.

Maybe he *had* acted too fast.

He liked Spain, but he was still a foreigner in a foreign country. The cost of living was noticeably lower than Sydney. The quality of the food and wine he could not fault. Even the weather he found so far to be as good as in Sydney. Once he had accepted the local customs, such as the siesta and the late dining hour, he found the people in the nearby village friendly and helpful. He even made an effort to learn Spanish. Contrary to the opinions of several Englishmen he had asked, Kay found the gardener, cleaner and tradesmen he employed perfectly satisfactory. In one area only did he have a problem. The local women were watched by someone at all times. Or so it seemed. Prudence dictated he tread carefully where Spanish women were concerned. As a result, pressure steadily built up inside him and the need for release became more and more difficult to ignore.

One day, not long after, he told his cleaner he was taking the Range Rover on business for three days in Barcelona. While there he purchased a number of items which a casual observer might find eclectic, but not of particular interest. One, made of specialty Toledo steel and designed to separate flesh from the backbone of fish, belonged in a gourmet fish kitchen. All were small enough to fit unnoticed in his overnight bag when he returned late on the third day

A week later, a well-camouflaged and silent observer watched the silver Range Rover exit the driveway. This time the observer saw two small suitcases loaded into the back of the vehicle. A longer stay. He would confirm that in the village. When he had waited an hour to be sure Kay did not return, Dragor Slavovic left the hide and stretched his legs. He lifted the vine off his pushbike and pedalled in the direction of the local tapas bar. As he rode he pressed SPEED DIAL.

"He's left at last, this time for a longer stay," he said. Then, in answer to a question from his client, "I'll find out where and how long in the village. I'll get entry to the house tomorrow once I confirm no one is scheduled to be there."

Another question.

"OK. I'll meet you at the airport."

He slipped the phone into his vest pocket, tightened the velcro strip for safety and continued into the village.

67

"The house is isolated. It stands at the top of a very steep slope with magnificent views down the valley. It can be approached from two sides without being seen, particularly if we are on foot," explained Slavovic as he drove the hire car out of the airport. His client nodded; she knew from experience Slavovic did his homework with thoroughness forged in the brutal war with Bosnia. They parked the vehicle out of sight, shouldered small day packs and walked across the field, just another two holiday makers. At the house, Slavovic knocked on the door to be certain, although the cleaner had told him she was not due for a week. Satisfied it was empty, they both checked for alarms and cameras.

"No alarm. It would be ignored in this area anyway," he said.

He spent an hour searching for signs of a camera system.

"I can see wires that could be waiting for an installation, but no camera. Maybe there is a camera inside so we wear masks until I am certain."

His client nodded and pulled on a ski balaclava. "I think Kay believes no one knows he is here," she said.

Half an hour later, finding no cameras, they relaxed. Slavovic stretched out on a chair on the patio overlooking the valley, careful not to move the chair's legs. His client carefully memorised the layout of the house and its dimensions. Although tempting, they decided a thorough search of the contents would not be a sensible idea. One small item misplaced and Kay would know there had been intruders. By mid-afternoon the house had returned to its empty, silent state. No sign of the visitors existed, no grains of dirt on the rugs, no footprints in the garden, all windows and doors locked.

As they approached the airport, Slavovic pulled off the road to authorise the electronic transfer of the balance of his fee to a Cyprus bank account. At the airport, while the car rental clerk processed the paper work, the woman, dressed in tailored woollen slacks and a matching three-quarter length coat, continued past the rental counter into the terminal. She totally ignored Slavovic and proceeded to check in at British Airways.

Only a small inner circle knew the full extent of Callaghan's fortune and he preferred to keep it that way. In order to protect his investments, Callaghan had developed a network of contacts and sources that rivalled many government intelligence services. Most were high level executives covering every major industry and business sector. Some held senior permanent positions in governments around the world. Very few knew the membership of more than one or two of the others in the network. That protected the integrity of all. Each member of the network, including Callaghan, exchanged information on a confidential, non-attributable basis. One breach of this rule and the individual was blacklisted, for life. No mistakes, no breaches, nothing in writing. To become a member of the network one had to be invited, and introduced gradually, based on performance. Once part of the network, which for obvious reasons had no name, one could obtain answers to an extraordinarily wide range of questions. However, inside information for personal use, or compromising the national security of a member's country also resulted in lifetime blacklisting. Someone always found out.

Following his takeover of Nestor Nankervis & Co., Callaghan decided to follow the money deposited by Clive Nestor into the account at First Bahamas Trust. Nestor believed the account to be his own, when in fact it was controlled by an unknown party. Callaghan told DS Rysakov he had lost the trail at Cyprus. He did so not to deliberately mislead the policeman, but to avoid Rysakov finding himself in a potentially compromising position. To trace the funds beyond that location meant using sources and technologies which breached laws in several jurisdictions through which the money passed. Once the money left Cyprus, it went far beyond anything an Australian law enforcement officer could touch. To tell them would have achieved nothing, in Callaghan's view. In reality, it may only have resulted in warning the party he tracked to hide more effectively. And then he would have lost them.

He knew few people outside the intelligence services could have acquired the information he had secured through his network. Information that had enabled him to identify who controlled the FBT account, who re-routed the three hundred million paid into that account, and where it now lay. He also felt confident he knew who sent him the cryptic message concerning Warren Kay. But that was only speculation.

Apart from Will, only Sarah Longhurst knew who he had traced.

Now, one of his network sources in Europe had suggested to him a possibility he considered too far left field to be credible. It was an astonishing proposition. The difficulty rested in the quality of the source and its assurance that the suggestion had some basis in fact. Not sufficient to make it conclusive, but enough to take the possibility seriously, Callaghan decided to work only with what he knew to be fact. He asked Sarah Longhurst to make direct contact with the person who controlled the FBT account, the person who now held three hundred million dollars in several bank accounts around the world. Despite the extent and quality of the network, their banking contacts had only been able to track down a phone number and the name of the corporation holding the account. Not the name of the individual who owned the account.

"Icon Investment Management manages its own funds. We don't manage any third party money," Sarah said after introducing herself as Managing Director of Icon.

"Then why are you calling me? I have no funds to invest." As she and Callaghan expected, the person who answered was a woman.

"We have an exceptional network of information sources and are always seeking possible new sources," said Sarah.

"I'm not interested." Then, after a pause, "How did you get this number?"

"One of our investments in Australia is Nestor Nankervis & Co., which we bought from Mr Nestor and Warren Kay. Clive

Nestor was murdered. Now Kay has disappeared from Australia. One of our young protégés recently witnessed Kay in suspicious circumstances and we believe was threatened by him in Sydney. Fortunately the young man is now in London, under our protection. Perhaps I could give you some background on Warren Kay."

"I know all about Mr Kay," said the woman on the other end of the telephone. There followed silence.

"Hullo, are you still there?" said Sarah, thinking she had suddenly been disconnected..

"Yes... you must have tracked me somehow." More silence. "Who do you work for?"

"Will Callaghan is our principal. We exchange information with people we trust and invest our own funds, nothing more," said Sarah. "Do you know where Kay is now?" she asked on the off chance.

"What is your name?" the woman asked.

"Sarah Longhurst. I'll give you my phone number," and she dictated the number. "And what is your name?" She received no response. "Well, can you at least give me your direct phone number?" asked Sarah.

Sarah sensed the woman at the other end of the call was making a decision. It didn't take long.

"I found out today that Kay is not in Spain, where he now lives. I don't know for sure, but I suspect he is in London. I was about to call Callaghan direct to warn him. Make sure he warns John Martin to be very careful. Tell Callaghan to make sure no harm comes to him."

Then the phone went dead.

When Callaghan heard Sarah's report of the conversation he immediately arranged to meet John Martin that night.

An hour later, Sarah received an SMS message consisting solely of a phone number. She assumed it to be the number she had requested and copied it to Callaghan.

68

Will Callaghan left his office late and took longer than he expected to get to the Rose & Thorn. It took more time again to find a parking space, finally walking in nearly an hour late. At the bar he saw John talking to two girls. All three burst out laughing as Martin ordered another round. Callaghan joined them, adding a glass of red wine to the order. Insisting on paying for the round, he asked the barmaid to hold a zip-around document case behind the bar until he left the pub. Twenty minutes later, after the girls drifted off to join friends, he and John went upstairs to the restaurant.

By mutual agreement all documents relating to the estate of Jack Martin were sent to Icon Investment Management. Although no decisions were made without John's approval, Icon had the staff to take action, if required.

"A bundle of papers relating to your father's estate arrived this week. They look OK to me, but you should read them. If you're happy to go the way suggested, sign them and get them back to my office. Sarah will know what to do with them."

Martin nodded.

"If you've got some decent coffee I'll come back to the house after dinner and go through them with you," said Callaghan. "There's money from the sale of your house, the balance in your father's superannuation fund, and a number of small assets to decide on, as well as what you would like to do with the proceeds."

Once they had ordered their meal, Callaghan told John of the phone call and the likelihood that Warren Kay was in London.

"I don't believe he's the holiday type, so if he's here the only reason I can think of is to do you or me some serious injury. After your Bahamas experience I suspect it is you. Of course I have no proof Kay is in London, but it won't hurt to be careful. Stick to crowded streets, don't open your front door until you know for certain who is there. Remember, he's in no way reluctant to kill."

The wine arrived, followed by dinner and the conversation turned to the soccer, rugby, the cricket and how much John enjoyed London. When they left the pub Callaghan said he would keep him company as they walked back to the townhouse. Halfway to Martin's residence Callaghan suddenly stopped.

"Bugger it. I've left the documents at the pub. I'll go back and get them. It won't take long. Why don't you go on ahead, it's too cold to stand around," he said.

"I'll get the coffee on," said Martin as Callaghan retraced their route at a fast pace.

Tension, caused by the unfamiliar environment and the excitement Kay always felt before he killed, tightened his muscles. The first two nights had been reconnoitring exercises, although had the opportunity arisen he would have seized it. He had settled on a dark narrow lane between two terraced houses that accessed the rear yard and a tiny studio flat. The houses themselves fronted directly onto the street. Fortuitously, the lane was over fifty metres from the nearest street lights, which themselves were low candle-power.

Kay leaned against the wall a metre into the lane and enveloped in shadow. Martin's usual route after leaving the Underground took him right past the entrance to the laneway. The atmosphere felt right tonight.

A cough startled him. It came from the wrong direction, away from the Underground. The footsteps turned into the laneway and headed toward him. He slid the knife out of the leather scabbard strapped to his ankle. He took care not to cut his hand on the razor sharp edge. Light, short steps, a female. He thought briefly of retreating down the right-of-way, but that offered no hiding place, only a door to the studio apartment. The woman would collide with him in seconds.

He stood blocking the lane, seeing her outline and height briefly against the faint backlighting from the street. Too late she sensed an alien presence before colliding with him. Kay's left hand grabbed her scarf and pulled her toward him. His right hand drove the thin blade into her neck with all his strength. It cut the carotid artery and partially severed her spinal column. The only sound from the woman was a strangled gurgle as she choked on the blood flowing down her throat.

Kay pressed her scarf hard against the fatal wound to prevent any arterial blood spurting onto his clothes and dragged the body further into the darkness. He carefully laid the dead woman on the ground and extracted his knife, cleaning it on her clothes. Exhilaration coursed through him. Confident he could not be seen, he stood just inside the laneway entrance, ready to strike the moment Martin moved one step past him.

Callaghan began to feel uneasy as he neared the Rose & Thorn. By the time he had retrieved the document case and made his way out through the pub crowd, his level of anxiety reached near panic. It was totally irrational, he knew, he just felt an overpowering need to be certain John was safe. He began to run.

Kay recognised Martin walking down the lane alone toward him. He tightened his grip on the knife. He noted the boy was as tall as himself with broad shoulders and an easy walk. He adjusted his stance slightly, ready to pounce. In seconds John Martin would be dead. One step past the lane, Kay sprang at his back. His left arm shot over Martin's left shoulder, grabbing his chin to expose the neck. The knife hand, a second behind, went for the carotid artery.

Callaghan turned the corner to see a tall shadow suddenly burst out of the blackness and attack John from behind. He doubled his speed, knowing that if it was Kay John Martin would be dead before he got there. At least he would make sure Kay did not get away.

I'll kill the bastard.

He saw John go down. Kay seemed to fall onto him.

Martin felt an arm brush his left shoulder and in a microsecond flash thought of Clive Nestor. He instantly propped, his knees bent, then straightening both legs, he pushed back with all the power of his rugby training. He felt the momentary surprise of his assailant, before the attack was remounted. Martin grabbed the man's left wrist and hauled down on it, collapsing the maul.

Martin's reaction threw Kay off balance. He struggled to regain control as he fell clumsily onto his victim. Then he heard the pounding feet of someone approaching at speed. He stabbed where he thought Martin's neck should be, before springing up to deal with the newcomer. Kay swung the knife into the oncoming body only to find his knife arm deflected and the air knocked out of his lungs by a shoulder charge. The power of the collision knocked him backwards and he hit the pavement heavily. When he saw the face of his opponent he knew he was in trouble.

He felt Callaghan grapple his right arm getting it in a lock. If he did not get it free it would break at the elbow. Kay fought for his life. He twisted his body with all his strength, momentarily freeing the arm. His knife free, he stabbed at Callaghan's chest. Callaghan's legs twisted Kay, giving him leverage on Kay's right arm. Callaghan immediately threw his weight backwards, totally dislocating the elbow joint and tearing the shoulder muscles.

Excruciating pain shot up Kay's arm. He dropped the knife and kicked with all his fading strength. He managed to stand with sufficient balance to aim a kick at Callaghan, freeing him momentarily from the grapple hold. He turned and ran, the silver Range Rover, a block away, his only hope. With every step razor sharp barbs shot down his dangling arm. Tears of pain filled his eyes.

As Callaghan scrambled up to pursuit Kay he heard John moan. Abandoning Kay, he knelt down to help. Once he was certain John was still alive, he set about investigating how badly he was injured. It was then he realised his hand had come in contact with a sticky wetness. Blood.

69

The police arrived first in response to Callaghan's emergency call. By the time the paramedics were on the scene one of the constables had found the woman's body.

"Looks like a modern Jack the Ripper," said the lead detective from the Murder Squad. "You say you know the identity of the attacker?" he asked Callaghan.

"Yes, it's Warren Kay. If you call DS Rysakov in Redfern, Sydney, he can give you all the background on this bastard. I'll give you his phone number. We heard he lived in Spain. I don't know where, or if he'll go back there now."

Both Martin and Callaghan had stab wounds in the shoulder and were taken to hospital for x-rays and sutures. The emergency doctor told John that his fast reaction to Kay's assault not only saved his life but restricted Kay's striking capacity.

"You are lucky. The knife penetrated deep into the shoulder touching the shoulder blade. From what you say, your backward momentum prevented the blade penetrating the lung. I've stitched it up, but you'll need it in a sling. I'm afraid it'll be painful for a few weeks. The bang on the head as you hit the pavement has given you a mild concussion, but no worse than you'd expect on the rugby field," the doctor said. Then to Callaghan, "Mr Callaghan, several stitches, nothing serious, no stress on the arm for ten days, OK?"

Martin remained in hospital for observation overnight. As Will made his way home he made a call to the number Sarah had given him.

"I thought I'd let you know," he said. "Your warning was very timely. Kay came very close to killing John tonight."

He explained what happened, how Kay had very painful injuries and how he had arranged fulltime security to guard John until Kay was caught.

"Thank you," said the woman at the other end.

After stopping at an all-night pharmacy to buy the strongest anti-inflammatory and pain relief drugs available over the counter, Kay drove to Dover in time for the early morning ferry to Calais. When he arrived at his house in Andalusia twenty-four hours later, his arm in a makeshift sling, he barely had the strength to get out of the vehicle. Once inside, he took a strong sleeping pill and lay back in an easy chair. It was far too painful to lie on a bed. Within minutes he had succumbed to exhaustion.

The next morning, working on the assumption that in a farming district dislocations were reasonably common, he called the local doctor.

"Hmm, that does not look good. Pretty painful, eh?" the doctor said in reasonably good English.

"Bloody painful. Can you fix it?" Kay asked.

"Maybe. I will need an assistant to help," the doctor said.

"Whatever you need, just get it done."

Fifteen minutes later the doctor had prepared two splints and explained to Kay what would be involved, when an old man walked in.

"This is Pablo. He has been helping the local doctors fix dislocated and broken bones for forty years. He only speaks Catalan," said the doctor. "Are you ready? You sure you refuse the morphine?"

Kay nodded and grasped the back of the wooden chair. No way could he risk going under to morphine, it would put him completely under their control. Kay clenched his teeth as Pablo took hold of his upper arm and the doctor took his wrist. Kay fortunately did not see the doctor nod to Pablo, then pull down hard on the wrist, both twisting slightly to realign the bones. The doctor then bent the elbow ready to bind the splints. The pain was so intense Kay passed out for several seconds. The doctor looked at Kay's face, white and covered in sweat.

"Is it done?" Kay asked through clenched teeth. He saw Pablo smiling. "What's so funny?"

"It is a long time since we see someone go without strong painkillers for this," said the doctor. "You one tough fella."

Once the splints were on and the arm in a sling, the doctor said, "It will take time to heal, even then you will not get full use and strength back. I will see you in a few days. Till then, rest, do nothing strenuous."

When he woke next morning the arm felt better, but still tender and useless. "Next time will be the last time for Callaghan," he said to himself.

Thinking about Callaghan forced Kay to face the facts. His days with a knife were over, or at best very limited. Callaghan had seen to that. To be certain of a kill in the future he had to use a gun.

"It'll be close and very personal," he said with a snarl. "A bullet through the knee to disable, then organ by organ, bullet by bullet I'll close the bastard down. And it will be very painful."

After eating whatever he could find as breakfast he walked slowly from room to room, making certain there had been no intruders in his absence. It took several hours. He needed frequent stops to rest and ease the pain. In each room he checked small objects left facing a certain way, pens on top of papers in a drawer, a hair across a cupboard door. Nothing had been disturbed.

Although his arm eased, it hurt far more than he expected if he rolled on it in bed, so he continued sleeping semi-upright in the easy chair. Cushions supported the arm. By the end of the week he figured he should be able to sleep in his bed again. He got the cleaner to help him set his laptop on a tray so he had access to the outside world. She also bought him a hot meal in the middle of the day, and he gratefully paid extra. The food was good.

He had acquired a Spanish made semi-automatic Astra A-80 and several boxes of nine millimetre cartridges soon after arriving in the village. He had understood why the farmer wanted to sell it; it was twenty-five years old and needed attention. But it worked. For close quarter disagreements it would kill as efficiently as any other weapon. He laid it on the tray, next to the laptop, the magazine full, one in the breach, and the safety off. Kay did not think he needed the gun. No one knew where he lived. However, in his present state, he could not afford to be wrong. After the debacle in Islington he wanted to be sure he remained safe, very sure. The attack by Callaghan and the injury he'd sustained had seriously unnerved him. He considered, for the first time in his life, the possibility he had met his match. The Astra tipped the balance.

Next day he spent on his feet doing what he could, researching on the internet and taking two long walks to tire himself. After reading for several hours he settled down in the easy chair for the night. Once, about four a.m., he woke suddenly. He thought he'd heard a noise and picked up the Astra, straining for any sound. Nothing, total silence. Within fifteen minutes he drifted off into a sound sleep again.

Kay startled awake, unsure what had disturbed him. He fumbled as he grasped for the Astra. The grip was facing away from him. *I didn't leave it like that*, he thought. He fought down a rising feeling of panic.

"Don't move Warren Kay, a Sig Sauer is inches from your head," said a woman's voice.

The sound of the voice shocked Kay awake. For the first time in his life he understood the meaning of terror, knowing he had no way of defending himself. Without thinking he began to swivel on his chair. As he did, he briefly glimpsed an image reflected in the wall mirror, before a nine millimetre slug shattered it, showering him with shards of glass. He had seen a female figure, average height, clad in close fitting black trousers, long sleeved shirt, with a black balaclava pulled up to expose the face. He couldn't exactly place the face, yet in the back of his mind he felt he should know it.

"The next shot will be through your good elbow. Keep very still."

Kay's mind slowly began to function. There had been no percussion so the Sig Sauer must have a suppressor. No chance of any passer by hearing the shots. He looked out the window. About an hour after dawn, he estimated. No one would come by until midday.

"What do you want?" he asked.

"To explain why I am here," she said.

"I'll understand better if I can see you."

"It depends how much you value your good elbow."

"Surely you're not ashamed to face me," he sneered.

While he had been speaking Kay's fingers had slowly turned the Astra around to where he could now grasp the grip.

"Pick up your gun and fire a shot," said the woman behind him.

Kay's heart sank, but he took a firm grip and squeezed the trigger. All he heard was a metallic click. He squeezed again and again. No good, the magazine was empty. Now he understood why the Astra had been facing the wrong way.

"This week you tried to kill two people in London. You also killed foolish Clive Nestor whose main fault was to believe his own hubris."

"Nestor stole a large amount of money using inside information. He should have shared it with other shareholders," said Kay.

"The money had been dealt with. Nestor received none. That was punishment enough. You were entitled to not one cent. You sold out of the company at a huge premium. Yet you still killed him."

Her voice struck a familiar chord. "I know you, don't I?" he said. "It's Alice Martin."

"I do not recognise that name. When you saw my reflection in the mirror, did you recognise me?"

Kay closed his eyes to recapture the image. "No, I did not. Faces can be changed, voices are more difficult." Even as he said it he was sure he had it right. The voice had a slight European accent. That could be practiced. It was Alice, he was certain.

"You asked me who I am. I will tell you. My true history I only discovered recently and that only because of an old man's conscience. My great grandmother was Anna Macek, sister to Yuri Morozov, the great grandfather of Will Callaghan. I have since determined that John Martin is also descended from Anna Macek. The two people you tried to kill in London are my cousins."

"I don't give a shit about your family history," Kay spat out. "Tell me what you want then fuck off."

"Your efforts to kill my relations were unsuccessful, I'm pleased to say."

"Callaghan attacked me without provocation. I had no argument with him," said Kay.

"So you admit John Martin was a target."

Kay remained silent.

"You killed Honey French for your own pleasure. She provided a service to a number of clients, not only you. She may have been a sad individual, but she did not deserve to die and be dumped in the forest," said the woman.

Kay noticed the woman did not say 'bush' as he would expect an Australian to do. Maybe it was not Alice. Kay decided to try another ploy. He had a throwing knife hidden next to his left thigh. While they had been talking his fingers had closed around the blade, ready to hurl it with all his strength at the woman. To succeed he needed two things to happen. First, he needed to turn around to face her. Second, he needed a distraction.

"My cleaner will arrive soon unless I leave an empty refuse bin on the front mat. It's my Do Not Disturb sign," he said, expecting the woman to look toward the door. He braced himself, and kicked the swivel around, raising the knife in a throwing action as he moved.

Before he had time to complete the throw a tremendous force hit his left leg. Wrenching pain pierced his left side like a red hot poker. A soft-nosed slug shattered the bone in his left knee. The knife clattered to the ground.

"I warned you," she said.

"Fuuuck!" Kay screamed. "Take what you want." Tears of pain rolled down his cheeks. He now expected to die.

"With the sale of your Nestor shares you have amassed a sizeable fortune. Congratulations. Now it is time to hand it over to more productive management, mine."

"Get fucked!" he said through clenched teeth.

"I expected you to say that. A pity, it might have been one of the few decent gestures you've made in your life."

"Ahhhrrr." Kay tried to rise and fell back in pain. When he

opened his eyes he thought the woman had gone. His hopes rose for a brief moment.

"I have access to expert forgers and banking experts. They have details of all your accounts and other assets. So, although you don't deserve it, I believe it a matter of common courtesy to inform you that by now, documents executed with your signature have transferred all of your assets to me. One of the documents appoints me to act for you under a power of attorney with no restrictions. Even this house will eventually be mine."

The voice came from immediately behind him. Kay heard a metallic noise, a click, then silence. The pain was now so intense he had gone beyond caring. He just wanted it to stop.

"One last thing, I made a mistake in not recognising how degenerate you truly are. You're a vicious, egocentric bastard. You have no redeeming features. Fortunately you have no offspring to carry your bad genes," said the woman. "It all ends now."

Before the people in the village began their day, the woman with the Sig Sauer locked the house and walked to her vehicle, a cheap rental. Once away from the house she changed out of the black into her tailored woollen slacks and three-quarter length woollen coat and drove to the airport at Malaga.

Not long after midday Callaghan received a phone call. A woman's voice began speaking without any preamble. "I thought you may be pleased to hear that Warren Kay is dead. Eventually the police will tell you. It'll probably be attributed to an intruder after some valuable art, bearer certificates, or some such. His laptop and personal papers including banking details will be found to be missing. The story being spread in the village says Kay stole from some rather nasty Romanians who found him and exacted retribution. For the CNP, that will sound authentic enough to cover his arrival and demise."

"Thanks for the call," said Callaghan. "Before you go, I would like confirmation as to who you are. You know who I am, and my family history."

"I assumed you had worked that out cousin," she said.

He now knew her identity, but wanted to be certain. "I imagine you want to keep your identity secret, for your own protection. My great grandfather was Yuri Morozov, his sister Anna migrated from Russia," said Callaghan.

"I can prove my lineage from Anna and Charles Macek, the Czech she married. Anna was Yuri's sister. I've seen letters written to Anna by Katya Morozov, clearly Anna's mother." After a pause she said, "Call me Anna."

"Thank you, Anna," said Callaghan

Two days later, Interpol received an anonymous tip. They in turn informed the CNP, the Spanish National Police Corp, who then discovered the body. Because they found an Australian passport, they advised the Homicide Squad in Sydney, the city of issue. Later that week, DSC Tom O'Leary called Nic Rysakov.

"G'day Nic, we've received some news from Spain. A Mr Warren Kay was found after a tipoff with a nine millimetre bullet though his head. Also had a gunshot to the leg and a buggered elbow wrapped around a splint. Clearly mixing with the wrong crowd."

"Couldn't have happened to a nicer bastard," said Rysakov. "Do they have any idea who did it?"

"Not a clue, though I got the feeling that after they'd received a copy of our file on Kay they won't be spending too much time on it."

70

"If we include that poor girl who had her throat cut in London, there have been ten deaths connected to Alice Martin. Those are the ones we know about. There may be others. Yet she still remains an enigma," Rysakov said to Ruby that night.

"Isn't that case closed?" asked Ruby, caressing her pregnant belly.

"Not yet, it becomes a cold case."

"But she's not dead?"

"Not according to Will Callaghan. He assures me she's very much alive," said Rysakov. "I'll add a note to that effect in the file. In due course it'll be closed."

"Do you think anyone will ever find her?" asked Ruby as she picked up a baby magazine and opened it.

"Not unless she wants to be found. That reminds me, I had an odd call today from Ann Stratton asking for the return of her hairbrush. Some family heirloom or other. Anyway, she said Alice had borrowed it about a month before she disappeared, said she wanted to get one like it in an antique shop. Stratton promptly forgot about it, having several other brushes. It wasn't until she saw the Martin family house for sale that she remembered the brush.

"I asked her to email me a description and I'd get John's lawyers to look for it. It turned out to have a very distinctive design on the back, a seated naked woman and a young satyr, with four hoofed legs and an erection, behind her brushing her hair."

"I can see how it would stay in your mind."

"Just as well it did, because it was in the Alice evidence box."

Ruby put the magazine down and looked up.

"This was the brush John Martin gave to the lab for DNA analysis on Alice, and where he got what he thought were Alice's hair samples. I sent someone around to pick up hair samples from Ann Stratton. I'll know in the morning, but I'll put money on it that our DNA analysis for Alice will turn out to be Ann Stratton's DNA. We didn't find any other sources that could give us a DNA sample for Alice. She made sure of that."

"If it is Ann Stratton's hair, could Alice really be John's mother?"

"It wouldn't surprise me if they are related. But who knows, little in this case is what it seems," said Rysakov. "If the hair is Ann Stratton's, we have no DNA for Alice."

"I wonder what Will Callaghan would make of that?"

They were both silent for a few minutes.

"She doesn't want to be found," said Ruby. "That way, if she's still alive, she can start a new life. That's a fantasy many people have at some time, but no one acts on, just remains an idle thought. There are usually too many reasons to prevent you running away."

The next day Rysakov asked Tom O'Leary, "What was Will Callaghan's reaction when you told him?"

"He said he had heard weeks ago. I thought you must have told him," said O'Leary.

"No, it wasn't me. I wonder how he found out?"

"One of his sources?"

"Must have been. Anyway, main thing is he knows," said Rysakov.

He resolved to ask Callaghan next time they met. In the meantime, he had a full timetable. His promotion to Detective Inspector came through and from the beginning of next week he would be very busy.

Tom O'Leary had several conversations with the Metropolitan Police Murder Squad in London. They said they had no forensic evidence tying Kay to the murder of the girl walking home down the laneway, only the statements of Callaghan and Martin that they were attacked by a person, whom they both identified as Kay. Neither actually saw him come out of the lane. However, based on the profile of Kay supplied by O'Leary everyone agreed it most improbable he could have hidden elsewhere. The Murder Squad set up a dragnet at every port, airport and police station in the UK, though, as they told O'Leary, once they received notification of Kay's death from the Spanish CNP, it would lapse.

Several weeks later Callaghan rang Anna.

"A couple of things still puzzle me. Firstly, why did you and Jack Martin adopt John? Secondly, did you know he was related to you at the time?"

"That was Heinrich Schmidt's idea. He believed it provided better deep cover. Because of things that happened to me around puberty I am unable to conceive, so it had to be adoption. Jack liked the idea, particularly if we adopted a boy. There were no shortages of candidates in Eastern Europe at that time," she said. She did not say anything for a short period.

"From what I have been able to piece together, some section in the Russian government, probably the secret police, the KGB or whoever, knew my family history and, incorrectly as it turned out, figured I might be useful to them. Since my own parents were dead or dysfunctional, I was taken away and trained. As for John, it probably appealed to some bureaucrat's warped sense of humour to have me adopt a relative. There's no way they wouldn't have known his family history."

"I would like to meet you one day. I'm certain John would like to see you again. You're his closest blood relative, and for as long as he can remember he looked upon you as his mother."

"In time. First, I have some issues to resolve with several individuals in Eastern Europe. It is my preference they think me dead for the time being," Anna said. "When that is done we will meet."

"I shall look forward to it. In the meantime, do not hesitate to call if I can assist in any way."

"Thank you, Will." The warmth of her tone gave him confidence he would see her in the near future.

In addition to his wealth he now had family, blood relations, with unique and desirable skills and abilities. An idea began to take shape. In due course he would bring them, and their skills, into the Nataliya Trust.

He pressed the buzzer on the door to Sarah's apartment. The

maître d'hôtel at the exclusive restaurant had guaranteed him a quiet table overlooking the Thames and assured him the best champagne had been put on ice. He had left nothing to chance. Tonight he was going to ask Sarah Longhurst to marry him.

So why did he feel so nervous?

About the Author

Born in Perth, Western Australia, Geoffrey Lambert grew up roaming through the bush in bare feet and body-surfing the Indian Ocean. Holidays were spent swimming, fishing, or on an uncle's sheep farm. Somehow he found time to learn to play the violin (badly).

He worked as an economist, investment banker and company advisor until he began writing.

The Morozov Inheritance

The Morozov Inheritance by Geoffrey Lambert
Book 1 of The Morozov Chronicles

DoctorZed Publishing 2012
www.doctorzed.com
ISBN: 978-0-9873244-1-2 (sc)
ISBN: 978-0-9873244-0-5 (e)

Genre: Fiction/ historical/ epic

"… one of the best stories I have read in a long time." – J D Briggs, Literary Consultant, Melbourne.

"Well-written, historically interesting, and an exciting story-line." – R Darroch, Journalist.

A banker's throat is cut in the driveway of his Sydney home, triggering a chain of events that had been set into motion one hundred years earlier on the other side of the world.

In Moscow at the turn of the twentieth century, Senior Investigator Maksim Rysakov is investigating the brutal murders of young women by a clever and psychopathic serial killer. From each victim, the murderer takes a gruesome trophy. The only clue is "a man who walks like a wolf."

Two World Wars and a Cold War later, The Morozov Inheritance is about to reach its devastating conclusion